Drop Dead, My Lovely

Drop Dead, My Lovely

Ellis Weiner

NEW AMERICAN LIBRARY

New American Library
Published by New American Library, a division of
Penguin Group (USA) Inc., 375 Hudson Street,
New York, New York 10014, U.S.A.
Penguin Books Ltd, 80 Strand,
London WC2R 0RL, England
Penguin Books Australia Ltd, 250 Camberwell Road,
Camberwell, Victoria 3124, Australia
Penguin Books Canada Ltd, 10 Alcorn Avenue,
Toronto, Ontario, Canada M4V 3B2
Penguin Books (N.Z.) Ltd, Cnr Rosedale and Airborne Roads,
Albany, Auckland 1310, New Zealand

Penguin Books Ltd, Registered Offices:
80 Strand, London WC2R 0RL, England

First published by New American Library,
a division of Penguin Group (USA) Inc.

First Printing, March 2004
10   9   8   7   6   5   4   3   2   1

⊕ REGISTERED TRADEMARK—MARCA REGISTRADA

LIBRARY OF CONGRESS CATALOGING-IN-PUBLICATION DATA:

Weiner, Ellis
    Drop dead, my lovely / Ellis Weiner.
    p. cm.
    ISBN 0-451-21117-0 (alk. paper)
    1.   Private investigators–New York (State)–New York–Fiction.   2.
New York (N.Y.)–Fiction   3.   Actresses–Fiction.   I. Title.
    PS3573.E39323D76 2004
    813'.54–dc22

                                                2003019343

Set in Bembo
Designed by Ginger Legato

Printed in the United States of America

PUBLISHER'S NOTE
This book is a work of fiction. Names, characters, places, and incidents either are the product of the author's imagination or are used fictitiously, and any resemblance to actual persons, living or dead, business establishments, events, or locales is entirely coincidental.

To my parents,
Jerry and Sheron Weiner,
for everything

ACKNOWLEDGMENTS

The author wishes to thank:

Paul Bresnick for optimism and savvy.
Doug Grad for a simpatico edit and a shared vision.
Tom Lutz for a central, defining insight.
Debbie Shulins for timely worrying and encouragement.
Ellen Tien for great notes and a crucially validating first reading.
Marsha Weiner for enthusiasm, suggestions, and love.
Laurie Winer for good ideas and an irreplaceable discussion.
David Yazbek for friendship, help, and knowing commentary.
Steve Zipperstein for legal smarts and consultation.

. . . and especially Barbara Davilman, for faith, empathy, thoughts, laughs, recommendations, alternate takes, and other things to which mere "Acknowledgments" can't do justice.

"People are always doing ridiculous things."

Ross Macdonald, *The Goodbye Look*

"This is the end of a perfect day, Jeeves. What's that thing of yours about larks?"

"Sir?"

"And, I rather think, snails."

"Oh, yes, sir. 'The year's at the spring, the day's at the morn, morning's at seven, the hillside's dew-pearled—' "

"But the larks, Jeeves? The snails? I'm pretty sure larks and snails entered into it."

"I am coming to the larks and snails, sir. 'The lark's on the wing, the snail's on the thorn—' "

"Now you're talking. And the tab line?"

" 'God's in His heaven, all's right with the world.' "

"That's it in a nutshell. I couldn't have put it better myself. And yet, Jeeves, there is just one thing. I do wish you would give me the inside facts about Eulalie."

P. G. Wodehouse, *The Code of the Woosters*

ONE

"Mr. Ingalls!" She was a tall skirt, maybe five eight, a nurse with long brown hair clipped up in the back and big brown eyes that had seen things. She came into the room and delivered a provokingly amused smile. "You're awake!"

"As never before, doll."

" 'Doll'? That's a first." She picked up a control and pushed a button, and the world held its breath while we waited for the bed to raise me up to a sitting position, halfway between bedtime reading and sleepy-time lights out. She held up a nasty-looking probe cabled to a digital display. "Open."

I played ball. She placed the business end of the item under my tongue and things threatened to get intimate. Then the technology beeped and the threat passed. She took it out. "Normal. Good." From a hanging apparatus on the wall nearby she swung a serious-looking rubber hose attached to a squeeze bulb. "Let's check your blood pressure."

I pulled back my sleeve. Sit-up bed, nurse, blood pressure: I made the place for a hospital. The thought brought a laugh. I must have been working a tough case. As she velcroed the cuff around my upper arm and pumped it tight, I said, "Maybe one day I can squeeze you back, sugar."

She smirked. "Aren't we frisky for a man who came in unconscious. . . ." She let the air gasp out and eyed the twitching gauge and checked her watch. "Excellent. The patient will live."

"Mr. Ingalls?"

In the doorway stood a slim Japanese woman in a doctor's lab coat. She had short dark hair, and her face was dominated by a pair of square, black, strictly business eyeglasses that make a woman look good when they come off. She carried one of those boxy clipboards that held a sheaf of pages. She floated over to the bed with that innate grace that all Asian women have, except for the clumsy ones. "How do you feel?"

"I could go a few rounds with Jersey Joe and not disgrace myself."

"Um . . . I'm sorry. Is that good?"

"That's tip-top, Doc. How long have I been here?"

"Two days." She skimmed some papers in the clipboard, frowning. "Mr. Ingalls, we did a comprehensive diagnostic EEG and got some interesting results. . . . do you feel up to talking with Dr. Gordon again?"

"Again?"

"He spoke to you yesterday. Don't you remember?"

"Lady, I can't recall anything I remember at this point. Not even the case that brought me here."

She glanced at the charts again and muttered, "Well, he said you might not. . . ." She flipped through some pages while the nurse lingered off to the side. "Dr. Gordon is our chief neuropathologist. He spoke with you and then took those readings— they can get very specific measurements from all over the brain, and they don't even have to shave your head. In any case, the way

Dr. Gordon interprets the data"—she fixed me with a full-disclosure stare, right through the big specs—"certain functions of your brain seem to have . . . migrated. Everything, um, 'works,' but some centers of function are in different places than they should be. Dr. Gordon wants to keep you here and administer a series of tests. But you would have to submit to these tests voluntarily. We can't compel you to take them."

That got my attention. "You mean I can go?"

"I'm afraid so." She looked rueful, as though the medicine gods had dealt from the bottom and busted her nice pending flush. "Your vital signs are all fine. Physically you are in very good health." She got up. "Let me get Dr. Gordon and he can explain it." The thought reminded her of something. "Oh. There are two men out there waiting to see you. Should I send them in?"

I laughed. I do that. "Depends, angel. Not if they're hard boys on assignment to play stickball with my skull."

"I'm sorry?"

"Sure, send them in. The more the merrier."

"Did you say 'angel'? I think I like that."

"Don't encourage him," the nurse said. And we laughed and laughed, and shared a merry moment, as though everything was a joke, and this was a house of healing, and Death wasn't out there in the solarium, paging through *Prevention* and waiting for his next client.

The gals dusted and I took stock. Whatever had put me in here, I felt fine. In fact, I felt more than fine. I felt new.

After a couple of whispers in the hall two men entered. One was around thirty, in black jeans and a thin sweatshirt with the logo of Squirt soda. He had longish hair, pale skin, and a wispy moustache that couldn't decide if it was romantic or just tired.

"Peter. Jeez. How do you feel?"

"Like a new penny, friend," I said. "P.S. Do I know you?"

He looked put-upon and answered acidly, "Yeah. I'm Nikola Tesla."

"Nick, a pleasure."

"Come on. Seriously. Leonard told me to come here and check on you."

"You may have the wrong room, Nick—"

"Stop it, Peter. It's Louis."

"Louis, Nick—let's make a decision. Then all we need is for me to know who Leonard is."

"Mr. Peter Ingalls!"

The second mug stepped forward. He was in his thirties, thickset in a decent gray suit, clean-shaven, with thinning hair and a wide, dissatisfied mouth and an air of annoyance. He made the mean mouth smile. "My name is Jason Burnick. I'm with the legal firm of Stanley, Fleischman, and Korn. We represent your employer, Seaside Books."

"Should I take notes, Burnick, or is this all covered in the *Playbill?*"

He flashed a courtesy smile. "I'm glad you can make jokes, Mr. Ingalls. It shows your recovery is complete." Before I could reply, he hoisted a briefcase onto the nearby rollable sickbed table, popped it open, and pulled out a two-page document and a business envelope. Then he shut the briefcase. "I won't take up any more of your time. I'm authorized to present you with this check in compensation for your injuries." He handed me the envelope.

"Peter," Louis said, "you might want to have someone look at that before you accept it."

"Relax, friend." I opened the envelope and extracted the contents, which proved to be a check made out to Mr. Peter Ingalls for a handsome sum of many dollars and no cents. I looked at the lawyer. "This could come in handy around Christmas time," I said. "What month is it now?"

"April."

"Close enough." I slid the check back into the envelope and gently placed it on my lap. "What else have we got?"

He handed me the document. "Just this release. Your signature here"—he flipped to the second page and showed me the little yellow and red SIGN HERE flag—"and I'm out of your hair and you're on your way to the bank."

I scanned the first page and caught the salient points. By accepting the above-referenced sum I absolved Seaside Books, Inc., and their issue and assigns and the rest of the human race, of all further liability for all injuries physical, psychological, and emotional, as currently diagnosed or to be diagnosed in the future, and so on and so on. "Whatever boilerplate your client needs, Burnick," I said. "And thank him for me. This is a bit more than my usual fee. Tell him I'm glad to be of service."

"Sir, uh . . ." He stopped and offered a polite little grin. "Sorry. That's funny. So yes, if you'll just sign the document . . ."

"Peter, are you sure you're okay?" Louis looked puzzled. "This isn't a fee. And what happened to you had nothing to do with being of service to Leonard and the store."

"We're all men of the world, aren't we, Louis? Then let's act like it." I looked at the lawyer. "If you've got a pen, Burnick, we can put this to bed. Meanwhile, whatever I did that made your client so happy, I hope he won't keep it a secret. I get most of my business through referrals."

The mouthpiece flashed a ballpoint like a bee presenting its stinger. I started to reach for it, but the young man in the Squirt sweat shirt intervened. "Wait—Peter, you do know that you got a pretty bad crack on the head, right? I mean, that's why you're here. Right?"

"If you say so, Lou," I said.

"It's not what I say. It's what happened. You suffered, like, a, a severe trauma to your head!"

I absorbed this and then looked at the lawyer. "That's a hell of a story," I said. "Maybe you can option it to the pictures."

"Well." Burnick smiled. "But it's hardly complete. The issue of exactly how the accident occurred was never resolved. We stipulate a certain percentage of culpability, to be sure. But I must tell you, I've polled the relevant witnesses who were present at the scene—"

In other words, he was saying what he was supposed to say. I gave one of my knowing nods and waved him quiet. Then I spoke to Louis, who didn't know whether to glower off to the side or just blow. "Listen, Lou," I said gently. "Let's all find the same key so we can sing together nice and sweet. I'm a private investigator—"

"What? That's nuts! You work in the bookstore!"

"—and I just did some confidential work for Mr. Burnick's client—"

"—and, no, and you met this woman—"

"And for some reason this work ended up with yours truly in the care of those pretty ladies out there."

"And you had this book—"

"And all this chatter about bookstores and culpability is a cute little cover story for your boss, and for Burnick's firm to hand out to the cops and the hospital and the press and the insurance boys, all the various parties who just need something to fill in their forms with so they can punch out and go home." I looked at the lawyer. "Right?"

He started to reply, then just winked and offered the pen again. I took it and signed the paper. He pulled a duplicate out of the briefcase. "This one's for you. We'll mail it back once it's been executed."

I inked that one, too, and handed it over. Burnick shoved the documents into his briefcase and snapped it shut with the crisp, efficient moves of a man who lives for signatures. "Thank you, Mr. Ingalls." He turned and left. He seemed to be in a hurry. Lawyers: when you bill by the hour, you give time a whip—and then wonder why you're covered with scars at the end of the day.

Burnick's exit changed the atmosphere and signaled that school was out. I put the check on the nightstand and began to get out of bed. Young Louis sent up a flare. "What are you doing?"

"Getting ready to blow, kid." My clothes were folded neatly on a nearby chair. I untied the hospital gown, pulled it off, and tossed it onto the rumpled sheet.

"The doctor said you had some tests to take."

As I climbed into my trousers I said, "She also said I was 1-A and cleared for takeoff." I shrugged into my shirt, then held up the insurance check in its envelope and, with ostentatious care, folded it in half and slid it into my shirt pocket. "Besides, when someone gives you one of these, you don't wait around for tests. You put it in the coffers before they change their mind."

"Jesus Christ, Peter, you really have gone nuts." Louis threw up his hands. "Which . . . okay, fine. I'm not getting involved in it. I gotta get back to work. Good luck with whatever." He started to add something, decided the hell with it, and bounced.

I was halfway down the corridor when I ran into the nice lady doctor and a tall, sharp-faced gent in a lab coat with a name tag reading "Dr. Robert Gordon." They weren't crazy about the prospect of my checking out but admitted there wasn't much they could do about it. Gordon gave me his card and urged me to get in touch if I experienced any "symptoms." I said sure. I kept to myself the observation that symptoms are all we've got.

The client's insurance would be billed for the tab, so I signed a few papers and a half-hour later I was on the street. When a cabby answered my hail I couldn't quite remember my new address, but the hospital must have gotten it off something in my wallet, because the receipt had it printed loud and clear. The keys in my pocket fit the front door and the apartment door, which is what they're supposed to do.

Inside, the place wasn't quite the way I remembered it and now, for some reason, it seemed inadequate. In fact, I decided, it was time to stop working out of my home. I decided I would need not only a proper office, but a new wardrobe, too.

I didn't mind. I had a five-figure check and wasn't afraid to use it. I was ready to get on with my life.

And one more thing. I would need a secretary.

PROLOGUE

On a Tuesday morning at around eleven o'clock, Maria Lopez, a chambermaid at the Hotel Urbane, a fading tourist rack off Broadway in the Nineties, pushed her service cart down the corridor toward Room 1214. She had a lot of things on her mind. Yeah, I know. Who doesn't? And maybe that's my point. We've all got things on our mind. We've all got service carts to push. We're all chambermaids in this hotel called Life, shuffling down the corridor as people all around us, sooner or later, but inevitably, Check Out.

The Urbane is a second-class establishment, which is tour guide code for "it could be worse." The hallways smell just as much of fruity air freshener as stale cigarette smoke; the windows are grimy, yeah, but they still open and close; and the plates in the coffee shop downstairs, under the tired tunas on toast and the enervated BLTs, are clean enough to eat off of.

The clientele are mainly tourists and transients—Europeans on bargain tours, students on a budget, business travelers who had flown coach and paid for it themselves. They all have one thing in common.

They're all from out of town.

That's why you had to wonder what a young woman named Olivia Cartwright had been doing there when she climbed the few steps up into the small, stifling lobby of the Urbane the day before. God knows who or what she expected to find. Yeah, sure. God knows. Think He's talking? Grow up.

Olivia was a class skirt, with the flexible standards of a romantic. She wasn't above staying in a "colorful" "budget" cave like the Urbane on a vacation to Italy or France, but the idea of actually sleeping in such a place here, in her native New York, was repulsive. It wasn't "nice." There was no complimentary letterhead stationery in the writing desks, no little bottles of shampoo and conditioner in the bathroom, no ten-sheet memo pad and cheapo ballpoint near the phone on the nightstand. Every drawer was empty, every bed covered with a spread of exhausted polyester, every faucet a source of banshee wails and air-hammer percussion. Everything was bare bones, past its prime, and tired, because what did you expect for eighty bucks a night?

But then, Olivia wasn't a guest at the hotel. She'd come to see someone who was.

Maria Lopez, meanwhile, would have felt privileged to stay in such a place, In fact, she felt lucky to work there. She knocked on the door of 1214 and called, "Housekeeping."

There was no reply. A DO NOT DISTURB sign hung on the knob, as it had all day Monday, but now its legitimacy had expired. Checkout time was noon, when the current guest's booking ran out. The room was reserved and had to be ready for a new arrival by three. Maria was by nature a patient broad, so it was with a rhythm of unhurried routine that she knocked again. "Housekeeping."

Maybe the guest had already checked out. Or was away at breakfast or business or shopping, or in the shower, or zoned out

chanting some one-word droning yoga-tune while tying himself
into a pretzel. Or just still asleep. In any case Maria had her job
to do. She produced a master key, fit it in the lock, and opened
the old, heavy metal door. She went into gloom and thick atmosphere, moving through the narrow passage between the bathroom and the closet that fed into the room itself. The place
smelled awful, of excrement and terror. The thick window
drapes were still shut from the night before. But the spill of day-
light angling in through the window above and below them, and
the wan light from the corridor, were sufficient to disclose the
reason why no one had answered her knock.

For one thing, the guest had indeed checked out—or skipped,
luggage and all. Oddly, the bed had either been remade with fa-
natical chambermaid exactitude, or it had not been slept in. And
while there was, in fact, an individual in the room, it was Olivia
Cartwright, and she was in no condition to open any doors, ever
again. She had been strangled.

She lay slumped on the floor between the bed and the lowboy
dressers. She was fully clothed. The body had voided itself before
the moment of death—something they traditionally haven't
shown in strangulation scenes on TV and in movies, although
now, with the amazing developments in computer graphics, that
should no longer be a problem.

Maria called the desk, the desk called the cops, and the M.E.
put the time of death at between twenty-four and thirty-six
hours previous. There were precious few clues. If the young
woman had had a purse, it was gone. It would take a canvass of
cab drop-offs and pickup locations, plus some plodding, patient
inquiries around the office buildings in the area, to enable them
to ID the corpse. There was no sign of sexual assault. The room
turned out to have been registered to one Robert Jones of
Columbus, Ohio. Mr. Jones had paid cash. The desk clerk

thought he remembered Jones as a pleasant man with a mous-tache and an Indians baseball cap. The whole thing was puzzling and mysterious and grossly illegal, but one thing was clear: Olivia Cartwright was quite dead.

Nice, eh? "Quite dead." Very elegant. Very British. And a lit-tle affected, coming from some. But not from me. My name's In-galls. Pete Ingalls, P.I. Some people think the P.I. stands for Pete Ingalls. Actually it stands for private investigator. That's what I am. It's what I do. And I couldn't be affected if I tried.

Not that I haven't. Believe me, I have tried, like crazy. "Go immediately to hell." "Kindly jump in a lake." "Drop quite dead." I've said them all, often when sober, but somehow I never get the boost in tone and the upgrade of respect I'm after. Not fair? A raw deal? Cue the string section and pass the Kleenex. Meanwhile, I'll be over here, not kidding myself.

I'd be involved in this case of the dead frail at the Hotel Ur-bane. And it would change my life forever. But that was okay. My life had already been changed forever, over and over again, from the day I was born. So yeah, my life would be changed forever. It was business as usual.

TWO

It started, the way it often does, with a phone call. That's why I love this business. You don't have to go looking for trouble. It finds you and calls you on the telephone. It asks to speak to you personally. It wants to thank you for being such a good customer in the past. And to show its appreciation, it wants to make you a special offer. It wants to offer you more trouble.

"Detective offices, how may I direct your call?"

The skirt I'd hired answered quickly, but the greeting was all wrong. Sure, I could understand her blowing smoke down the line—there was only one office, just as there was only one detective, but it couldn't hurt to make the operation sound big and teeming and corporate.

Still, she was having problems with the preferred greeting. I went to my office doorway and looked out into the reception area. I caught the gal's eye and said, "I got it, sugar."

"Wait a minute." She sat back. The hand with the receiver fell into her lap in a gesture somewhere between I-give-up and you-must-be-kidding. Apparently someone had said something provocative. " 'Sugar'?"

"It's an expression." I hustled back to my desk and grabbed the extension. "Ingalls."

The voice that came back was throaty for a woman, deep and husky and knowing. "Is this, um, Pete Ingalls, P.I.?"

"The same."

"Mr. Ingalls, I saw your ad, and I think I may have a job for you."

"I'm all ears, Miss . . . ? Or should it be Ms.? Or Mrs.?" Call me a P.C. sap, but I respect women's preferences in the way they want to be addressed. After ten million years of patriarchy, I happen to think dolls are entitled to a few little symbolic courtesies.

"Ms. Vroman. It doesn't matter." She laughed. It was an empty laugh, a mirthless laugh, as though at something deeply not funny. I could relate. "The thing is, I can't come to your office. I'm on a tight schedule. Could we meet at a restaurant for dinner tonight?"

"Just tell me where and when. I'll be the one looking discreet."

She gave me the specs and we set it for eight. Then I went back up front, where my receptionist could be found snapping her way in disgust through the pages of *Back Stage*.

"Look, doll, when you grab the horn—"

"Jesus Christ. 'Doll'?"

"Just—"

" 'Grab the horn'?"

"—please say 'Pete Ingalls, P.I.' Got it?"

She put the paper down. It felt like a small triumph. "What did I say?"

"Detective offices."

She hit me with a poker pan and a distinct lack of remorse. "That's what they say at law firms. Instead of having to spit out all those names."

"This isn't a law firm. And there's only one name."

I.e., mine. Hers was Stephanie Constantino. Mark her down as a medium-tall looker from Chi-town. She was twenty-six, slim, with nice curves and nothing too underdeveloped or overwhelming up front. Her face was not half bad, with strong cheekbones and a straight nose and a well-sculpted chin. Her eyes were wide apart and green, maybe hazel, one of those nonblue, nonbrown colors. The face was framed by short, straight reddish brown hair that stopped at a nice, lean jawline with lots of shine and bounce and manageability. The hair, not the jaw. No, the jaw and the mouth that came with it already gave signs of lacking manageability, at least by yours truly.

Stephanie now composed herself as though making an effort. "Fine. 'Pete Ingalls, blah blah blah.'" She pointed at me. "But you're kidding with that suit, right?"

Oh, yeah. She also had opinions.

Which is generally jake with me. I'm not going to bust a clavicle patting myself on the back for it, but it so happens I approve of women having ideas of their own. When you consider the fact that women are the only minority that outnumber men, it makes the whole package easier to swallow.

I'd put an ad in the *Village Voice* for a part-time receptionist and she'd shown up before the press run was dry. Turned out she was an actress—yeah, I know: who isn't?—in need of a day gig between classes, auditions, and nervous breakdowns. Or is it nervous breaks-down? Court martial, attorney general, time immemorial, Nutty Buddy—some words are like people. They get perverse in the plural. From times immemorial, after courts martial, attorneys general traditionally enjoy Nuttys Buddy and have nervous breaks-down.

"I'm dead serious," I said. "It so happens I take great care with my appearance. And everything else, angel."

"Um . . . Pete."

There it was. That "um." I'd been hearing it all my life. The party of the second part was about to pop some frequently asked questions. "What? You're on the air, kid."

"Seriously. What's up with you?"

"Come again, doll?"

"That. The way you talk. With all these 'dolls' and 'angels.' And these zoot-suity clothes. And the hat. This whole hard-boiled thing. Are you serious or what?"

"Yeah, people ask me that all the time."

"So? What do you say?"

"I say I'm just a guy trying to stay clean in a dirty world. I'm a professional, and I wear what the professionals wear. Anybody who doesn't like it can send an e-mail to their congressman."

Stephanie suddenly looked sly. She said, one con artist to another, "Come on, Pete. You can tell me. This is a put-on, right?"

"Lady," I said, "you're looking at a man who doesn't do put-ons. Why? In self-defense. Because life as we know it is a put-on. The more you learn about the world, the more they change it into something else while you're in bed reading *The New Yorker*. The more convinced you are that you know the score, the bigger the pie they're baking to hit you in the face with out on the street. All a mug can do in a world like this is be as deliberate as possible. In everything. Which brings us to the present conversation."

She widened her eyes and recoiled a bit, and I thought, Well, well, Ingalls. Maybe you touched a nerve. Maybe this slice of the boss's worldview hit home. Then she said, "Wow. You're even more fucked up than I am." She went quiet and looked away and started chewing on her lip.

Speaking of which, it was a nice lip. I know guys that wouldn't have minded chewing on it themselves. As for me, let's leave it at: I wasn't in the market. So I repeated, "Just answer the phone in the specified manner and we'll get along like hot dogs and mustard. And clean up the language."

She stopped chewing and shrugged. "Fine. Whatever. Who was the call?"

"A client. She saw the ad."

"No shit."

"Please?"

"Sorry. So. The ad! Fuck me. . . ."

I'd written it myself two weeks before:

GUMSHOE...DICK...SHAMUS...FLATFOOT

Put Them All Together, They Spell

PETER INGALLS, P.I.

A Private Investigator

For when you need that Certain Someone
To Find Out *or* **Do** *Those*
Certain Things
• NYC •

Plus phone, e-mail, and street address. It took hours of hard labor at the keyboard to achieve the right tone. I was proud of the ad.

Then, this morning, when Stephanie arrived for her debut at the salt mines, I showed it to her and solicited a sincere evaluation.

"It's . . . fine," she said.

"Fine?" I scanned the ad. There were no typos. The layout was to spec. It was perfect. "It's better than fine. It's highly clever and media-savvy."

She studied it. "I wouldn't call it media-savvy, but it's fine. Totally adequate."

"'Fine,' 'adequate'—correct me if I'm wrong, angel, but this is the lingo of euphemism and I-hate-it."

"Just check with me next time before you send in copy. Okay?" Then she added, "I mean, no offense."

Call me overly sensitive, but I find that wounding. People say the worst things they can think of—"you talk funny," "you're insane," "your ad's not media-savvy"—and then try to salve the hurt with "no offense." Memo to the world: "no offense" isn't good enough.

Now, though, the ad had paid off and Ingalls graciously declined to twist the knife. Instead I merely said, "Yeah, it worked. So give me a little credit, and answer the phone like I asked you to."

Maybe I was coming down a bit hard on the kid. But she just shrugged. "Sure, Pete. No problem." Women: their fantastic resiliency, their unexpected guts, their stealth moxie. They'll outlive us all.

The phone rang. My assistant picked it up, her eyes unblinkingly on mine. "Pete Ingalls, P.I."

I gave her the thumbs-up. Ms. Stephanie Constantino just might work out.

The restaurant Ms. Vroman had selected was called Buggsy's Bistro. Loud wasn't the word. Or maybe it was. You'd never know because you couldn't hear a thing. The place was about the size of a rec room, with a tiled floor and hard walls; a man could go deaf just sitting there eating an olive. The chatter of the patrons, the clang and hiss and splash from the cook, the relentless tinny yammer of the utterly superfluous music on the PA—the noise level was just below that of a boiler factory. Now, like you, I've never set foot in a boiler factory. I have my doubts as to whether they exist anymore and I certainly have no idea what one sounds like. So let's just say they're loud.

I wore a tan gabardine double-breasted suit and a snap-brim fedora, a white shirt and maroon rep tie, and dark brown socks and brown wing tips. But then, I always do. Two harried young women in white aprons hustled in and out from behind the tiny bar, while a beefy guy in whites and a headband slammed large frying pans and vat-sized pots on the constantly burning stove top in the efficiency-sized kitchen in the back. The place was too small for conducting a decent Ping-Pong game. Still, the customers seemed happy and the joint was full.

I looked around for a single dame and finally spotted her in a corner. It wasn't easy; the place was dark, the only sources of light being a couple of dim flood bulbs above and a single small candle on each table. I eased through the congestion of people and chairs until I reached my client in the rear.

She extended a hand. "Mr. Ingalls. Celeste Vroman." Her shake was firm. Ms. Celeste Vroman was a solid woman in her forties with a big-boned, regal-nosed sort of face. She had curled, set, jet-black hair and wore a black long-sleeved mock turtleneck sweater over whatever else she was wearing that the table obscured. I sat.

"Thanks for meeting me," she said, and with a girlish flutter let her lightly opened hand come to rest on her throat. "I've been fairly busy lately." We traded the usual small talk. Turned out she lived in Atlantic City but spent a lot of time up here. When I asked what she did for a living, she said, "I'm a marketing consultant. I mainly work out of my home."

Then I asked how I could be of service. She opened a purse and withdrew a color snapshot. "I want you to find this man."

I took a look: In the snap, a short, trim gent in his mid-forties wearing a plain white T-shirt and khaki shorts, no socks, and sneakers, stood squinting in the sun. The pic had been taken on a boardwalk, presumably in Atlantic City, with the beach and ocean in the background. The man was smiling. He was clean-shaven, balding, and had the kind of focused attentiveness that intelligent people can't lose and stupid people can't fake. "His name is Jeffrey Litman," she said. "I've been having an affair with him."

"By 'affair,' do you mean—?"

"I mean he's married, and not to me." She smiled. "I hope this doesn't offend you."

"Nothing offends me," I said. Then I realized it wasn't true. A lot of things offend me. I decided not to go into it and pulled out a pack of Princeton Indigos. "Cigarette?"

"Well, it's not allowed in here. And no, thank you, I don't smoke."

"Smart girl. Neither do I." I put the pack away and examined the picture. "Who took this? You?" She nodded. "When?"

"A few months ago. Jeffrey and I have been seeing each other for about six months. Usually in Atlantic City but sometimes here, too. We met at a casino. He'd become fond of gambling, and we got to talking over a blackjack table." She shut her purse. "You can keep it."

I took out a pad and pen from my inner jacket pocket. "What's he do for a living?"

"He's an attorney. Actually he's a partner at Hoffman, Ratner, Litman, and John."

I laughed. "What's John's problem? Doesn't he have a last name?"

"John is his last name. Wendell John."

People kill me. Nine months to think about it, then they get to the delivery room. The doc holds up Baby. It's a boy. Mom turns to Hubby, suggests that since his last name is a first name, let's make his first name a last name. Think I expressed this observation to Ms. Vroman? Think again. Ingalls stands for nothing if not self-control. Instead, I asked how long he'd been missing.

"About a week. He doesn't call, and when I call him at the office they say he isn't in."

"Do they say he's missing? 'Not in' doesn't mean 'disappeared.'"

"They don't know where he is."

Something occurred to me. It happens a lot and I'm used to it. "Why don't you try speaking to his wife? You can pretend you're someone else. You know—'Hi, Mrs. Litman? I'm just some telemarketer, so is Jeffrey there?'"

She forced a wan smile. "I don't dare go near his wife." She looked at her watch. We hadn't ordered our food yet. "What do you charge, Mr. Ingalls? And should I pay you a retainer?"

I told her my rate was a hundred dollars a day plus expenses, that a retainer of three hundred would be nice, and that I'd need a phone number where I could reach her. She wrote a number on a slip of paper. "If I'm not there, you'll get voice mail. I'll return it pretty fast." She looked hopeful. "Then you'll take the job?"

"It's my job to take jobs, lady." She handed me the number, then wrote out a check as I asked, "Does Mr. Litman have any enemies that you know about? Someone who might wish him harm?"

She looked away and thought. I admired her profile, to the extent that I could see it. "I suppose all attorneys do," she said finally. "But he never spoke of anyone in particular."

I nodded. There was a delicate issue pending. I said, "You realize that I'll probably have to talk to his wife."

"Oh my God. No, you mustn't."

"It can hardly be avoided. But I can assure you that your identity will remain confidential."

"Promise me you won't speak to her unless all else fails. And that you'll check with me first."

"Fair enough."

"Good. And please start as soon as you can. I'm worried about Jeffrey." Then she looked at her watch and stood up. "Mr. Ingalls, I have an important appointment uptown. Please, order whatever you want and bill it to me. I am sorry." I rose and we shook hands. "Thank you."

I reached into my breast pocket and pulled out one of my business cards. I gave it to her. She looked at it without expression. Did it irk me? Yeah, it irked me. You want people to like your card. I swallowed it. "I'll be in touch, Ms. Vroman," I said. And she walked out of the restaurant into the night.

If I had only known then what I know now . . . well, nuts to that. The only people who knew then what they know now are clairvoyants and time travelers. The rest of us have to stagger along in the customary manner, finding out things the hard way, one rude awakening at a time.

Besides, I don't believe in "regrets." Life is hard enough in the present without having to compound the difficulty by looking to the past. Who was it who said "Be here now"? Some impatient, demanding bastard. Still, he had a point. Be here now, and if you can't be here now, be here as soon as you can. But leave your regrets at home.

THREE

The next morning featured a chat with a certain Catherine Flonger. The system worked. She phoned for an appointment, was greeted with "Pete Ingalls, P.I.," and showed up an hour later.

You might recognize the name. Mrs. Flonger, née Catherine Binney, was the second and current wife of Darius Flonger, the famously confrontational network newsman. Darius was renowned for his aggressiveness at White House press conferences and impromptu photo ops. He'd parlayed an unpleasant personality and a surplus of ego into a career of notoriety as the bad boy truth–teller, or at least truth–asker, on the beat. The fact that he never uncovered anything important seemed, to him, at least, like a debater's point for soreheads. Or so reviewers had alluded to regarding his best-selling memoir, *Query: Confessions of an Obnoxious Man*. In response, he'd published two more successful books, *Truth to Power: An Obnoxious Man Speaks with World Leaders*, and *Having a Nice Day: The Obnoxious Man's Secrets for a Happy Life*.

Then, last year, in an effort to goose their ratings, the network brought Flonger up from D.C. and installed him as a nightly commentator on their flagship newscast. Darius and spouse moved to the Apple, where hubby thrived and the missus was having problems.

I could hear it from my vantage point in the back room: Catherine, Darius Flonger's wife, was barely hanging on by her glossy, well-shaped nails. "Catherine Flonger to see Mr. Ingalls," she said as she entered. Then, "Is . . . could I trouble you for some bottled water? And perhaps a piece of fruit?"

Stephanie bristled. I could hear that in the back room, too. Like I said, she was an actress. She had waited her share of tables and probably thought that was all behind her now. "Excuse me? Fruit?"

The reply was chilly. "It's a reasonable request."

"Yeah. For a deli."

The visitor's voice tightened as though someone had adjusted it with a wrench. "Look, miss, I have had a very trying day—"

Stephanie pushed her chair back and got up. "Excuse me, please."

She appeared in my doorway in her chic-burglar outfit, black jeans and sleeveless black tank top. She rolled her eyes, pointed into her mouth with an index finger, and made with the gagging. Then, with vamp-heavy lids which brought out her cheekbones, she deadpanned, "Boss? A Ms. Flonger to see you."

"Aces, Miss Constantino. Show her in."

Catherine Flonger wore a charcoal gray business suit and black flat shoes and carried a briefcase. Her face was oval and shapely, under dark brown hair cut short in sweeps and waves. It was a nice face, with a high, smooth forehead and pale blue eyes under fine, arched eyebrows. Its nose was thin and straight, its mouth was narrow but not without a hint of sensuality. It was the kind of face you'd call an aristocratic face, if you were the kind of person who believed in an aristocracy of faces and went around gassing off about it. "Thank you," she said to Stephanie, and bestowed a wan smile.

"No problem." Constantino's smile was as phony as maitre d's laugh. "Would you like some water? Forget the fruit."

"Yes, please."

I motioned for her to sit, and we traded chitchat to get settled. "Flonger," I pondered. "What is that . . . Dutch?" I always say that. Nobody is ever Dutch, so the other party has to respond with some content and oomph.

"Flemish, actually," she said. Then she forced a brave little smile and said, "Does it matter?"

"You tell me."

"I like to think it does."

"You probably like a lot of things," I said. "If I know you."

"But you don't know me—"

"I said 'if.'"

Then Stephanie breezed in with a small bottle of water and a plastic tumbler, handed them to the client, and gave me a look as she left. The client poured the water and took a sip and made an effort to compose herself.

"You've heard of my husband?" She put the cup down and meshed her fingers into a solid wall and placed them on her leg, parade rest for a careful woman. "Darius Flonger, the network reporter?"

"Sure," I said. "I watch TV as much as the next guy." It seemed inadequate. I elaborated, "I'm not saying I watch what the next guy watches. I wouldn't know. I've never met the man."

"You mean my husband?"

"Him, yeah, or any other citizen I don't know."

"I'm sorry . . ." She frowned. Maybe we were going into places she would rather not have gone. Maybe in my own quiet way I was opening secret doors. "Are you telling me you've never met a man you didn't know?"

I leaned back in my chair and looked coolly amused. It's a look I work on, in a mirror, usually after shaving. It gets results. "Oh, I wouldn't say that, Catherine. May I call you Catherine?"

"I'd rather you didn't."

"I wouldn't say that, Mrs. Flonger. I think I might put it the other way around. I've never known a man I didn't meet."

She pressed her lips together. "I'm sure you mean something intelligible, Mr. Ingalls. I apologize if it escapes me. I've been under a great deal of stress. You see, I think my husband is having an affair."

I nodded. "What makes you say that?"

"The way he smells."

I took a moment to marvel at yet another aspect of this thing we call women—their sense of smell, the advanced, complex, mysterious naso-chemical ability they have to detect and discern scent, to be moved by it, to manipulate it, to care about it. Men are lucky if they can sniff out if dinner's ready or the house is on fire, but women have a sixth sense for fragrance.

Stephanie appeared in the doorway. "Mr. Ingalls? I'm sorry to interrupt. But I have a question about that FBI matter. It'll just take a moment."

I excused myself and joined my assistant out front. "What FBI matter?" I was peeved. "Nobody tells me anything."

"There isn't any." She spoke in an excited whisper. "But I heard what she said. It's very interesting! Let me come in and listen."

"Absolutely not. This is business."

"Come on. I'm into this kind of thing. I'll sit quietly and take notes."

"Nix it was and nix it is. Now do your job and let me do mine."

"Please?"

I silenced her with a look and rejoined Catherine Flonger, apologized for the interruption, and got back on track. "Now, where were we? . . . Oh. Yeah. Your husband. He doesn't smell right. You mean from perfume? He smells of another woman's fragrance?"

"No, I mean, he smells like he just took a shower."

"Is that . . . you know . . . bad?"

"No, of course not. Not per se." She blushed and looked away. "Forgive me, Mr. Ingalls—"

"Hey. Pete."

"Pete, forgive me; this is very difficult for me to discuss."

"Mrs. Flonger—"

"Please. Catherine."

I smiled. "Catherine—"

"No. I'm sorry. Mrs. Flonger."

"Fine, all right, Mrs. Flonger—"

"I'm sorry, Pete, I—"

"Mr. Ingalls."

"Yes, all right. Mr. Ingalls." She looked vexed. I didn't blame her. I probably looked vexed, too. Yeah, I know—so what? Outside there were eight million people looking vexed. Deal with it, I thought. She asked, "What were we talking about?"

"Your husband," I said. "The way he smells."

"Yes. Thank you. He smells like he's just showered when it's eight o'clock at night. After a whole day's work. He comes home at the end of the day, and he smells like he does when he leaves in the morning. That's unusual. And it . . . implies certain things."

I knew damn well what it implied. But in this business you

have to chew up the mundane appetizers before you can sink your teeth into the meat. "Maybe he goes to the gym during the day."

"Darius?" A faint smile played about her lips, got tired of playing, and went home. "Please. His idea of exercise is opening the wine."

I thought, looked around, gestured. "He's a big star. He must have a fancy office. With a shower. So he freshens up before he comes home."

From the outer room came a "hah!" We, two adults with self-control, ignored it.

"That's what I'm afraid of." Catherine Flonger sighed. "At the office, or somewhere else. But why?"

I shrugged. "For you."

Somebody in the outer room snorted, "Yeah, right." Somebody who sounded as though she needed a quick career-advancement tip. I excused myself and went to the reception room, shutting the office door behind me.

Constantino made no effort to look busy. She sat there as though expecting me, like a kid caught painting graffiti—apprehended but not all that sorry. "What?"

"I'm a professional," I said, "conducting an interview. You are my professional assistant. Your job is to sit here and field the horn. And not crack wise with helpful little value-judgment sound effects from the observation deck."

"Then let me sit in! Come on. She's a woman, I'm a woman—I understand her in a way that you can't!" She leaned in close and said softly, *entre nous*, "The guy's all showered and nice because he's fooling around on the side."

I didn't play back. "I think I can deduce that without your help."

"Okay, fine," she said. "But then, why?"

"Why what?"

"Why take a shower? It's so obvious. He *wants* to get caught."

I looked away. Somewhere outside a car horn honked. Lucky bastard—to be in a car, honking a horn, instead of here. "Thanks for your interest in our project," I said. "Now just shut up and pipe down or you're out."

She laughed. "You're going to *fire* me? Forget it! I'll quit!"

"That can be arranged."

"Yeah okay fine."

I went back into the office, where Catherine Flonger was gazing at the walls with the look of a woman who had suddenly found herself in a precinct detention cell. "I'm sorry, Mrs. Flonger," I said, sitting. "I was suggesting that your husband showers in order to freshen up before seeing you."

She gave me a look of something like pity. In fact, it was pity. And it was great. I like being pitied. I don't understand the standard beef about pity, where in a movie a guy will say, "I don't want your pity!" or some broad with an English accent will weep, "I'd rather die than be the subject of your pity." What gives? What's wrong with pity? People feel sorry for you, they treat you nice, they bring you a drink, they help with your problems. What's the catch? "Are you married, Mr. Ingalls?"

"No."

"Obviously. After twenty years of marriage, the notion of my husband taking time out of his day to freshen up for me is almost laughable."

"I notice you're not laughing."

She stood up, nervous as a virgin on her wedding night. Or at least as nervous as virgins used to be on their wedding nights, back when brides were still virgins. "No, Mr. Ingalls, I'm not laughing." She started wandering around the office, speaking as much to herself as to me. "Half the time these days, I'm crying.

My life is falling apart. We both know what I'm saying. I'm convinced my husband is having an affair with another woman and is taking showers to conceal it." She walked back toward me. "And that's something he's never done before."

"Had an affair?" I tried another angle. "Taken a shower?"

"Tried to conceal it." The phone rang. I ignored it. "Look, Darius is a big star with a huge ego," she said. "He's had flings. And somehow I've managed to live with it. Either he's been right when he's said they mean nothing, or I've just gotten used to them. . . ." She sighed and shook her head, perhaps in a brief reverie of disgust or defeat. Then she sat back down and said, her eyes seeking out mine, "But he's never acted this secretively before." Her expression started to melt into hopeless misery and her cool blue eyes swam with tears. "He may actually leave me. And it's not fair."

The phone rang again, and I wondered where Stephanie was, and why she wasn't picking up. I said, "No, it's not fair. But love has nothing to do with fair. It wasn't 'fair' that he loved you in the first place. Assuming he did. But let's say he did."

She looked at me with loathing. Or so I thought. Believe me, it hasn't happened so much that I can instantly recognize it when it happens and think, Oh, look, there's loathing again. Then she composed her hands into that wall of fingers and said, "Well, Mr. Ingalls, I suppose I have to let you talk to me that way."

"What way is that, Mrs. Flonger? In terms of a little thing called 'the truth'?"

"You know, I hesitated before coming here." She looked away. They always look away. Then they look back. She looked back. "I suppose I was worried about telling you all my secrets. I guess I thought it might be humiliating."

"Thanks, but being humiliated's part of the job. I can deal with it."

"No, I meant humiliating to me." She laughed. It was a bad laugh, a laugh that tried to fend off panic by pretending that everything was terribly, terribly funny. "Then again, some days it feels like I pour my heart out to every stranger I meet. I tell people on line at Starbucks that my husband is leaving me, but I can't discuss it with my therapist. I live in absolute fear of that bitch. Isn't that terrible? But she's so . . . judgmental."

The phone rang yet again. I said, "Excuse me," grabbed the receiver, and snapped, "Pete Ingalls, P.I."

"Pete, come on! Let me come in. Please!"

I slammed the phone down and said, "Meanwhile, I'm saying, it's not fair, what may be going on with your husband. But it happens."

I was shocked at the vehemence with which she replied, "Well, it's not supposed to happen to me! I am not the kind of person these sleazy tragedies happen to! I've done all the right things!" She looked away, jaw working, pinioned between outrage and despair.

I said, "All the 'right' things? And what things would they be?"

"I've been smart," she said, staring at the floor, eyes burning. "I've been *aware*. I haven't been naive or idealistic or a fool. I got good grades and went to Vassar. I got a good job and married a TV star who makes millions. My daughter will graduate Princeton next year. I keep in shape. I'm still attractive. I've thrown dinner parties for twenty, and I've written book reviews for the *Washington Post*. I have done everything I'm supposed to do! And it's all falling apart!"

She started weeping. The wall of fingers came apart and her hands clutched, her nose ran, she sobbed. I stared dispassionately, unaffected by the fact that I didn't know what to do. Then Stephanie appeared out of nowhere with a box of tissues, gently placed it beside her on the desk, and floated away.

"I don't know what that means, everything you're supposed to do," I said.

"Of course you don't!" She grabbed at the tissues and blew her nose. "Look at you! Look at this place!"

"Hey!" The cry came from the doorway: Stephanie was standing there, glaring. "There is no need to insult the detective. He's a professional conducting an interview. You're the one who's a fucking mess."

"Stephanie?" I said.

She recoiled a little, stung, then raised her petite nose an indignant inch and said, coolly, "Sorry, Mr. Ingalls. Shall I remain, in case I'm needed?"

"That won't be necessary."

"It's no trouble."

"Kindly dust, with my thanks."

"As you wish, sir." She winked at me, spun in a way that made her hair shimmer, and bounced, closing the door behind her.

"I'm sorry, Mrs. Flonger," I said. "She just started working here and is arguably somewhat mouthy."

"No, she's right. Look at me. You're all nice and calm, doing your job, and I'm ready to collapse. And"—she spread her hands, taking in the office—"this is exactly what I had in mind."

"Meaning—?"

"I wanted a private investigator who I was sure none of our friends would know. Someone completely out of our social circle."

"I see."

"We know a lot of people with money and taste and great intelligence and refinement and sophistication. I wanted someone far removed from all that."

"Well"—I indulged in a little smile—"I like to think—"

"So, obviously, I did this right." She gave a bitter smirk. "It's everything else I've been wrong about." Grimly, with tight-lipped purpose, she opened her briefcase. "I want you to follow Darius and get me proof of whether he's seeing someone. I mean, of course he is. I want to see who." She withdrew a manila envelope. "Here's a picture in case you need it." From the envelope she extracted an eight-by-ten black-and-white glossy photograph of Darius Flonger in a smart dark suit. The photo showed him from the knot in his tie on up, smiling genially against a neutral, flattering backdrop. It was the standard-issue head shot put out by the PR department, complete with the network logo and the man's name in formal print, the kind of thing you see on deli walls and at book signings. This one had something handwritten on it: "To my good friend Pete Ingalls. Best wishes, Darius Flonger."

I was baffled. I looked at the wife. "You mean, I do know him?"

"I needed a picture, so I said you were a friend of a friend who wanted an autograph. Don't take it personally." She took out a checkbook and sniffled. "When can you start?"

I handed her my card. She looked at it and sighed.

When I returned from lunch, Stephanie was tapping away at the computer. She immediately made the program get small so I couldn't see what it was. I pointed to the screen. "Ms. Constantino. We don't keep secrets in this office. We uncover them. What gives?"

"Oh, all right . . ." She brought it up: on some arty layout program she had assembled my name, address, and phone numbers in a little letterhead configuration. "I'm designing you a new card."

"I already have a card."

"I know." She held one up and made a face. "But, I mean, ick. It so sucks."

I headed to my desk in the back. "I don't need a new card."

"Yes, you do!" She followed me back. "Come on. At no extra charge."

"Easy, sugar. There are human feelings at stake. I designed this myself."

"I know. That's why it's so bad. You're not a designer."

"Neither are you."

"I'm artistic. I designed posters for the drama club. I mean Christ, Pete. A box of cards costs thirty bucks, big fucking deal."

"Please? Now forget it. Back to work. Answer the phone."

I checked my e-mail, skimmed the paper, and then hit the street. I grabbed a subway uptown to the address Celeste Vroman had given me, to the offices of Hoffman, Ratner, Litman, and John. I had Jeffrey Litman's photo in my pocket and a nice sharp sense of moment and occasion.

I had decided there were two tacks I could take to find the missing attorney: through home or through work. I nixed kicking it off with the wife. First, for obvious reasons: my client was the Other Woman. I couldn't very well dance into Litman's home and tell the missus I was searching for her husband on behalf of a person who chose to remain anonymous. Besides, a man goes missing for many reasons, not all of them personal. In any case, it was my responsibility to, if at all possible, find Litman without revealing either myself or my client to his wife.

So I began at the workplace.

I walked into a tall building on Lex in the Forties and read on the address board that the law firm occupied the third and fourth floors. I took the elevator to Reception on Four. When the doors opened I had to dodge and weave around an obstacle course of overturned desks on dollies and small citadels of cartons marked HRLJ—FILES. The gal at the reception kiosk smiled with mechanical dependability.

I held back. I hit the brakes. On-the-job jitters? Performance anxiety? Try due diligence and sensible professional caution. Litman might be missing, and his colleagues might have their own sheaf of reasons for wanting him found . . . but they'd have a larger stake in maintaining a facade of normalcy, which is not really a word, but people use it instead of normality. So delicacy, or delicality, was called for. This office full of savvy pros would be well versed in the fine art of giving a mug like Ingalls the big stall and the endless runaround. Getting face time with a person who knew where Litman might be would prove as difficult as actually finding the man, a project requiring as much finesse as persistence. I steeled myself for some tricky maneuvering.

The receptionist, a cute youngster in a big black blouse, a tiny gold hoop through her right ear, perked, "Hi," as I eased up to her command post. I smiled in a restrained way.

"I'm looking for a certain individual," I said. I pulled Celeste Vroman's photo of Litman out of my jacket pocket and showed it to her. I had the sudden sensation of standing at the base of a large mountain, preparing to embark on an arduous climb. "His name is Jeffrey Litman. Do you know him?"

"Jeff? Sure."

"I don't suppose you've seen him lately," I began. "But I'd appreciate anything you can remember about where and when you last did see him. And do you have any idea at all about where he might be now?"

She pointed toward a man standing in a corridor behind her, farther in. "He's right there."

FOUR

I didn't move. I gave the skirt a tight smile and a courtesy laugh. "Come on, sister. Let go my leg. Give."

"Huh?"

"Where's Litman? Or should I mention to Mr. John Wendell that you've been less than cooperative?"

"Who? You mean Wendell John? Look, I am being coopera-tive." Once again she pointed. "That's Jeffrey Litman over there."

"Do tell. And suppose I said that I have it on decent authority that the lad is missing, whereabouts unknown."

She rolled her eyes. Cute? Let's review the bidding. Ingalls gets his chain yanked. He's the yank-ee. This doll at the PBX is the yank-er—and she's the one giving him the body-lingo high sign for exasperation. Memo to God: try handing out less irony and more fairness when you do the sequel. "When you say 'miss-ing,' you mean, like, he was at lunch?" she said. "He was. But he just got b—oh, Jesus—Jeff? Mr. Litman?"

I looked up. The gent she'd specified came walking toward me through the entrance to the rear offices. He was a short, well-built joe in a slate gray suit. Balding, clean-shaven, athletic-

looking, alert, with a trim upper body like he lifted weights or
spent more than the usual amount of time on the shot-put range:
he was virtually identical to the man in my snapshot. Coincidence?

"What's up, Cheryl?"

The receptionist pointed a glossy pink frosted talon at me.
"There's a guy who talks weird who says you're missing and
wants to know where you are."

The man reached us and gave me an appraising look. That's
fine. I don't mind being appraised. If it's good enough for an-
tiques, it's good enough for Ingalls. "Can I help you?"

"Are you Jeffrey Litman?" I asked.

"Yes . . ." He spoke with the tentative caution of a man willing to give out name, rank, and serial number for free, then make
you pay for anything more.

"Can we talk privately?"

"Do you have an appointment?"

"In a manner of speaking," I said. Then I drew him aside just
as the elevators bonged, the doors slid open, and a team of moving guys in jumpsuits spilled out and scrambled over the desks on
their dollies. I took advantage of the bustle to show him the
photo and murmur, tête-à-tête, "A friend of yours gave me this."

Litman looked at me with sudden comprehension and released a little exhale of beleaguered rue. "Come on." He escorted me past the receptionist, waved at her and called, "Thanks,
Cheryl. I'll take it from here," and ushered me into the inner
sanctum.

The joint was a shambles. What seemed to have once been a
cozy club room of secretary desks, bookcases, and tufted leather
chairs was a chaos zone of mover boxes, books stacked like pan-
cakes, and distracted paralegals and associates edging past each
other with open irritation. Everyone devoted half their attention

to not getting dust on their creamy white blouses or chalk-striped navy suits. Phones rang at their own risk. Gorillas from the moving company hugged computer monitors to their chests like looters, then lurched their way through the congestion toward the elevators.

"You know," I began, leavening it with a chuckle. "I—"

"Not here." He gestured with his eyes to the people all around. "In my office."

He steered me into a corner suite with a view of other swank buildings and their corner suites. Then he shut the door. For all the tumult outside, his office was undisturbed: near the door, leather chairs and a matching couch formed a placid conversation area around a heavy, handsome glass-and-chrome coffee table. Across the thick beige-and-blue Persian carpet was his desk, a walnut monster gleaming and neatly furnished with a blotter, keyboard, monitor, desk items, and an angular matte-black mantis of an Italian lamp. A small, ornate gold picture frame stood beneath it, with a woman's picture inside. She was pretty, chic, and professionally posed.

At his gesture I sat on the couch. He fell into one of the chairs and leaned forward, speaking quietly. "Look, I know who you've come from. Celeste sent you, didn't she?"

I flashed a polite nonsmile. "I'm not at liberty to disclose the identity of my client."

He shrugged. "All right, then, let's play a little game. I'll pretend I don't know Celeste sent you looking for me. And you'll pretend I don't know, too. The first one to die of boredom loses."

"Fine, counselor. I like games."

He sat for a moment, fingertips together, mulling over something. Then he said, "I don't suppose I can ask you to keep this confidential. I mean you're working for her, I know, but . . ."

Suddenly he stopped, struck by a thought. He looked at me. "How much is she paying you?"

"My usual fee. A hundred a day plus expenses."

"Suppose I double it if you say you couldn't find me."

"Sorry, Litman. I'm a professional. I don't do things for money."

"What?"

"I mean I don't betray clients for money."

He nodded in disgust. "Forget I asked. I'm not exactly proud of it." Then he bounded to his feet and walked across the room. "Look, I'm avoiding her, okay? I don't call her, I don't take her calls, and I've asked everyone around here to say they don't know where I am."

"That isn't what young Cheryl said," I replied. "She pointed you out right off the bat."

"Well, I mean, I was standing right there and you had a picture. She had to." He added, "Look, I don't even know your name."

"Pete Ingalls, P.I."

"Mr. Ingalls. Celeste and I have had a relationship for a few months. It so happens I'm married. She knows that. I told her at the start I couldn't promise anything and I refused to be held to anything. Those were the terms and she accepted them knowingly. Now I want to end it, and she's been hounding me. That wasn't part of the deal and, frankly, she's gone a bit over the edge."

"What edge is that, Mr. Litman?"

"What do you mean, what edge? The sanity edge. The edge of what's reasonable between consenting adults."

"I wouldn't know. I've never met a consenting adult."

"I—" He held out his hands, open and slack, at a loss. "I don't know what the hell that means."

"Never mind, friend. As long as I do." The truth was, I didn't either. It just seemed smart to parry his rhetorical move at that moment. And it worked: he shuffled to the main chair behind the desk and fell into it, as though seeking sanctuary. From me? From guilt? From . . . himself?

"She's a passionate woman," he said. "But she has a temper. I knew that. Shit, it was part of what attracted me to her. That fire. We did things"—he shook his head—"I mean, I even helped to buy her a boat. But that was a while ago, and I guess I jumped in too deep, too soon. Now she keeps pushing and pushing and calling and insisting. . . . I know I can't avoid her forever. But I just needed a break from it. So I pretended I wasn't here."

"You did a fine job, Mr. Litman," I said. "She hired a private dick to find you."

He sighed, looked away. "I guess you think I'm a wimp. Hiding from my girlfriend. Lying to her. Getting others to lie."

"It doesn't matter what I think, pal."

"Meanwhile, in the middle of all this, I still have to work. Things are nuts around here, as you can see."

"Remodeling?"

He smiled. "Sort of. And now I'm up half the night worrying. Is she going to start calling my home? Speaking to my wife? You can see how I'd want to avoid that."

"All the more reason to talk to her," I said. "I don't know much about the law, counselor, but I do know something about women. They'd rather know the truth than be forced to live in limbo."

He looked suddenly a bit more alert, even hopeful, not so much the hangdog perp as a guy possibly presented with a way out. "You think so?"

I shook my head. "Not really. It's bushwa. *They* think so.

They think they'd rather know the truth. Then, when you tell them the truth, they don't say, 'Thank you. At least you told me the truth.' They say, 'How can you tell me that?'"

"But—"

"And sometimes they even say, 'I wish you hadn't told me.'" I allowed myself a bitter laugh that spoke volumes no one would ever have time to read. "Dames. Ask for 'em by name."

Litman sighed. Apparently someone had lit the philosophy lamp. "I should have your job," he said. "Get out of the office, meet a different class of people, and just generally . . ." He paused. He was speaking to himself more than to me, but I wondered: was he listening? ". . . just spend your time digging up the truth instead of burying it."

"Don't kid yourself," I sneered. "You can't dig something up without getting your hands dirty. Unless you wear gloves. But there's one thing I don't get."

"What's that?"

"Why you're giving her the gate. Why now? It's obviously unilateral. She wasn't expecting it. So what's the proximate cause?"

He looked away, unable to meet my gaze. "It was just time to end it, that's all."

I looked grave. "This is your business, friend," I said. "But carrying your answer back is mine. And I don't relish trying to get that consignment of guff past customs. What does that mean, 'It was time'?"

"Relationships are living things," Litman said. He was suddenly seized by a great impulse to earnestness and sensitivity. Yeah—that old gag. "They're born, they grow, they get old, they die. You know that. Everybody knows that."

"I know a lot of things," I said. "Everybody knows a lot of

things—about a lot of things. Things and people. A lot of people know a lot of things about everybody, Litman."

"What?"

"But sometimes, when somebody doesn't know something about someone, it's because someone is hiding something about something. Is that it?"

"Is what what?"

"Are you hiding something? From Celeste? From me?"

He started and looked self-conscious. I'd touched a nerve, and it was saying ouch. "No. Of course not. What would I have to hide?"

"You tell me."

"If I told you, I wouldn't be hiding it."

"Exactly."

"What 'exactly'—?"

"You're going back to your wife."

"I, no—"

"Someone else's wife."

"Hardly."

"You're gay. Someone else is gay."

"Look, Ingalls—"

"There's another woman. No, Celeste is the other woman." I snapped my fingers. "There's another other woman."

Silence descended like snow that nobody can hear when it falls. He seemed to deflate, shrinking to a small, worried man in the immensity of the tufted leather armchair. He made a noise of self-disgust. "I'm pleading for understanding from you as though if you give it to me, it'll mean that Celeste will give it to me. I'm such an asshole."

I said nothing. Try it sometimes. It's easy, it's free, and it offers a refreshing change of pace from saying something. He got up and sighed, worked his jaw, walked idly to the window, and stared out. He was obviously weighing something and reaching a decision. I was about to find out what.

"Okay," he said. "I should tell her myself, but as long as you're here, maybe this is her way of making it easier on both of us. . . ." He stopped, walked quickly back to where I was, and sat. He spoke in a whisper. "The truth is, I am seeing someone else."

"She's going to ask me who."

He got up and shut the door. "Her name is Olivia Cartwright. She works at Taylor and Tackett. It's a small publishing house in Chelsea. She's an editor of nonfiction. We met . . . Do you really need to hear this?"

"Not how you met, no. And what does your wife think of all this?"

"That's pretty much none of your business, is it?"

I held up open hands in surrender. "Agreed."

He sighed. "So, what are you going to do?"

I got up. "I'm going to call Ms. Vroman tomorrow, tell her I found you right here, in your very own office, and advise her to sit down with you and face whatever facts there are to be faced. Then my job will be done."

He got up and walked over to me. He held out his hand. "You're right. You have your job to do, and I guess I have mine, too. This isn't your problem." We shook. He had a firm handshake. I like that in a man. Or a woman. Or a dog—I know a black Lab out on the Island, you say "Shake," he doesn't just hold out the item in question to be admired, he slaps his paw in yours and he pumps.

Litman suddenly gave a little private chuckle and, as he escorted me into the main room, murmured, "I can see you've been around the block once or twice, Ingalls. I'll tell you—and this *is* confidential—for all that woman's volatility, the shrieking, and the threats—she still gets to me. I mean, I *dream* about her, for Chrissake."

A young man looked up from a phone. "Jeff? Caldwell on line three."

"I have to take that," Litman said. "Tad? Would you take Mr. Ingalls to the elevator?" He slapped me on the shoulder and was gone.

Tad looked sour as he threaded through the jumbled furniture. "This way," he snarled, and led on. He was a thickset plug of a lad, in a plain navy blue suit, with a football player's neck and thin, wavy brown hair. His complexion was the color of oatmeal. I caught up to him.

"Out with the old, in with the new, eh?" I said.

He gave a bitter laugh. "Yeah, right. Try vice versa."

"Come again, friend?"

"Fuckin' place is imploding. See all this shit? Going into storage. Office is squishing down from two floors into one."

"And why would it do that?"

"Why?" he barked, as though the answer were obvious. "Why do you think? The head guys fucked up, man. Big time. The firm is having its ass sued off. Malicious prosecution. Fuck, don't you read the papers? So, of course, the partners circle the wagons and start throwing people to the wolves."

"Like you?"

He nodded. "Me, other associates, partners who can't eat what they kill. Fucking Litman calls me into his office two weeks ago: 'We're not going to have need of your services.' I said, 'Fuck, man, I've been here seven years! I'm supposed to be *on track*! I should be making partner! Not out on the street hustling my resume.' 'We're sorry, but the firm is contracting in size. Take a month. Use the Xerox machines.' Fuck *him*. Dickhead."

We had reached the lobby. The floor space was still crowded with furniture and cartons. I said thanks to Tad and had taken a step away, when he took light hold of my arm. "Hey, you're not an attorney too, are you?" he said. He produced a business card and I took it. "I'm whack on contracts but do primo litigation."

I withdrew a careful inch, and scrutinized the kid anew. Whack on contracts? Such nasty talk, from such a nice young man. "Keep it under your hat, chum," I said softly. "If I need hired muscle, I have other sources."

"Huh?"

"Besides, murder for hire's not exactly on the menu at Chez Ingalls."

"Fuck, you're psycho, Jack." He backed off, shuddered, and trooped toward the offices. Then he stopped and came back. "I'll send you my resume. You got a card?" I gave him one. He scrutinized it and laughed. "This sucks ass, man. Later."

That night, back at my place, I had a Stouffer's in the oven and a glass in my hand when the phone rang.

"Ingalls."

"Peter? Is that you?"

It was a woman's voice—older, slightly nasal, with a certain Gaelic lilt neutralized by an undertone of disappointment. "Why didn't you call? I've been leaving messages."

"Call who?"

"Call who. Well, if you can't even be bothered to phone your own mother, then I'm calling you."

"Lady, you've got the wrong number."

"Please, Peter, I'm very tired. It took a hundred phone calls to track you down. I talked to that nice man at the bookstore, what is it . . . Fish? And what is this he tells me about the hospital?"

"Ma'am? Do us both a favor. Write down this address."

"Let me get a pencil. . . ." She murmured my specs back as I recited them. "That's more like it," she said. "Where is this, your new apartment?"

"It's my office, ma'am. Drop by during business hours and you'll tell me what I can do for you."

"Oh, he has an office, now, does he—"

"And now excuse me. I've got a hot date with a frozen lasagna."

After I hung up I took a few snorts and walked around the kitchen several times. You have to when someone tells you they're your mother.

FIVE

I arrived at the office the next day with two items on my dance card. First, call Celeste Vroman and drop the bomb that her boyfriend Jeffrey was appearing live and in person at his place of employment. Then I planned to begin preliminary stakeout on Darius Flonger.

The contrast in the two tasks appealed to me. One of the chief attractions of this job is its variety. Everyone thinks of private investigators as operatives hired to uncover the hidden and restore the missing—and, yeah, get drugged, arrested, or beaten up if the occasion calls for it. All of which is true. We do the things you think we do, and it's our pleasure: tracking down the missing spouse, recovering the stolen heirloom, getting the goods on the cabana boy who has caught, if you're lucky, just your daughter's eye.

But we flatfoots—that's right, "foots." Flatfeet is the mailman's headache—we flatfoots do a lot more than merely pry and spy. We deliver ransom money when your tycoon uncle's been snatched by ruthless thugs. We keep tabs on your drunken nympho niece at the country club reception for the Japanese investors, so nobody loses any of the various forms of face. We play temp bodyguard and watch your back on those unfortunate occasions when your regular muscle is home with a child-care problem, jury duty, or the flu. We do whatever's called for, whenever the need arises, and we do it promptly, courteously, and for a fair price. We go by many names: private eye, peeper, flatfoot, gumshoe, private talent, P.I., shamus, dick. We're America's private detectives. And we're just a phone call away.

Sorry. A brief, unintended excursion through the Ingalls poetic soul. I can't promise it'll never happen again.

Stephanie had already arrived and was unpacking groceries from a swank supermarket's shopping bag as I walked through the door. To make amends for her ill manners and foul language of the day before, I assumed. Was this the dawning of a new era of civility, discretion, and class?

"Fucking jerkoff at the Food Fucking Emporium short-changed me." She wore a man's blue Oxford shirt and a pair of untight jeans. Plus sneakers and no makeup. Her hair, normally lively and glimmering, was a hank of tired, defeatist rust. She gestured to the goods. "Milanos, o.j., and coffee. So we can use that coffeemaker."

"Good," I said. "Make me a double, black, please."

"Am I doing it? I'm doing it, aren't I? So just wait. Please."

"Thank you so very much." You could hear the frost in my tone. And with cause: she was showing up for work in a professional office dressed like a student en route to the Laundromat. Did it matter? Put it this way: I had harbored fantasies of a front-office gal in a trim, tailored suit, high heels like the St. Louis arch, hair done up in that muss-me-darling way, plus eyes decorated like Fabergé eggs and enough high-reflectivity lip gloss to guide ships to safety off Montauk. Who doesn't? So was this really the gal I wanted to quarterback Mission Control?

"Oh shit, I forgot filters."

By now the attentive reader is thinking, "Hey. Ingalls. Give this daffy frail the gate and hire some nice sharp lad out of college. Or get on the blower to young Tad uptown, and keep his murder-for-hire skills as an ace up the P.I. sleeve." Believe me, the thought had occurred. I considered it.

Considered and rejected. The attentive reader has apparently never worked in an office. First rule of office life: have women. An all-male office is a grim place. Sure, at first it's all comradely us-guys joshing, with bottles of brew and bags of chips, and shoulder-punching and high-fiving, and the telling of racy jokes and the creation of Western civilization. Then one day somebody says, "By the way, gents, from now on I'm Pharaoh," and it all goes bad. Then existence itself becomes a slugfest for courtside seats on the totem pole.

Now have someone come over with some women. The mood changes. Nature awakens. Men take their hands from around each other's throats and decide it might be nice to start a chamber music society. Everyone has a slice of pie. The children are born. And the rest is history—the history of elegance itself.

"Fuck it, I'll use paper towels. I'll pick up some filters when I go out for lunch."

So the front office had to feature a woman in a significant speaking role—in which respect Stephanie was at least superficially qualified. It was in other departments that she seemed to be gimping and hobbling around the track—professional comportment, performs assigned tasks satisfactorily, doesn't talk like a hoodlum. I adopted a wait-and-see attitude.

The paper towels worked just fine. A few minutes later

Stephanie shuffled in, grim-faced in her care not to spill a steam-ing mug of jamoke. I leaned back and decided to permit her a glimpse of her employer's thought process, summarizing my fairly surprising experience the day before in discovering that the missing Jeffrey Litman was in fact completely present and ac-counted for. And that he was seeing a woman named Olivia Cartwright, who was apparently to supplant my client in Mr. Litman's extramarital affections. Celeste Vroman wasn't going to like that news.

"She must love the guy," I said, referring to the client.

"Whatever that means," Stephanie said.

I raised my eyebrows. I can do that. "Don't you believe in love, angel?"

She shrugged and sat on the edge of the desk, toying with a paper clip. Her legs, somewhere inside the baggy denim, were a distant memory. "I guess. Anyway, I just think they're both a bit weird. Celeste and her boyfriend, what's-his-name. Litman."

"Weird?" I sipped the joe. "Pretty strong language, doll. Care to back it up?"

"First of all, 'weird' is not strong language. But look at it. Why is she hiring a private detective? Because he's not returning her calls? So fucking what? Like it doesn't happen every day? You think someone's disappeared or missing just because they blow you off? Plus, did she try calling him at home?" I said I didn't think so. Not yet. She continued, "And him. I mean, you can avoid someone for a while, but not forever. Why not just tell her it's over? What's he afraid of? He's a big midtown lawyer. You think his feelings are so sensitive and delicate he can't stand some conflict? And if they are, he shouldn't be going through this serial adultery thing with the new one. Olivia. Jesus, what a prick."

Something about this hit me wrong. I wasn't so sure a man's

secretary should have such strong opinions. "Careful, kid," I said. "Calling the client's boyfriend names—may have to put the ki- bosh on that."

"Whatever. You're the one who has to deal with these peo- ple. I just think some of this is a little strange." She widened her eyes to encompass me and the office and said, "Among other things."

She went back up front to her desk. I allowed myself a brief chuckle at the naivete of youth, then reached for the number Celeste Vroman had given me, with its Atlantic City area code. After two rings I got voice mail in her sultry, dark tones. I left a message. "It's Pete Ingalls, Ms. Vroman. I have news. Call me." I left two numbers, the office and the cell.

Sooner or later, each of us ends up asking himself, "How do you tail a celebrity without getting caught?" It was my turn to dwell on it later that afternoon, when I took the train up to the net- work HQ and cased the immediate environs for a way to shadow Darius Flonger.

Several basic techniques suggested themselves. Wait until he came out of the building, then follow him from the rear. Wait until he came out of the building, then move in front of him and "follow" him by continually looking back to make sure he was still there. Wait until he came out of the building, then hail a cab and instruct it to drive slowly, slowly, along the street, behind him, as he walked. And I could take a few chances, because my alibi was set. If they put the arm on me all I had to say was, "I have his wife's permission."

I decided to start in the newsstand off the lobby. I took up a position that afforded a view of the elevators, then grabbed a copy of *This Man,* one of those men's lifestyle rags that some ad- vertisers apparently believe somebody is reading. I pretended to skim as I scanned the area. A familiar face came and went, some weatherman whose name I didn't remember. They all look alike anyway, don't they? Weathermen. Then I told myself that they didn't look anything alike. The job was getting to me.

I pretended to find an article very amusing. I pretended to find it hilarious. I pretended to laugh—noisily, heedlessly, because that's what you do when you read a funny article, you laugh out loud, and if you're not laughing out loud, then it's not really funny, is it? And if it's not really funny, then maybe you aren't really reading it.

"Please do not read." The lug was Pakistani, or Indian, one of those subcontinent birds who for some reason run all the news-stands in town. "Do you wish to purchase the item?"

"Beats me, soldier," I said. "How do I know if I wish to purchase the item if I don't read what's in it first?"

"Reading the contents would obviate any necessity to purchase the item," he replied. "Thus your comment is superfluous and absurd on its face. Please, this is not a lending library."

I was about to crack wise when Darius Flonger emerged from an elevator and walked, alone, across the lobby. He was maybe twenty feet from me and looked much like his head shot, only older. He was tall and thin, with that short, toupeelike haircut and those court-assassin eyebrows the satire shows mimic when someone plays him in a sketch. He looked relaxed but a little pre-occupied as he headed for the street. I gave the newsstand guy five bucks, put the magazine back where I found it, and followed. It wouldn't be until the following Tuesday that I would realize my mistake.

Outside, Flonger stopped and glanced around. The air had that late-afternoon tinge of melancholy, when the morning's hope has come and gone, and the night's excitement is still a hypothesis yet to be established. Traffic had picked up, the pre-rush-hour rush hour, as drivers hit their horns, buses hit their brakes, and a million engines idled, waiting, waiting. It was then that I felt a suspicious trembling in my pocket, a brief insistent flutter against my leg. For a mad moment I contemplated the possibility that the newsstand guy had somehow dropped a frog into my pants. Never mind *how*—when people have perverse lit-tle missions to accomplish, they find a way.

I reached into my pocket, ready to throttle the frog and shove it into the face of its overarticulate owner. Instead, I pulled out my cell phone, vibrating with an urgent call. I flicked it on, and said, "Yeah?" as I watched Flonger get into a cab and cruise off.

"Mr. Ingalls?" a throaty voice said against a background of grinding trucks. "Celeste Vroman. I hope this isn't a bad time."

"Not anymore, Ms. Vroman. It just got better."

"You said you had news for me."

"What? I can't hear you. Where are you?"

"I'll talk louder."

"What?"

"I said I'll talk louder. I'm on the street."

"You'll have to talk louder. I can't hear you. I'm on the street."

"What?"

"I have news for you."

"Is this a bad time?"

"What? Wait a minute."

I went back into the building. The lobby, with its hard glossy floor and polished marble walls, amplified the noise of the scurry and bustle as people left for the day. I needed a place with some kind of sonic insulation and found it in the newsstand. I pressed myself into a corner of the area, amid the racks of sound-absorbing magazines, and resumed the conversation.

"I'm back, Ms. Vroman. As I said, I have news for you."

"Did you get a lead on Jeffrey?"

"Do not conduct your personal conversations here, please."

"I, yes, wait—" I looked at the newsstand man. He was standing before me. He wore a tired white shirt . . . never mind. It doesn't matter what he wore. "Gimme a break, pal. I just need a minute of quiet here."

"This is not a telephone booth," he said, his dark, round face devoid of humor or compassion.

"It's a public place. I'm a member of the public."

"It is a place of business. You are not purchasing anything."

"I'm browsing."

"You are abusing your right to occupy a space that is explicitly designated for commercial purposes. Kindly leave the area."

"Mr. Ingalls? Are you there?"

"Hang on."

I took the phone outside and started walking, somewhere, anywhere, just to have a peaceful conversation. "Okay, Ms. Vroman, prepare yourself for a shock. I found Jeffrey at his office, going about his business."

From the phone came the sounds of a woman's stunned silence, and the city's mad twilight square dance. "Then he must have just gotten back," Celeste Vroman said at last.

"Actually he never left," I said. "He says he's been there all along. He's, ah, avoiding you."

There was another pensive moment of silence, or another moment of pensive silence. You decide. Then she said, "But I went there, and everybody said they hadn't seen him for a week."

"He got them to cover for him. He's been lying low."

Again she paused, and when she spoke it was with a great weariness. "Then I don't know what to think."

"There's something else."

I don't know what I hesitated for or what I was trying to hear from the other end. Perhaps some hint that she was steeled, girded, ready to absorb what I knew would be a blow. "Yes . . ." she said.

"He's seeing another woman. Some editor named Olivia Cartwright at a small publishing outfit in Chelsea." I ransacked my brain for something to soften the impact. I came up empty. "I'm sorry, Celeste."

"That son of a bitch," she began to herself. Then she said sharply to me, "He's dumping me for someone else? That shit! Maybe his wife would like to hear about this."

"Celeste—"

"I want you to find her, Mr. Ingalls."

"Ms. Vroman—"

"Immediately. Now."

"Now? It's late—"

"Then tomorrow. Find this Olivia slut and ask her if she is aware of me. Now that I'm fucking aware of her."

"All right. I'll find her and tell her about you. Is there anything else?"

"You're goddamn right there's something else." Her tone was hot and reckless. "You find her, and you tell her to stay away from Jeffrey! Do you hear me?"

"Celeste, try to calm down—"

"Don't tell me to calm down! That cowardly worm! That shit!"

"Just a minute." I took a breath. "Is this a request, an order, or a threat? Because if—"

"It's a fucking command! Tell her!"

"—really better off being handled by you and Jeffrey, in a room. It's not really this woman's role—"

"I'm paying you, Mr. Ingalls. Now do what I said. It's your job. Now do it!"

I sighed. "All right, Ms. Vroman. It's your money."

"That's correct, Mr. Ingalls. It's my money. Thank you. I'll be waiting for your call."

I stopped back at the office before punching out for the day. Stephanie said "some old guy" called and would try again soon. Then she dusted and I had a moment of quiet reflection.

There was something about Celeste Vroman I didn't like. And it wasn't that she was romantically involved with another woman's husband. That didn't faze me. I try not to "approve" or "disapprove" of other people's behavior, so long as I don't find anything objectionable in it.

No, it was her manner that rubbed me the wrong way. All that heat, all that anger, all that cursing. Put it this way: I have a problem with big emoters. They spew like Vesuvius and the rest of us get buried alive. Yeah, I know—"It's called self-expression, Pete." Maybe. Or maybe some selves shouldn't be expressed. Maybe some selves should either zip it tight or tell it to the Marines.

The phone rang, snapping me out of my spiraling reverie.

"Peter? Leonard Fish." The mug's tones were soft, and sounded inviting, until you actually tried to accept the invitation. "I wanted to check on you. I know it's a couple weeks now, but Louis said you, ah . . . you didn't seem completely recovered. . . ."

"Do I know you, Fish?"

"Ah, ha-ha, anyway, I assume you're back to normal. Mr. Burnick said we concluded our business, very happy to hear that, so everybody's claims and liabilities are all straightened out. Do you have an address, in case we have to send you any paperwork?"

With one half of my brain I gave him the office address, while the other half worked on what he'd just said. Then the veil fell. "Burnick, eh? You're the client."

"I, well, I suppose. The store is his client. Oh, also, just so you know, we found something of yours, a notebook or something, in Oversized Children's—"

"Hold the wire." Some urgent alarm went off in my mind and the rest of my faculties responded. I didn't like the phrase "oversized children." I didn't like what it suggested—the casual trafficking in minors for purposes for which innocent youngsters came in "sizes." And I liked even less the possibility that, in working for Fish through Burnick, I'd been complicit in it. If I remembered what work I'd done for this clown it would be one thing, but I didn't, and it bothered me. And in any case it wasn't clear what his game was. So I vamped. "The notebook . . . yes, I'd like to get it back, if you have no need for it—"

"It'll be at the main desk when you come to pick it up," he said.

I bet it will, I thought. Just to play out the hand I said, "And where's the, uh, 'store,' Mr. Fish?"

"Where it's always been." He chuckled. "I don't know what you think you have to gain with this play-acting, Peter. This masquerade. But we're quits. When you endorsed that check you gave up all further rights and recourse. Do you understand?"

I wanted to tell him what I thought of him. I wanted to tell him that any man who deals in children, whether regular or over-sized, deserved a fate much worse than any feeble destiny Pete Ingalls could dish out. But I had to get possession of that notebook. So I volleyed back. "Sure thing, Fish," I said. "I'll be around."

I had just managed to put the phone back on the hook when I heard a rap on the office door. I went out and opened it. Standing there was a tall, heavyset middle-aged woman in a light-weight beige raincoat, a massive black purse on her left wrist. "Good Lord," she drawled. "Peter, look at you. What kind of outfit do you call this? Who dresses like that in this day and age? Dear Lord . . ." When she moved past me into the front room, it was slowly and with an aggrieved air. She looked around. "And how is it that you've come to have a real office?"

I made the voice. It was the woman from the phone. "Ma'am, is there something I can help you with?"

"Please, Peter, not now. I've been on my feet all day. Elaine Delaney and I went to the Metropolitan Museum. The mob—I don't know what half those people think they're looking at. . . ." She turned to face me. She was a big, heavy-featured woman, with a strong nose and mannish chin and small, skeptical blue eyes. Her gray hair was medium-length, set, and unremarkable. She squinted, studying my face. "You shaved the beard off. It's about time. Haven't I been telling you to shave it off for the past ten years? But no, don't listen to me. Where can I sit down?"

I ushered her into my office in the back and steered her into the customer's chair. I then sat in my own, pulled out a pad and a pen for notes, and said, "Now. What can I do for you?"

"What can you do for me? You can tell me what you're about with all this. I call the bookstore and you're not there. You go to the hospital and nobody tells me a word. Now I find you wearing these fancy clothes in an office. . . ."

"Lady—"

"And where did you get the money for it all?" She looked around. "What are you, some kind of pretend lawyer? Lord knows you're never going to be a real one."

"Miss . . . what is your name?"

"My name? My name is your mother, that's my name." She sighed. "My name, my job, my affliction . . ."

She was loony as two waltzing mice. It was time to stop the music. "Sure, honey. Whatever you say. But, for the record, I'm a private eye. People hire me to do things for them."

"Things? What does that mean? Dirty things? Dirty things for hire? Shame! Shame on you, Peter!"

"No. Not dirty things. Clean things."

She shook her head dismissively and spoke mainly to herself. "I thought, when you moved out, you were going to start a real life. Get out of your room and away from all those books, and meet a nice girl and start a family. Now you're telling me you sit here in your office, in your fancy suit, waiting for people to hire you to do dirty things. Like what? I want to know! No, don't tell me. It's disgraceful and I won't listen." She sat back and sighed. I was adding as much to this exchange as a cigar store Indian. "But I can't say I'm surprised. It's another disappointment. Just like your father. It's the wages of love, I always say. Disappointment is the wages of love."

I nodded. "That and worse." I tried a sympathetic tone. "Mrs. Ingalls, you've got me confused with a different Peter Ingalls. It's happening all over town lately, and you're in good company."

"Now you stop. With your games. With your games and your secrets and your diaries and your books. As if I don't know my own son." She shook her head. "At least you're alive." She looked at her watch. "Elaine Delaney is waiting for me downstairs and we're going for dinner at the Brasserie. I just hope we can get a cab."

Apparently the interview was over. She rose and made her way out into the front office. She turned and looked at me—or rather, through me, her eyes focused on something beyond my actual expressions and reactions. "If you want all your books and old papers and things, come out and get them. I want to redo your room, maybe sell the house. Will you at least do that for me?"

"Sweetheart," I said, "I don't know what the hell you're talking about."

SIX

Stephanie was already there when I arrived the next morning, hunched at her desk and looking smart in a white long-sleeved blouse and a pair of khaki chinos, or are they called chino khakis? Whatever. She was studying a paperback and barely glanced my way. "'I left no ring with her. What means this lady?'"

"Come again?"

She held up the book: Shakespeare. "*Twelfth Night.* I have a scene next week. I'm playing Viola."

"While you're doing the scene?"

She frowned. "Huh?"

"Playing the fiddle while you're acting?"

"The fid—oh, Jesus."

"Any calls?"

She shook her head, then turned back to the play. "'Fortune forbid my outside have not charmed her. . . .'"

There was a small white box about the size of a brick on my desk. It was heavy. Who, I wondered, would want to send me a boxed brick? A naked, unwrapped brick, maybe flung through a window as a thinly veiled threat of violence, to chase me off a case, yeah; or, if I didn't play ball, dropped from a height, as a thinly veiled way of bashing my head in. Those I could comprehend. This, though, was a puzzle. I opened the box.

I summoned Stephanie and dealt a high hard one down the middle. "I thought I told you that I don't need a new card."

"I know." She smirked. "But admit it. Aren't they great?"

I examined them. Finally I said, "I don't see the improvement."

"Of course you don't. Everybody else will." She plucked up a little stack from the box and more or less shoved it into my hand. "Here. Give these out. People will fall down." It was then that the phone rang.

Stephanie answered ("Pete Ingalls, P.I."), spoke for a moment, then handed me the line. "It's her. Flonger."

I took it as she rolled her eyes and drifted off. "Mrs. Flonger? How are you?"

"I have information for you, Mr. Ingalls." Her voice was dull, dead. It was the voice of a woman who had lost the will to live, or at least the will to make her voice sound alive. "Can you meet me for lunch?"

"Why don't you tell me now? Then I can get on it right away."

"No. It has to be at lunch."

She recited the place and the time in a tone that made you think of sacks of flour and sleeping manatees and other big inert lumpy things that don't move a whole lot. It struck me that maybe she had been drinking. It was nine thirty in the morning. It was time for some tough love.

Then I thought, Nix, Ingalls. This wasn't a question of love. A man in my business was in no position to be distributing love, tough or otherwise, to clients, no matter how needy they were, or how attractive, or how possibly available given their domestic and personal circumstances. No, this wasn't a question of love. It was a question of toughness. It was time for some tough toughness.

"Mrs. Flonger, you sound lousy. Few too many mimosas with your toasted English?"

"You mean, have I been drinking?" She gave a dry little laugh. "You'll find out at lunch."

It was an Italian joint a flight down from Sixty-first off Third, a cozy and, of course, windowless room, where they place your thick white napkin on your lap with a dainty little gesture, and you say "thank you," and they say *"prego,"* and everyone beams and twinkles and pretends the whole transaction isn't just a little bit obscene. I came early, on purpose, but so had she, earlier. It looked like she was nursing a vodka tonic, but you never know. She might have been providing intensive care, and it might not have been her first patient of the afternoon. I gave her a tight smile and a nod, and sat. "Mrs. Flonger."

"Hello, Mr. Ingalls." She didn't smile. She wore a pair of tight black pants, a loose-fitting gray linen blouse, and an elegant silver necklace of tiny links. Her makeup was just right, her short, dark brown hair neatly combed. And yet she looked as though some- one, just before I'd arrived, had smacked her on the head with a two-by-four, albeit internally.

"How have you been?" I asked.

"That's the question, isn't it." Offhandedly she added, "I seem to be falling apart."

"Drinking won't help."

"Spoken like someone who's never fallen apart." She forced a wan smile and referred to her drink. "Don't worry. This is my first and only."

The waiter appeared and asked if I wanted something from

the bar. Sure I did. I wanted a double Chivas and a water back. But drinking during the day, even a beer, makes me sleepy. I yawn a lot. My eyes tear. I have to take a nap. And that's not a thing a P.I. can do gracefully. "Sorry, pal, I gotta dust. Nap time." "Gimme a rain check, doll. I need a quick snooze." "Might as well put that gat up, friend. In thirty seconds I'll be asleep anyway." So I asked for club soda with lime.

Then we ordered some high-priced pasta. I found myself wondering how much better it could be than a box of Ronzoni and a jar of Paul Newman's Sockarooni. But the menu said "a delightful blend of shrimp, saffron, cream, and sherry," and there was no apparent reason to think it was lying. "So, Mrs. Flonger." I toyed with a breadstick. "What is this information you have for me?"

"In a minute," she said. "Can't we talk first?"

"I was born talking. What shall we talk about?"

"About me." She seemed to settle in. "I've been thinking about our first meeting," she said. "About what we said. When I said that I had done everything right, and this wasn't supposed to happen." I nodded. "But it did happen. Didn't it."

"I can't say yet. I've just begun the investigation."

"It has. I'm sure of it. And so what does that mean? Well . . ." She offered a fake smile. "It means that I *haven't* done everything right. Maybe I've done one or two things wrong." She suddenly made eye contact. Her icy blues met my baby blues. "Or maybe I've done everything wrong."

"Not so fast, Mrs. Flonger—"

"Call me Catherine." It came out in a rush, a moment of pure impulse.

"Fine, okay. If you're talking about your husband, he may still love you."

"Really?"

"Yeah, really. This may be one of his flings. You mentioned them yourself, Catherine."

"No, call me Ceecee."

"What?"

"Ceecee. It was my nickname when I was a child."

"Ceecee. Got it."

"You're a good listener, Mr. Ingalls."

"It's part of my job, Ceecee."

"Oh God, no. Call me Mrs. Flonger." She added, "As long as I still am that."

The waiter brought my club soda. Sticking up out of it were two of those tiny, thin red stir straws they give you, the ones you're never sure whether they are for drinking or just stirring. So you take a chance and try to suck something up, and your throat collapses like a crushed beer can. I tossed them aside. When I finally took a long pull, manually, the bubbles were abrasive going down. It felt good. It made me wonder why other things weren't carbonated, like coffee and milk and turkey gravy.

Catherine Flonger suddenly leaned toward me across the table and spoke with a kind of pleading urgency. "I knew these things happened to women like me. That husbands left them for one reason or another. I've seen it happen to women I know. But I truly thought I was *exempt* from that. Because I was so special."

I said nothing. I waited.

"The real point is," she continued, "not that I thought these things were *unlikely* to happen to me. It's that it never occurred to me that it was even possible. And now here we are. I was wrong about myself and about the world." She sat back, depleted. "Sometimes it's exciting, to be detached from your whole life and your whole self. It's exhilarating. Then the exhilaration passes and your life is this . . . *chasm* . . . this frightening abyss that you're constantly falling into. Do you understand?"

I looked wise and said, "I think so."

She drank some water. "It doesn't matter whether you do or not." She leaned toward me and reached out and took my hand in both of hers. It was a gesture of sincerity, not passion. That was okay by me. "Mr. Ingalls, I've never spoken this way to anyone before, because I've always been afraid of what they would think of me. But with you, I just don't care! God, what a relief!" Then she sat back and meshed her fingers into that little wall and placed it on the table.

In the back of my mind, where the important things happen, I thought: Easy, Ingalls. This doll trusts you—a lot. Maybe too much. Time to get the kid gloves back from the dry cleaners. "When you say you don't care what I think—"

"Because how can I?" She smiled. Everything was turning out hunky-dory now that Ingalls was the topic. "You're so absurd! I mean, I'm sure you're competent at your job, and so forth. . . ."

I wasn't crazy about her presumption. "Don't be so sure, lady—"

"So, I talk in your presence. But that's all. I mean it's not as though I'm asking for advice from you."

I'd had enough. It was time to blow the whistle. "Okay, but maybe I have some anyway. You need a hobby, Mrs. Flonger."

She started, then actually laughed. "You mean, like stamp collecting? Needlepoint?"

"Too small. Too fussy. I had in mind something bigger. Like fossil hunting. Or rock climbing."

"In Manhattan."

"Jersey is just a PATH ride away."

She laughed again. I was hilarious today. "Mr. Ingalls, I truly can't tell whether you're very wise or a complete lunatic."

"Want my opinion?"

"No. I don't think you know, either."

We were interrupted by the arrival of the food. We ate and exchanged desultory small talk about Italian parsley, and the size of pasta bowls, and other terribly interesting subjects. Catherine Flonger ate as though by force of will. I was less reluctant. My dish was delightful. It wasn't until the plates had been cleared and coffee had been served that I reminded her I was there to get some information she had for me.

She reached into her purse and produced a new book of matches. "I found this on Darius's night table." She handed it to me. It was for a restaurant called Les Deux Chats. I'd never heard of it but I could guess the gist of the theme.

"French, of course," I murmured, studying the matchbook cover. "Interesting. A religious motif. 'The Chats with God.' No, sorry, probably something like 'God Speaks' or 'God Converses.' And with these two kittens on the logo, I'm going to say Egyptian. They worshipped tabbies, didn't they?"

"Actually—"

"An Egyptian café run by French-speaking disciples of Ra. It could mean something." I speculated freely. "Perhaps it goes back to your husband's experience during the war."

She frowned. "What war?"

"The last good war, sugar. World War Two. Was Darius in Europe at that time?"

"Darius was in junior high school. Actually this means The Two Cats." I acknowledged the correction and asked her about its significance. "We never go there," she sighed. "Darius hates it. We both do. So do all our friends."

I nodded. "So you think he's taking Ms. X there, knowing he won't be made."

"Something like that."

"For lunch or dinner?"

"Oh, lunch. He comes home for dinner." She sighed. "All showered and sweet."

"Can I keep this? Or will he miss it?"

"You'd better give it back. Do you want to write it down?"

I smiled. "I'll remember. You were right, Mrs. Flonger. It's a decent lead. I'll stake it out, take some pictures. . . . Of course . . ." I trailed off provocatively.

"Yes? Of course what?"

"Say I come back with snaps of some gorgeous young bimbo hanging on Darius's every word," I said gently. "Have you thought about what you'll do then?"

She gave a bitter laugh. "You mean apart from killing myself? No, not really."

"It's none of my business, Mrs. Flonger, but in my experience, suicide doesn't solve anything."

"How would you know?"

I fell silent. And I mean hard—I plummeted silent. It was a good point. There was a stern, unsparing logic in the need to personally commit suicide in order to entertain a valid opinion about it. I reached into my jacket pocket and came up with some cards—the new ones, hot off the presses. "Here. Just so you have it."

"You already gave me your card."

"Take this one, too."

She looked at it and made a face of surprised admiration. "This is nice," she said. "Much better than the other one."

The offices of Taylor and Tackett occupied a floor of one of the giant cast-iron buildings in Chelsea, huge ornate castles with curvy decorations over the main entrance and swirly ornamentation around the ledges along the front. These are buildings with big spacious floors, with wide windows and fancy elaborate carved-looking things in the corners. Maybe now's the time to state that I don't know much about architecture.

I got off the elevator and presented myself to the receptionist. I asked if Ms. Olivia Cartwright was in. Who wants to know, the gal more or less said.

"Tell her Jeff Litman told me about her."

The message was conveyed, and I was ordered to wait. I sat in one of several black-leather-and-chrome chairs that surrounded a glass coffee table holding copies of *Publishers Weekly* and *The New York Review of Books*. I started to page idly through one of them. Then it struck me that it was enough work to read a book or a magazine; to read a magazine about books seemed to be pushing it. So I gave that up and concentrated on sitting quietly and keeping my hands to myself.

Presently a mature gentleman of at least twenty-two, in black pants, a white dress shirt, and a Batman tie, emerged from the offices and flashed a genial smile. "Hi! You're here for Olivia?" I nodded. "This way."

I followed him down a hushed, carpeted corridor, past small offices in which vaguely worried men and women sat behind desks too large for the space allotted and frowned at computer screens. Framed book covers and awards lined the passage. The corridor occasionally widened into an office area, where editorial assistants sat at cluttered desks and worked the phones. Each office had a name plate at eye level, beside the door. When we reached one that said OLIVIA CARTWRIGHT, Junior gestured me in.

She was small and thin and intense, with an angelic, pale face, long, thin light brown hair tied in a frizzy ponytail, and black, thin-rimmed, smart-girl glasses. No makeup. Small pearl earrings. She wore a black silk suit that somehow seemed a size too big. It shimmered with a moire sheen over a demure, off-white plain silk blouse. She looked like a dame who knew she looked like a hip spinster, but also knew it was just a look. If Celeste Vroman represented Jeffrey Litman's type—or one of them, apart from his wife—I could see how this petite frail might offer a stimulating contrast.

She stood up to a height of five four, tops, and held out a slim, manicured hand. "Hello. I'm Olivia Cartwright. You're—actually, did you say your name?"

"Pete Ingalls." Her handshake was a cool squeeze of presence, without competitive crunch or passive-aggressive mush. She sat and indicated the visitor's chair. As I got comfy she said, "Thanks, Randy," and, with a nod, asked her assistant to shut the door. He did, and we were alone.

"So," she said, leaning back in her big leather chair. "You're a friend of Jeffrey's?"

I didn't get a chance to answer. After a quick double knock, the door opened and a thin, dapper, heavy-lidded gent in a white suit and a maroon bow tie leaned in. His geniality was as phony as a telemarketer's greeting. "Sorry. Olivia? You can't be serious."

The dame was unperturbed. She must have been expecting this. "Not now, Dylan."

"But you promised." Dylan glanced at me as though I were one of those life-sized photo standups of celebs you pose with for a gag snapshot on the street: realistic and compelling for a second, then disappointing and, in the end, inanimate. "Jesus, listen to me, I'm reduced to sounding like a child. But you did."

"I did not promise. I said we'd consider it."

"But I told him yes."

"You exceeded your authority."

"I did *not* exceed my authority! You told me—"

"Dylan, I told you the proposal had merit but was problematic. You jumped the gun."

"You led me to believe—"

She reddened; her nostrils flared. "No. You misinterpreted what I said. Maybe deliberately. Who knows, maybe for your own reasons—"

"Oh, spare me—"

"You heard what you wanted to hear, not what I said. Can we discuss this later?"

"You always do this! Now I have to go back to him—"

"Can we discuss this later?"

Dylan stopped and gave a petulant exhale. "Fine." He shut the door louder than was strictly necessary.

Olivia Cartwright shook her head. I said nothing and let her cool down. "Sorry," she muttered. "I'm director of nonfiction. He brought us a proposal that he wants to acquire but that we're going to turn down."

"He seemed upset."

"The author is someone I think he may be having a relation-ship with. Or hoping to . . . Never mind. You don't want to hear about this." She forced a smile. "So, you're a friend of Jeffrey's." The question had become a statement.

"Not exactly . . ." I pulled out a pack of Peterson's Invinci-bles. "Cigarette?"

"Actually, there's no smoking in the building. But I don't smoke anyway, thanks."

"Neither do I." I put the pack away. Then I explained that I had met Jeffrey Litman through a third party, that Jeffrey had told me about her, and I had come to discuss a certain matter. I kept it vague to scope her reaction.

She surprised me with a giggly, girlish smile. "You're not the investment guy, are you? Jeff said he was going to sic you on me. I must say, I'm impressed, you coming all the way here—"

"No, Ms. Cartwright, I'm not the investment guy. I'm a pri-vate investigator. I represent a woman named Celeste Vroman."

It was as though I'd slapped her with a sturgeon. The girlish pleasure vanished and was replaced by a stern, wary, chilly formality. "I know the name," she said, and clamped her thin lips shut.

"Then you know that Ms. Vroman and Mr. Litman have lately been . . . involved," I said.

"I have no interest whatsoever in the affairs of Celeste Vroman," she replied.

The door opened. Another man stood there, a short, feisty little operator in a snappy pinstriped charcoal suit, and thick, waved dark hair. Behind him Randy spread his open hands in helplessness. "Livvy, Jesus, what's going on?"

"Richard—" She appealed beyond him. "Randy? Don't I get any privacy?"

Randy rushed forward. "Sorry, Olivia, he just—"

Richard shouldered past the stammering assistant, shut the door. "Dylan is in a snit and says you lied to him."

"Oh, that manipulative little queen!" Olivia Cartwright spat. "I told him it was pending the committee's approval."

"That's not what he says happened. . . ." Richard was immensely solicitous. He held out an open hand and looked as though he had to restrain himself from taking her face in it. "And I'm not so sure that's what I heard either, Livvy."

"Goddamn it—"

"Okay, look. Look." He practically bent over her in supplication. "You know I'm here for you. I'll tell Dylan whatever you want."

"It's not whatever I want! It's what I really said!" She took her glasses off and rubbed her eyes—dame-speak for: I'm aggravated. You're dismissed. "I cannot deal with this now." She gestured toward me. "I'm in a meeting . . . ?"

He retreated, holding up open hands of surrender and backing toward the door. "Okay. You're right. I apologize." He sighed.

He was trying to help. "Dylan is huffing and puffing, but he'll calm down." To me he said, "Sorry." Before he left he turned back to her and added, "But you do know I'm here for you."

"I know, Richard. Thank you."

It was cool and formal, but it was all he was going to get. He nodded and shut the door. Olivia Cartwright shook her head in disgust and flipped her glasses onto the desk.

I said, "I had no idea publishing was so exciting."

She wasn't going to play back. Fun time was over. "Mr. Ingraham, why are you here?"

I played it straight. "Ingalls. I'm here to convey a message from Ms. Vroman. She asks me to tell you to stop seeing Mr. Litman."

She looked startled for a second, then burst into laughter that sounded sincere. "Or what?" she mocked. "She'll call me a hussy and pull out my hair?"

"Or nothing," I said. "There is no threat."

"Thank God for small favors," she sighed. "Well, when it rains it pours. It's Lunatic Day at T and T."

"Ms. Cartwright—"

"You know, Jeffrey has told me about her."

For some reason that threw me. "He did?"

"Oh, he talks about her all the time. I know he was seeing her. And I also know he's stopped seeing her. He actually seems kind of scared of her. Not that I blame him. She sounds horrible. I mean, I've never met her. But these phone calls he was getting . . . And now look! She sent you here! No offense, Mr. Inglenook, but, I mean, a private detective, my God."

"Ingalls." I pulled out a card and handed it to her. "Pete Ingalls. No offense taken."

She glanced at it. "This is nice."

"Thanks. I have a gal, does my graphics for me."

"Look," she said. "Jeffrey and this Celeste person had a relationship, and then he met me, and he broke up with her. The End."

"Mind if I ask how you and Jeffrey met?"

"Yes, I do mind."

That's what kills me about rhetorical questions. You never know when the other guy is going to take them literally. What could I do? I played a hunch.

"Okay, so you mind. Feel like telling me anyway?"

"No, not remotely." She put her glasses back on, like a catcher after a mound conference pulling down the mask, returning to work. "Is there anything else?"

I said, "No, Ms. Cartwright, I think that's it. I've said what I was hired to say."

She stood. "Then please go tell your client that I will most definitely not stop seeing Jeffrey. Tell her I suggest she accept his decision and leave us alone so we can get on with our lives. Now excuse me, Mr. Ingalls. You can see I have a lot of fires to put out around here."

I thanked her and left her office. Out in the main area I looked to nod to young Randy, but he was across the way, huddled with sighing, head-shaking Dylan and sharing what sounded like a series of disdainful sniggers. Some feet off, vaguely in their orbit but wounded and steaming on his own, slouched Richard. Our eyes met for half a second. He didn't look like he wanted me to have a nice day.

I retraced my steps toward the elevators. I drew some fishy stares from the staff as I went, probably for my air of thoughtful distraction. But that happens all the time. I draw stares even when I'm not thoughtfully distracted.

Why? Maybe because the world recognizes an honest man when it finally sees one. Then it likes to stare, because maybe there aren't a lot of honest men walking around these days. Then the world can go home and say, "Hey, honey, guess what? I saw an honest man today." Yeah, and then honey can say, "Don't kid yourself. That guy's soul was just as mortgaged to expediency and selfishness as yours or mine. Now let's eat takeout and watch television." And the big wheel keeps on turning.

SEVEN

I hit the office the next day with my head full of women. Sound like fun? Try it sometime. The view is nice, but the atmosphere gets thick.

I summoned Ms. Stephanie Constantino to the Ingalls desk for a straight-talk debrief about her questionable performance on the job. First, though, I had to call Celeste Vroman and upload the skinny about Olivia Cartwright. As expected, I got my client's voice mail. I left a message at the beep. I always do.

"What's shakin', Pete?" Stephanie stood in my office doorway. She wore a men's blue dress shirt that fell, untucked, over loose-fitting denim jeans. She leaned against the door frame and slurped java from a mug that said CATS: NOW AND FOREVER. Sez you, I thought with a vicious irony. Nothing is forever.

"Look, doll." I started out slow. "When the dogface grunts ignore the word from upstairs, the system gets FUBAR. And the brass get peeved."

"Huh? Shit, man, half the time I can't understand you."

I ignored the scatology and volleyed back, "Then reach for

the Q-Tips, sugar. I'm teaching you a lesson in management and excellence."

"Q-Tips? . . . What—?"

"To clean out your ears. All the better to hear me with, Grandma."

She laughed. I had to give her points for moxie. "You're not supposed to put Q-Tips in your ears, Pete. Didn't your mother ever tell you that?"

I indulged in a world-weary sigh. "You're not supposed to put a lot of things in your ears, kid."

"Look, never mind," she said—a neat switcheroo, you'll note, since I was the one who supposedly had the floor. "Just tell me, how was your lunch with what's-her-name?"

I summarized my meeting with Catherine Flonger, and the life crisis she was in, and how nothing I said or thought about her mattered a damn. The tale elicited a sympathetic pursing of the mouth and nodding of the head from young Stephanie, which I found surprisingly touching. Then I thought: easy, Ingalls. The girl's an actress. You're supposed to find her surprisingly touching.

After that I detailed my streetside cell confab with the livid Celeste and described my visit to the offices of Taylor and Tackett, and my encounter with Olivia Cartwright. My assistant's expression morphed fast from sympathy to suspicion.

"This is a small company, right?" Stephanie said. She came into the office and pulled up the customer's chair. "She's a non-fiction editor with a ponytail?"

I spread my hands. It sounded like the setup for a brain teaser. Which, I realized, is exactly what it was. "Yes to all," I said. "Your point being—?"

"She's not exactly a babe," Stephanie said. "I mean, that job, that hair."

"So—"

"So what's a hot stud like Litman doing with her? Celeste, okay. She's a dragon. He wants to slay the fiery beast. Some men are into that. But this mousy little thing?"

"Now that is exactly what I mean." I brought it down like a sap and I didn't care if she felt it. "Who are you to say something like that? How do you know she's mousy?"

"Is she?"

I shrugged. "Some mice are cute."

"But all mice are mousy. Plus, Pete, the real thing is, does Olivia know Litman is married?"

An interesting silence descended. It was the sound of me realizing that that was what had irked me as I left the T and T offices yesterday. Olivia Cartwright kept alluding to herself and Litman as an exclusive item, threatened only by the now-discarded Celeste. "We can get on with our lives. . . ." she had said.

"I don't know if she knew or not." I went on: Olivia Cartwright could simply have been speaking optimistically, deliberately ignoring the existence of Litman's wife in an effort to convince herself that it didn't matter. "And so what if she doesn't know? What does that prove?"

"It doesn't prove dick. But—"

"Can't you say, 'it doesn't prove anything'?"

She sighed. "Okay, Pete, sorry, look: It doesn't prove *anything*. But Celeste knows Litman is married. Now we're saying Olivia doesn't. It's just another—"

The phone rang. We both looked at it, then at each other. It rang again. You can see the ambiguity in the situation: she was waiting for me to pick up my phone; I was waiting for her to do her job. We reached an impromptu compromise. I picked it up and handed it to her. She said, on cue, "Pete Ingalls, P.I. How may I direct your call?" Then Stephanie gave me a heavy-lidded, deadpan look and said, loudly, "It's for you, sir. Celeste Vroman."

She handed me the phone, twiddled her fingers in a facetious toodle-oo, and dusted.

"Ms. Vroman—"

"What do you have for me, Mr. Ingalls?"

Her voice was husky. If she was expecting bad news, I wasn't going to disappoint her. "I met Olivia Cartwright," I said. "Thin, small woman. Looks fragile. I'd call her mousy, yeah, but with some steel in her spine."

"How nice," my client said evenly. "And—?"

"Well, in brief, she rejected your request. She doesn't intend to stop seeing Litman."

"Oh really!" She fought for self-control like a stock car racer on a spinout. "And had she known about me?"

"Vaguely. Her position was that Litman and you were splitsville, and now it was her turn."

The car slammed into a wall. "That bitch! That fucking cunt!"

"Celeste—"

"Give me a moment." I listened to her breathing. A sound caught my attention and I looked up: Stephanie was leaning in the doorway, shooting me a series of skeptical looks like paper clips off a rubber band. I waved her away. She failed to take the hint. "I'll tell you something, Mr. Ingalls," Celeste Vroman now said in tone that advertised, discreetly, its poise. "You could say that this . . . this event, this fucking betrayal, has nothing to do with little Miss Olivia at all. She's not doing a thing to me."

"Meaning—"

"Meaning, of course, that it's Jeffrey who's destroying me. Jeffrey's the one sticking the knife in my heart."

"I don't know, lady." I was getting a sense of why certain P.I.'s won't take marital cases. Or maybe that's a myth, some cocktail of nostalgia and romanticism, like the longing for the days when the mob didn't touch horse. "I do know one thing," I said. It sort of came out, prodded by some vague desire to make her feel better. "I talked to Litman the other day, and he told me he still dreams about you."

I didn't like saying that. It wasn't any of my business. But it *was* my business to tell this woman about her unfaithful lover. So it was my business to tell people things that weren't any of my business. No wonder P.I.'s drink.

In this case, I could have saved myself the distress. What I'd thought might soothe the abrasion on Celeste Vroman's wounded ego only made the stinging worse. "He *dreams* about me? And he's still dumping me for this skinny little editor bitch?"

"He, uh—"

"I want to see you, Mr. Ingalls. Lunch. This Monday. I'll call in the morning and tell you where."

"Fine. Can—?"

She hung up with a slam.

I put the receiver down gently as Stephanie breezed in and looked triumphant. "I know she's your client, Pete, but I don't like that woman. I don't trust her, if you must know."

I allowed a small, amused smile to play about my face. "Do tell," I said. Then playtime was over, and the smile went inside to learn how to read the writing next time it appeared on the wall. "And what do you base that on? Your dame's intuition?"

Stephanie turned chilly. "No," she said. "Not my 'dame's intuition.' Jesus, who talks like that? Never mind. I don't trust her because I just don't."

"Ever hear the word 'tautology,' doll?"

"What? No." Then she said, "Because she hired you to find some guy who wasn't missing. I mean, I still don't get that."

I laughed and shook my head. "It's really fairly simple, Stephanie."

Her mouth dropped open. "Are you laughing at me? Because you think I'm stupid?"

"I wouldn't say that—"

"Because I'm an actress?"

"Some actresses are quite intelligent."

"No shit. . . . Oh. Of course." She favored me with a fake smile. "It's because I'm a woman. A broad, a skirt, a dame—what else did you say once? A quail?"

"A frail?"

"Yeah. Jesus. Like you're not nuts?"

"Hold the phone, sister—"

"You know what? I don't need this shit. If I want to put up with condescending assholes, I'll wait tables and make more money."

"Okay, now I'm sure you think you have a good reason for thinking I'm condescending—"

"Plus, who are you to talk? With this whole Raymond Chandler thing. Because I'll tell you something, Pete. If you're kidding then it's, like, sociopathic. And if you're serious then it's totally *fucked*. And you're going to lecture me on how to behave? I don't think so." She marched out of my office into the front room and called, "Mail me my check. I am so out of here." I heard the door slam.

And all this before lunch.

I had to admit I was surprised. I'd pegged our Ms. Constantino as one of those actors wise to the ploys you need in order to smuggle a self through the world while living to talk about it. Or don't such people exist? Maybe I made them up. It wouldn't be the first time.

I was now without an assistant. It meant I'd have to make my own coffee. But there wasn't much time to cry about it, because I

was due uptown pronto to stake out the eatery Catherine
Flonger had said hubby might frequent with his new paramour.
I'd deal with human resource problems later.

Le Chat d'Or was fairly unremarkable, just like every other
underlit French place where I could get six oysters and some
dunking sauce for what Con Ed charges me per month. I took
the worst table on the floor, a single jammed against the wall
near the kitchen door, and spent a good half-hour eating rolls,
reading the menu, and popping off discreet snapshots with a
small camera that fit in the palm. My client had suggested the
joint was somehow infra dig for her media star husband and their
set, and I could see why: there was an unstylish, matinee-crowd
feel to the clientele. These rich broads and distracted-looking
suits were here because they'd read about it in the *Times*, in arti-
cles that in terms of trendiness and heat had the effect of obitu-
aries.

I settled on the Asian chicken salad, knowing that I could
nurse something cold for as long as necessary without attracting
comment. I ate slowly, asked the dealer to hit me again and again
with bread and iced tea, and watched as parties of two came and
went with no sign of Darius Flonger.

Two and a half hours later the lunch rush had come and gone.
I was stalling over a third coffee refill when a sudden thought
brought a spasm of irritation. I summoned the waiter and asked
him the name of the restaurant. The lad was a pro. Without missing a beat he said, "Le Chat d'Or, monsieur."

"What's that translate to, soldier?" I asked. "The Shot Door?
Some French Revolution thing like that?"

"It mean, The Gold Cat."

"Nothing about God in that? The God Cat? The Cat God?
Two cats?"

"Two cats? There exist another restaurant, Les Deux Chats."

I thanked him and paid the bill, goosing the tip for his help-fulness. Then I hit the pavement. Restaurant ambiguity: you live in an international city, it's an occupational hazard.

I used the cell to check my voice mail and heard the tense, urgent voice of none other than Jeffrey Litman. And he wasn't happy. "Ingalls," he said. He spoke softly, as though not to be overheard. "Jeff Litman. Look . . . Celeste was just here. Call me at the office."

He left a number, and I called him back. He answered immediately. When I ID'd myself, he sounded relieved. "Okay. Thanks for calling back. I mean, I know I'm not your client, but Jesus . . ."

"She came to your office, Mr. Litman?"

"No, of course not. She had me meet her in a coffee shop. Christ, she was insane. Furious. Out of control." He paused, then added, accusingly, "About Olivia."

"Don't shoot the messenger, pal. It's your bed."

"I know, look, I'm sorry . . . it's just that I've never seen her that angry before."

"Maybe she never knew she had competition before."

"Yeah. But she threatened to tell my wife!"

"Don't they always?"

He yelled, "How do I know?" Then he lowered his tone. "I'm sorry. I'm taking this out on you, and it's not your fault. But look, Ingalls, you've met Celeste. You've spent time with her, you know how she's been feeling about this whole business. I have to ask you a question."

"I can't promise I can answer it, Litman. My loyalty is to her."

"I know, but just . . . do you think she's capable of . . . you know. Doing anything?"

I pretended I didn't know what he meant, and then realized that, in fact, I didn't know what he meant. "Meaning what?"

"You know. Meaning . . . is she capable of violence?"

I stalled with a rhetorical question, like a chess player marking time by castling. "Let me put it this way, pal. Is any of us capable of violence?"

He snorted and captured my rook. "Well, yeah, some people are. Probably most people are, if the right thing is at stake."

"Touché. But Celeste Vroman? I don't know. And frankly, I wouldn't tell you if I did. Unless the answer was no. Which I'm not saying it isn't. I'm not saying it is, either. I'm just not saying. Although if it was no, I think I wouldn't say anyway—"

"All right, Ingalls—"

"Because I shouldn't say. That's all I know. I don't know. And that's all I'm saying."

"Thanks for your time."

We hung up, probably both with the same thought: it wouldn't have surprised me to learn that Celeste Vroman was indeed capable of violence—against Litman, against Olivia Cartwright, against someone.

Little did I know then that—well, nuts to that. Life is an unbroken parade of little-did-I-know moments. And there isn't much you can do about it except stand along the curb, waving and applauding and waiting for the rain.

EIGHT

The weekend came and went, like—well, let's just say, like a New York weekend. Saturdays you walk the streets and get asphyxiated by the pressure to have fun. Expectation fills the air like tear gas, only it doesn't dissipate. You see the world as you need to see it, and hope to get what you want. You don't, of course. Then you give up, blame yourself, and go home.

Sunday is a tightrope walk across a valley of ennui, and nobody gets to the other side without falling in. By then Saturday's distractions have faded and all that hope has decomposed into disappointment. Listen very carefully and you can hear eight million souls shrivel like lizards too close to the heat lamp, as the population looks down the business end of religion, bad movies, and relatives.

On Monday I arrived to an empty office and had to remind myself that my assistant had quit. That was just fine. I'd made my own coffee before and I could do it again. Then the phone rang. I went to the receptionist's desk in the front and picked up.

"Pete Ingalls, P.I."

"Ingalls? Jeff Litman. Look, I know it may be a little iffy, my calling you, but I just wanted you to know that I saw Celeste over the weekend and she was a doll."

"Color me surprised, chum. I was under the impression she hated your guts."

He laughed. "You know your business, Ingalls. She did. But we hashed things out and she was sweet and terrific. And, in fact, you were right. I said I'd stop seeing Olivia and that's what she wanted. She was affectionate and positive, and it was just great."

"Well, I'm supposed to meet her for lunch today. I assume she'll tell me all about it."

"Good. I hope she does. I really think we have a chance. Anyway, thanks for . . . I don't know . . . for listening. Take care."

He hung up and I marveled, once again, at the human organism. It was a sap. But it was all we had.

It was then that young Stephanie Constantino breezed in, fetchingly but respectfully clad in dark slacks and a crisp white blouse. The short, bouncy hair gleamed, and she wore just enough makeup to look very, very nice. "Morning, boss," she said, and made herself at home.

I got up to relinquish the chair, but said, "I thought you quit."

"I did." She sat and bustled with things to reclaim the turf.

"Then what are you doing here?"

"I unquit. Want some coffee?"

"You called me an asshole, as I recall."

"Did I? Yeah, I probably did. Sorry."

"Plus nuts, psycho, and sociopathic."

"Well, I was provoked. You called me stupid."

"No, I didn't. You accused me—"

"Okay, look. Does it really matter? I want this job. It's getting interesting. And you *need* me in this job. Plus"—she looked coy—"wait 'til you hear what I did after I left on Friday."

"Ms. Constantino, it may shock you to learn that I couldn't care l—"

"I met with Olivia Cartwright."

I squinted at her. "Why?"

She leaped up, pleased with herself, signaled for me to follow, and went into the little kitchenette. "Because I was so goddamn curious." As she made the coffee, she explained.

She presented herself as an associate of mine and of Jeff Litman. It was half half-truth and half outright lie, but it worked: Olivia Cartwright invited her in and gave her ten minutes, during which Stephanie managed to drop the bombshell that Litman was married. "Which she didn't know," Stephanie said. "And she did this, like, internal rage thing. Very still, very collected, outwardly all 'I'm coping,' but she's this thin, pale woman—like this Joan Didion type—suddenly turning purple. She says, 'What else don't I know?' I just wrapped up whatever bullshit query I came to ask and got the hell out of Dodge."

I digested this like a bad mussel. Why, I asked her, did she take it upon herself to do this? What possible use could this be to our—my—client? "I did it to help the client," Stephanie said. "If Olivia knows all this, she'll probably tell Litman to get his ass out of there and never see her again. Then he'll go crawling back to Celeste. Isn't that what she wants?"

"Maybe—"

"Trust me, Pete. It is. If she gets him back she'll thank you and pay in cash." She batted her pea-green peepers at me and, with an actress's killer smile, said, "So didn't I do good?"

"No comment."

"And can I have my job back?"

I gave a tentative yes and warned her to watch her language. She danced over, kissed me on the cheek, and tripped off to answer the phone.

I had just enough time to make it back to my office when she called, "Some guy named Tad on two." It was Tad Phillips, the disgruntled young man from Litman's office.

"Mr. Phillips, to what do I owe th—"

"Listen." He was whispering. I heard corporate noises in the background. "Greg Higgins is like mega-steamed at Jeffy. I don't know why, but it's Defcon Four in there."

"Higgins is—?"

"One of the partners, man. Megan is pissed, too. Megan Loomis. Senior Partner Bitch Supreme. They wanted to talk to him but he, like, turns a deaf ear and is, like, 'Later, dudes,' and walks fucking out!"

"Where'd he go?"

"Fuck me."

I took this to mean, "I don't know." I asked Phillips why he was telling me this. He laughed. "'Cause I hate this fucking place and I want it to go *down*, man." Then he said, abruptly, "Later," and hung up.

So Litman was being hammered at work as well as at play. It made you wonder what his life was like at home. It also, if you were like me, made you wonder about the human capacity to assume first and ask questions, if ever, later. When I first spotted Litman at the law firm I instinctively sized him up as one of God's favorites: confident, healthy, vigorous, with a sweet job, a looker wife, and a hot-cha mistress. But reports from the fronts indicated discord, crisis, and *agita*. Even this new pact with Celeste Vroman sounded fraught and strained and a little too good to be true. Memo to self: don't believe in appearances.

Then again, Litman wasn't my problem. No, my problem was a certain tough, compelling dame with whom I had a one thirty lunch date. I told Stephanie I'd be back in a few hours. When she asked where I was going, I told her.

She stood up and reached for her purse. "I'm going with you."

"The hell you are."

"Come on, Pete. I want to meet Celeste. Don't you think I've earned it? After my meeting with Olivia?"

"That was unauthorized. And I'm telling you not to do it again."

"Okay, but still. Please?"

"Nix. Now man the horn and keep your nose clean."

She arranged her puss into a theatrical frown and an accusatory pout. I left with a slam. The contemporary American broad: what gives? Does it violate her personhood to take no for an answer? Is there something in all this bottled water they drink that makes them unable to say "Yes, sir"?

I was well immersed in these and similar musings as I left the building and stepped pensively down the stairs to the sidewalk—so pensively that I failed to spot the short, anxious gent waiting at the bottom.

"Ingalls. Hold it." His tone was equal parts anger and fear. Half fight, half flight—they cancel each other out. You stand your ground and hope for the best. "I have to ask you something."

He was five five, maybe five six, thin, in a lightweight suit of self-effacing gray. He had the pale, smooth skin of a man who went outside principally to hail cabs. He looked familiar, but some days everybody does.

"Make it fast," I said. "I have a lunch date, and I'm actually hungry."

He took a step closer, making it all the more obvious that I had six inches and thirty pounds on him. Still, he was a plucky little bantam. Any fear he had would be swamped by his little man's perpetual indignation at being small. He lifted his chin. It looked like a dare. "I want to know what your business is with Olivia Cartwright."

"Who's asking?"

"Don't fuck with me, Ingalls. I saw you visit her at the office last week. And afterwards she refused to tell me what it was about."

"Then why should I tell you?"

"Because you're not leaving here until you do. Olivia didn't come to work this morning. She didn't call in sick, and she isn't home. She never does that. Where is she?"

I laughed. "Friend, I have no idea, but believe me, I wouldn't tell you if I knew."

"What did you talk to her about the other day? Who are you working for?"

"Excuse me. I have an engagement with a dame who could eat your boss on toast points and still have room for dessert."

I put out my arm to shove past him and somehow ended up sprawled on the sidewalk. On the heel of my left hand, where skin used to be, there was now a pretty speckle pattern of red, and pain. "Neat," I said. "What do you call that move?"

"Where's Olivia, damn it!"

"Pete!"

From my cozy reclining posture on the sidewalk I looked up: Stephanie had come quick-stepping down the stairs and now squared off against my assailant. I could tell she was one of those women who was beautiful when she was angry, because she was angry. "What the *fuck* are you doing?" she snarled, and slammed a hand into the lad's shoulder, shoving him backward.

He recovered the lost territory and looked defiant. "Just an-swer my question," he said—to her, as though that made sense. But the confidence he'd shown with me began to erode. Maybe because he couldn't let himself strong-arm a woman. "I just want to know where is Olivia Cartwright and what's this guy's connection to her."

Stephanie looked hard at him. "I know you. You're Richard. From the office."

"And who are you?" he asked her. "His partner?"

"Yeah. Which means I'm authorized to kick your ass into next week if you don't leave *now*."

Probably I should have made an effort to get to my feet and contribute to the exchange, but then Stephanie produced, out of nowhere, a cell phone, punched a couple buttons, and said into it, "Janie? Get me Lieutenant Garbus, will you? ASAP. Thanks."

Richard looked apprehensive. "Hey, wait a minute. Come on. There's no need for that."

She kept her eyes on his and said into the phone, "And also call Kevin. I want to look into suing Taylor and Tackett for the actions of one of their employees."

"Okay, I lost my temper. Besides, he made a move toward me first." Richard stuck his open hand down toward me. "Look, sorry, okay?"

"Sure." I took it and he hauled me to my feet. "Thanks," I said, and dealt him a hard one to the solar plexus. It felt satisfying, at first. You could hear the air pump out of him as he reeled backward into a light pole. I went to do it again, but Stephanie put her hand on my cocked fist.

"Pete, stop. It's not worth it."

We watched as Richard gasped and wheezed his way back to normal respiration. I checked my watch to demonstrate to him that I was a mildly inconvenienced professional. Finally he said, "I just want to be sure that Olivia is okay," added, "Oh, fuck you people," and turned and limped off down the street.

I turned to my assistant. "Better tell Janie to cancel the calls."

"Who?" Then she saw the phone in her hand and laughed. "Yeah, right. Like I know people in the police department." She held it up toward me. "It's my voice mail. No messages. Fucking agents. Maybe you better wash that hand."

I told her I was late for lunch and would deal with my superficial injuries later. I hailed a passing hack. As it pulled up she said, "Can I come?" I started to protest. Then I held the door open.

We stopped at a small Indian joint on Third Avenue. Outside it might have been glaring high noon, but inside it was dark and cozy and two-thirds full. Celeste hadn't arrived yet. We took up a position in a corner table facing the room, like gangsters. Then I excused myself and squeezed into the men's room. It was larger than a coffin and the sink worked. I washed the blood and street grime off my hands and paused to think deeply.

It had been an interesting morning. I knew when I went into this racket that I'd have to be prepared to serve up and take delivery of various helpings of rough stuff. It came with the territory. The literature was full of it—fistfights and blackjack beatings, the skillfully administered hammerlock and the regretfully broken thumb, and odd assorted pharmaceutical surprises administered via hypo, herbal tea, and Mickey Finn. So I embraced today's tussle. It made me feel that I was what I thought I was. It made me feel alive.

I rejoined Stephanie at the table. She was surveying the joint and squinting. "Is this what you call atmosphere?" she muttered. "Or is it just dark?" We scanned the menus. It meant angling them as close as possible to the little candle without actually setting them on fire. Then she glanced up, and her expression froze. "Uh-oh."

Moving toward us across the restaurant was Celeste Vroman.

She looked lousy. Outwardly you could say everything was in order, sure: the gleaming black hair, shoulder length in a gentle inward curl, perfectly in place; the black slacks, maroon cotton turtleneck, and charcoal herringbone sport jacket, all set off with tastefully minimal gold jewelry. Her face was as I'd recalled it, too, all deep hollows and dramatic eye makeup and strong bones. The only discordant note was the purse. Because it wasn't a purse. It was an oversized tote bag, zipped up tight and bulging.

But what caught our eye was the way she moved. It was as though she'd just been hit by a truck that had somehow left no external marks but had still done damage in deep. Her steps were slow and deliberate, her head frequently swiveling from side to side as though warding off intruders. All this while continually adjusting her expression, mastering her presentation, *composing* herself. You didn't have to like the woman to feel sorry about whatever trauma she'd just apparently suffered.

Then she saw Stephanie, and it was our turn for trauma.

"What the hell is she doing here?" Her voice was that deep, throaty growl I remembered. "Ingalls, who is this?"

"Celeste Vroman, Stephanie Constantino. Ms. Constantino is my assistant."

Celeste reached her chair and stopped. We'd stood, more out of apprehension than manners. So we were all at the same level. Celeste looked at me and seemed to try to shy away from Stephanie. "I thought this was confidential," she said. "Damn it, it's just supposed to be you and me."

"It is confidential. Ms. Constantino helps me and I trust her implicitly. Now let's sit. You look like you could use a drink."

"I can't stay," Celeste said, even while she pulled out her chair and sat. Then she said, "A drink, Christ, what a good idea." She looked behind her, toward the room, and called for the waiter. The Indian gent toddled up, and Celeste ordered a Stoli and lime. I played it straight with club soda.

The waiter looked expectantly at Stephanie. She turned to me and said, "Pete, if you want, I can leave." I waved that away. She looked pleased and ordered iced tea.

Then I leaned toward my client. "What's the matter? This morning your boyfriend called and said everything was sunshine and lollipops."

"It is. . . ." She shifted in her seat, looked around, then grabbed a menu and held it up in front of her face like a commuter behind a newspaper. "Where the hell is that drink?"

Stephanie said, "You seem upset, Ms. Vroman."

"I am upset."

Then, nothing. Stephanie looked at me and rolled her eyes. I shook my head. "Celeste, are you eating? You said you can't stay."

"I can't stay. I'm looking at the menu. And waiting for that fucking drink."

Then the waiter floated up and placed the glass before her. As he put our tumblers in front of us, Celeste lowered the menu, grabbed her glass, and knocked back the whole thing in a few relentless gulps. She handed it back to the deadpan gent and said, "One more." He bowed slightly and drifted off.

Celeste raised the menu again and spoke in a voice tense with an effort at control, "I don't mean to be rude, Mr. Ingalls, but I'd appreciate it if you and Miss Constantino here wouldn't stare at me."

"Sorry," Stephanie said.

"I wasn't aware that we were staring," I said. "Ask me, I thought we were waiting."

"For what?"

"For you to come out from your cave and deal me a hand I can bet on."

"Ah, meaning—?"

"Meaning, what are we doing? What's going on?"

"Nothing's going on. We're at a restaurant. I'm looking at the menu."

"You can't possibly read it in that shadow. And you said you're not staying anyway. I found Litman. You and he are happily reunited. So why are we here?"

The waiter returned and set down the next drink. Celeste lowered the menu and said, "I'm sorry. It's just that this morning I had to do something I didn't want to do, and it's painful to me. I had to fire someone and I hate doing that. Maybe you know the feeling."

"Not really," I said. "My employees generally quit. Then they come back and we start over." Stephanie gave me a subtle kick under the table. I ignored it and played through the pain.

Celeste drained the second drink and put the glass back on the table with a sharp knock and a rattle of ice cubes. "Anyway, I apologize for my behavior. Miss Constantino, you must think I'm a very rude woman. I promise you, normally I'm not."

"You don't have to apologize," Stephanie said. "We all have bad days."

"That's very nice of you." She reached down and opened the big tote bag. "In any case, Ingalls, I wanted to thank you for a job well done. Jeffrey and I are back together, and you had a lot to do with it. In fact . . ." She took a multi-compartment wallet from the bag, opened it, and produced a check. "Do you remember that boat he helped me buy? When I leave here I'm going to Atlantic City. Jeffrey will be joining me on it for a few days. So thank you." She handed me the check.

I took it and looked at that little box where you get the good, bad, or indifferent news. I whistled. "This is more than we agreed on, Celeste."

"You earned it." She took a deep breath, her full bosom heaving under the turtleneck and jacket. Then she stood. "I feel better. Miss Constantino, thank you for understanding." She held out her hand to me. "Mr. Ingalls . . . Pete . . . send me the check for lunch. I'm sorry, I'd love to stay, but this event this morning has forced me to change around my whole schedule today." We shook hands. I appreciated the heft and pressure she brought to it. "I'll be in touch, but for now I think our business is concluded."

"Do you mind if we tell people?" Stephanie asked.

Celeste Vroman stopped and her jaw went slack. She looked slapped. She turned to my assistant and said, with scrupulous care, "Tell who? Tell them what?"

"You know. Like a reference. Tell people you're a satisfied client."

Celeste sighed in what looked like relief. "By all means. Tell whomever you want. Tell everybody! And now I really have to run." She hoisted the bag and left at a much brisker pace than when she'd arrived.

I gazed with contentment at the check. "Another satisfied customer."

"Mm-hmm . . . whatever."

I looked at her: Stephanie was staring frozen at the place where Celeste had last stood. "What? Come on, doll. Shake it up and pour it."

"She never answered your question."

"Sure she did. What question?"

"About why she was looking at the menu."

I gestured to signify reasonableness. I was getting good at it, with this gal. "She thought she might eat."

"She knew she wasn't staying."

"Maybe she was looking to be tempted to change her mind. Or to find something to nibble on with the drink."

"You said so yourself. She couldn't see a thing back there. No way she could read that."

"Then what are you saying?"

"I don't know."

"You do know. Just say it."

"Say what?"

"How do I know?"

"Then what are you talking about?"

"What are *you* talking about?"

"I'm saying, Pete, that something's extremely weird about your Celeste Vroman."

"Weird, doll? Check your statistics. That adjective applies to ninety percent of the people you meet in this city."

She smirked. "What about the other ten percent?"

"They're in Bellevue."

"Just . . . just . . ." She shook her splayed–open hands in frustration. "I'm sorry, I've got this radar about people and with her it goes way off the scale."

I folded the payment and put it in my pocket. "As long as the check clears."

"Yeah, well, don't count on that, either."

I paused to appreciate the snappy little vaudeville routine we'd perfected. I also tried to savor the girl's audacity, but I kept getting a bitter taste. Bear in mind that she'd displayed, on the job, equal parts mouthiness and presumption; add to that the list of pungent names she'd applied to her boss; and fold in gently the fact that I'd taken her back with hardly a reprimand. When I did the math it came out one way: she'd clean up her act, or she'd be back on unemployment with the rest of Equity.

The trilling of my cell phone spared me the necessity of actually having to say this. I pulled it out and said, "Ingalls."

"Can you hear me, Mr. Ingalls? It's Catherine Flonger."

"I hear you fine, Mrs. Flonger. Where are you?"

"Broadway and Sixty-eighth. I'm climbing."

"Actually I think we've got a bad connection, Mrs. Flonger. It sounded like you said you were climbing."

"I did. I'm rock climbing. I took your suggestion. At this indoor place near the noodle shop."

Stephanie prodded my arm. "What? Who is it?"

I covered the phone, irritated. "It's Catherine Flonger. She's rock climbing near a noodle shop."

"Mr. Ingalls," Catherine said. Some commotion around her began to obscure her voice. She said, loudly, "I have another clue for you. How soon can you get here?"

"Why can't you tell me on the phone?" I called. I was receiving dirty looks from the surrounding diners. I scanned the entire room, making reassuring eye contact with everyone, and spoke to them. "It's business," I explained.

"Who cares?!" some woman yelled. "Take it outside!"

"I'm almost done."

"Hey, Slick," a man called. "We're trying to eat lunch."

"So am I," I sneered. I looked around for the waiter. "Can we please give our order—?"

"Mr. Ingalls—?"

"Cath—Mrs. Flonger, just tell me."

"Shut up and go outside!"

"I want to tell you in person."

"Fine, I'll be right there."

"What? Mr. Ingalls—"

"I said I'll be right there!"

"WILL YOU SHUT UP?!"

"Sir, I must ask you to kindly turn off the cell phone or exit the restaurant."

It was the waiter. I said, "I don't have to exit, I'm leaving anyway." I leaned down toward Stephanie and said, "I'll eat later. Get something and I'll see you back at the office."

"I need some money."

I dropped a twenty onto the table and hustled toward the door. There were a few people loitering near the register, waiting for takeout orders. As I raced past I thought one of them looked like our boy Richard from Olivia Cartwright's office. But, I reasoned, it couldn't be. Like I said, some days everybody looks familiar.

Ten or twenty years ago some genius looked around New York and decided that, for all its attractions and diversions and cultural offerings, one thing the city needed was an artificial cliff face for people to scale. Maybe he decided that certain citizens weren't climbing the walls enough in their personal and professional lives.

Now we had this: a three-story expanse of hand-grabs and toeholds and obtruding knobs, just right for hoisting yourself onto or slipping off of. Presumably the idea is to make you feel like you're in Utah. Of course, you're not in Utah. You're in Manhattan. You came here to see a show or make a million or get a job or paint a picture or do any of the other ten thousand legitimate, doable things besides rock climbing that people come here for. You came to New York because it wasn't Utah. Not that you asked, but here's the Ingalls philosophy on urban rock climbing: don't do it. Go to where real rocks are, and climb them.

The climbing facility was part of an ambiguous indoor-outdoor place along Broadway, open to the street, beside a noodle joint that itself looked half like a public atrium and half like a private food shop. I didn't like it. I didn't like not knowing whether I was welcome as a customer or tolerated as a member of "the public." A small cluster of people stood around the base of the climbing wall as a young man in skintight cyclist-type clothes helped a middle-aged woman into a harness that didn't look all that different from a straitjacket. The woman was Catherine Flonger.

She was wearing gray sweat clothes, the expensive kind that make you want to go to sleep in them, and black leg warmers. That, plus the harness she had just put on. She wore no makeup and her short brown hair looked not so much brushed as yelled at and intimidated. There was something both defeatist and yet oddly serene about her manner as the instructor explained the basics and clipped the guide wires to the harness. I walked up and greeted her.

"Oh good, you're here," she said, dispensing with the formality of being nice. As before with this dame, I didn't know whether to be flattered or insulted by her presumptive intimacy. Just as I didn't know how to react when she turned to the instructor and, indicating me, said, "We'll be going up together."

"That'll be the day," I said.

But she wasn't laughing. "I want you to. Please, Mr. Ingalls. It was your idea. And I'll tell you something. I'm on what I admit is a very strange journey, and I need you along. I'll pay you, naturally."

The public was watching. "You're the client."

The instructor held up another harness but hesitated. "He's not exactly dressed for it," the kid said.

He had a point. I was wearing a brown double-breasted, a fedora, and wing tips. Catherine Flonger waved away this objection and the kid shrugged. I let him put the harness over my jacket.

I had a provocative thought. "Mrs. Flonger—"

"Please. Catherine."

"Fine. Catherine."

"No. I'm sorry . . . what do you think of Ms. Binney?"

"Heard of her. Some kind of children's television character, right?"

"It's my maiden name. Do you think I can go back to being a maiden, Mr. Ingalls?"

"Well," I laughed, "maybe if—"

"And may I call you Peter?"

"I . . . actually, no. I don't like Peter."

"You like Pete, don't you?"

"Yeah. I'm funny that way."

"I don't care for Pete."

"Good thing it isn't your name."

"I'm going to call you Mr. Ingalls."

"Ms. Binney, please, can—"

"Oh dear God, no. Call me Mrs. Flonger."

"Yes, all right. Mrs. Flonger." Whatever provocative thought I'd had, it was gone. "Can we just get on with it?"

The instructor, a solemn lad by the name of Justin, gave us a basic intro, and we set up at the base of the wall. I felt like a marionette, connected by ropes and pulleys to distant, invisible centers of power and control. Justin would anchor Catherine and his helper, a beefy, friendly young woman named Tracy, would handle my lines.

We started up. I fit the hard, gleaming toes of my wing tips onto the little outcroppings and into the little dents in the artificial surface of the wall, grabbed handholds on similar blocks and cuts above, and began the slow ascent. I kept an eye on Catherine Flonger and admired the way she moved. Maybe she had done this before. Maybe she was a natural. She hoisted herself a good foot farther up, her long, trim body moving gracefully amid the gray folds of her clothes and the safety ropes. "So," I said. "This clue. Skim it and give me the cream."

"Not yet," she said. She paused and looked over at me. "First I want to tell you how I've been since we had lunch."

"You look good." I stepped up eight inches or so and reestablished myself. I was eight feet off the ground and it was already a different world.

"I look terrible. And I've been terrible."

"Condolences, doll. But about hubby's girlfriend. Is—"

"I feel like I'm losing everything." She suddenly swung laterally to her left, with a creak of ropes and a squeak of pulleys, and found a new toehold. I didn't know you could do that. "Not just Darius, but everything. Friends. Causes I used to work for. Interests." She offered a wan smile. "I'm no longer interested in my interests."

"Uh-huh." I tried reaching for the next handhold up, but it was three inches beyond my stretched fingers. I could feel my right foot skidding off whatever miserable little nub it was on.

"And the funny thing is," Catherine Flonger said, "I don't *care*."

"Aces—" I looked to either side. Catherine was to my left, blocking any hope of finding a new position there. There was a little ledge three feet to my right. If I swung over like she had, the arc of the swing could raise me up enough to nab it with my right foot. I got ready.

"I'm not depressed," she went on, as much to herself or her god or her conscience as to me. "I'm not suicidal. I'm not even particularly unhappy. Isn't that funny, Mr. Ingalls?"

I decided I needed some outward momentum as well as some sideways push. I eyeballed the approximate angle and distance I'd have to propel myself outward and over. "Hilarious."

"I feel like all my opinions and reactions and positions are like the clothes in my closet. All of which I hate, by the way. I just want to get rid of them all."

"Good idea. Okay, just a sec." I kicked back and pushed off and leaned away from the wall into what I'd hoped would be a smooth arc, stopping at the foothold to the right. For a moment I hung suspended out from the wall. Tracy down below was slowing my motion but not stopping it.

"My daughter calls," Catherine Flonger went on. "And I can barely talk to her. I care about her, I suppose. I mean, of course I do. But these days . . ." She watched me float away from the wall and said, "Are you appalled?"

I had misjudged the jump. I had given it too much outward force and not enough lateral force. Result: I came slamming back to where I'd started from, into the wall. It didn't hurt, at least physically. I scrambled for a foothold, and managed to find one. "What? Appalled? I'm never appalled, doll."

Tracy called up from the floor, "You okay?"

I looked down. "Fine. This is my meat." I looked to my left: Catherine was gone. Then I looked up and saw that she'd reached the top.

I gave up trying to establish toeholds by going straight in. The tips of my shoes were too narrow and the sole leather too slippery. Instead I put my instep up against the wall and rested most of my arch on the blocks and knobs. It played hell with my pants. But I felt better established. Sure, at some points it looked like I was humping the wall. But you accept that, in wall climbing. People know you're not really humping the wall. Then again, don't ask me what people know.

Catherine Flonger had paused at the top and was there when I arrived. "I'm impressed, Mr. Ingalls. I didn't think you'd make it."

I was breathing hard. Twenty feet below, a little group of on-lookers offered some semi-facetious applause. "How about that info," I managed to gasp.

Catherine Flonger looked at me and said nothing. Then she pushed herself off the top foothold and floated a foot or so from the wall. Down below, Justin looked strangely amused. But then, that was what his generation did. Risk their necks in dangerous sports and look strangely amused. He called up to her, "I'm going to lower you down." He started feeding back rope to the pulleys, and she descended about two feet. Then she stopped with a little jolt and bounced a bit, gently, her hands lightly holding the ropes, utterly serene. Yes, "utterly."

"The line's kinked or something," Justin called.

"Have you ever heard of people going through this?" Catherine said. "Becoming detached from everything in their lives? Relationships, job, religion . . . everything. Oh, who knows what *you've* heard of. But how am I supposed to react? Am I supposed to panic? Or mourn? Or drink? Or get suicidal? But I think I like it. And it's all so obvious from up here."

Now Justin looked worried and called up, "Are you okay?"

"I'm fine. . . . Mr. Ingalls, I owe you an apology. Not that it matters, of course. I insulted you—before, at lunch—but you're the reason I'm up here." She went quiet.

Frankly, I was glad. I had my hands full with the return trip, which was harder than going up. When you pull you've got some measure of control. When you let gravity do the work, you're at the mercy of its schedule.

"Who knows what other wisdom you have access to?" Catherine Flonger said. "My God, what next? I completely give up."

Then I figured, the hell with it. I called down to Tracy. "Lower away, kid. I'm quits." I kicked out lightly from the wall and floated down to the floor like Peter Pan. I got out of the harness and looked up. Catherine was still hovering there. Another instructor had climbed up and was dickering with the lines and pulleys. Then he waved to Justin, who lowered the lady down. There was a small flurry of concern from the staff and the on-lookers, but she smiled and tamped it out.

I took her aside. "You had your fun," I said. "Now, is there something I should know?"

"My husband and his lover will be having lunch the day after tomorrow at one o'clock at the Marlin Room at the Jubilee Arms Hotel. They may be with another couple."

"And you know this how—?"

"I heard him on the phone." She displayed a kind of serenity I found myself envying, provided it wasn't symptomatic of a complete mental breakdown. "You might want to bring a camera."

"If you know this, why not just be there yourself?"

"I don't want to confront anyone. I just want to see who he's with."

I thanked her for the info and started to leave. She stopped me and said, "Mr. Ingalls? I appreciate your suggesting this. In your own strange way, you were right."

"It happens," I said. "Want some other ideas? Trumpet lessons. Study calligraphy at home. Learn tap dancing in your spare time—"

She said she'd think about it and said good-bye, and I bounced.

NINE

The next afternoon I was at my desk taking stock. The Catherine Flonger case was frozen in place until tomorrow at lunch. And the Celeste Vroman case was concluded. She and her boyfriend were off on a pleasure cruise, I was paid in full, and one tiny piece of this sad world's chaos had been cleaned, pressed, and stowed in the drawer marked "solved."

Or so I thought. Then young Stephanie appeared in the doorway, trim and attractive in black jeans and some kind of girly pink pullover. She looked disturbed. "Um, there's a guy here from the police."

She ushered in a huge, pale, shuffling mug in a cream-colored suit that someone, not necessarily the current owner, had slept in. The thin chartreuse tie was loose. His shoes were standard issue cop black but scuffed as though covered with hieroglyphics. He was maybe thirty-five, and his smooth white face was immense: very clean-shaven, very pale, two huge expanses of cheek against which the thin, small mouth and narrow, slitlike eyes were mere landmarks. His hair was thinning, a sandy brown that flopped down onto a half acre of forehead. He moved with a tentative shuffle, as though in a dream. A bad dream.

"Mr. Pete Ingalls," he said. His voice was a shallow baritone; he used it the way a nasty kid uses a slingshot. "Just what we need—another independent snoop." He scratched an eyebrow, grimacing. His main attention, if he had any, was elsewhere. "How come I haven't heard of you?"

"I was born yesterday." I gestured toward one of the client chairs. "And you are—?"

"Henry D. Thoreau. Detective. Homicide." He got settled and added, "The D stands for David. No relation."

"My sympathies," I said. "No siblings, or cousins, or uncles or aunts—that's gotta be tough. Especially come Thanksgiving. Sitting around that big table, with the turkey and the trimmings, and it's just you and the dog."

"I don't mean I don't have any relations. I mean I'm not related to Henry David Thoreau." Then he spoke to an invisible friend, and the two of them seemed to get upset and perturbed, which Thoreau expressed in a harsh sneer: "Which everybody asks about to where it fucking just *burns my ass*." He looked back at me. "Got some questions." He thumbed toward the door and the outer area. "Your secretary's cute. She married?"

"Not that I know of. Are you?"

He shrugged, then grinned horribly. "Not necessarily." He flopped a loose hand against several places around his chest. At first I took it to be some kind of involuntary palsy. Then I decided it was, in fact, a religious gesture. He was symbolically flagellating himself, probably cued by our vague intimation of his adultery with Stephanie. Then he said, "Got any cigarettes?"

I brought a pack of Parker Impresarios out of my jacket and offered one. He put it in his mouth with too much care, as though hand-feeding a dangerous animal, then slapped himself again for matches. I tossed him a pack. He grunted thanks and lit up, then looked around.

"Ashtray?"

"Sorry, Detective. I don't smoke."

He nodded—smokers are used to that; they take the news and soldier on—and dropped the match onto the floor. He took a drag, squinting, and sat back, a great pale shapeless hulk of a cop.

Then I remembered something. "Hold it. What do you mean, homicide?"

"We'll get there." He drew on the cig. "First, tell me, Lew Archer . . ." For a second his face took on some shape and character, but it dissolved into the smoke he blew off to the side. "What do you know about a woman named Olivia Cartwright?"

"I know her a little. Small broad, fine-boned. Smart. Nonfiction editor, works at—"

"Taylor and Tackett, yeah. I just came from there."

"Why?"

"She was found dead this morning. At the Hotel Urbane. Semicheap tourist place on upper Br—"

There was a big crash of crockery from the doorway. Stephanie stood there, mouth half open in shock, the shattered remnants of her coffee mug and the splashed remnants of her coffee dispersed across the floor. "Olivia's dead?" Her face was white.

Thoreau didn't turn all the way around to address her. That would have required too much effort. Instead he spoke across his right shoulder in her general direction. "The chambermaid at the hotel found her this morning. ME places death at late yesterday morning, plus or minus." He turned back to me. "How did you know her, if you don't mind my asking?"

"Who—"

He snickered and added, "Or even if you do mind."

"Who says I did know her?" I said.

"You did. Just now."

"Well, yeah. I did know her slightly. I only met her recently. And of course I didn't know her before I met her."

"Uh-hu . . ." He grimaced and I heard a clatter. Then he leaned forward as though to touch his toes. I peered over my desk and saw that he'd kicked off a shoe and was kneading his foot. "Fucking athlete's foot," he said—chattily, aggrievedly, to a supposed fellow sufferer in this vale of tears. "You use the creams, but it's like helping the damn fungus breed itself stronger."

"Things are tough all over."

Stephanie took a couple of steps into the room and stared. She had tears in her eyes. "Who would want to kill—ew, gross!"

"Sorry." Thoreau snaked his foot back into his shoe. "I understand you were at T and T last Friday."

She nodded. "Olivia was having an affair with this lawyer. Jeffrey Litman. She didn't know he was married. I went to tell her."

"And why did you do that? Go to tell her this Litman was married."

She looked at me. I jumped in. "As a service to a client of mine. Who shall remain nameless."

"Oh good." He dropped the cigarette butt onto the floor and smashed it out. "Does your nameless client have anything to hide?"

"Don't we all? Actually, I don't think so. But I'm ethically required to withhold a client's name unless legally compelled to disclose it."

"According to—?"

I gestured vaguely. "Common knowledge. Tradecraft. It's in all the books."

His eyelids drooped; he looked half-asleep. "And you don't want the commission crawling up your ass to take your license away, probably."

I smirked. "Nice try, Thoreau. But this has nothing to do with driving."

"I don't mean your driver's license. I mean your private investigator's license."

I was given pause. "Stop, you're killing me."

"P.I.'s are licensed by the State of New York. You have one, right, Mr. Gittes?" He started snickering and muttered to his invisible friend, "Or maybe he doesn't!"

Some fast thinking was called for. I said, "Let's just say the dog ate it."

"Do you have a dog?"

"I can get one."

"Mm-hmm." He smacked his lips, then looked up at Stephanie. She was watching him with a kind of fascinated loathing. He said, "Do you have any juice?"

"No," she said, all ice. "But would you like to hear our specials?"

"Would you like to suck my dick?"

"People," I said. "Let's call that a practice round and start over. Ms. Constantino, if you'll get the detective here some coffee, he'll can the spicy patter and everything'll be jakeloo."

Thoreau sighed and waved a hand in airy assent. Stephanie flushed red and stomped off. The cop then began using an index finger to carve grime out from his other nails, working avidly, as though autistic. Without looking up from it he said, "This Olivia Cartwright. Do you know if she had any enemies?"

"None that would want to kill her. But I wouldn't know."

A look of faint amusement flickered on his big preoccupied face. " 'No, but I don't know.' Fuck me."

Stephanie returned with a mug of hot black java, which she practically threw at him. "Here. Get your own milk and sugar."

"Thanks, this is fine." He looked at her and said, somewhat respectfully, "Tell me about your visit last Friday."

Cool and controlled, she described her visit to the T and T offices, and how she had told Olivia both about Litman's being married and his still seeing our client, whose name Stephanie alertly didn't mention. Thoreau took all this in while blowing on and noisily slurping his joe. He barely blinked. Finally, when she had finished, he turned to me and asked what I could add.

I described my visit, including the cameo appearances by the outraged Dylan and the still-smitten Richard. I also commented on how Richard had managed to deck me outside the office. It wasn't exactly a motive for murder, but it hinted at the strong passions running around the nonfiction department. I was careful not to mention Celeste's name, or the fact that she'd hired me to find Litman. I kept to myself anything that didn't directly touch on Olivia Cartwright.

"You want a suspect and a motive, Thoreau, ask about Dylan's friend," I suggested. "Olivia was about to turn him down for a book deal."

Stephanie said, "Are there any clues?"

Thoreau turned to her, jaw slack, nodding slightly. "Just a few dozen fingerprints in the room, which won't mean *shit*." These outbursts were sudden and seemed unpredictable even to him. "The killer's prints could be sitting there in Day-Glo, but if he isn't in the system, we don't have dick. Or she. Or it'll be some chambermaid or a tourist from Belgium from two weeks ago. Plus the bed hadn't been slept in. And the toilet seat was up."

"Suggesting a man had been in the room," I said. "And therefore that the killer is a man."

"Or that the guy who stayed in the room used the john and then left before the killer got there," Stephanie said. "Or that the killer is a woman who left the seat that way on purpose." I shot her a look that suggested she shut up.

Thoreau shrugged. "She was a small woman. Olivia. She could have been fairly easy to choke. A woman could have done it." He put the mug on my desk and stood up. "Thanks. I'll probably be back." He held out a hand, and I shook it. It was like grasping a warm fish. "And think about getting a license, Ingalls. I don't give a fuck, but somebody in Albany does." He started to walk out.

"Who do you think killed her?" Stephanie asked.

He stopped, a giant white whale on two feet. "Hell if I know. Maybe we'll find out, maybe we won't." As an afterthought he pulled out his wallet and handed each of us a card. "Call me if you think of something."

I looked at it and tried not to laugh. "Nice card," I said.

He snorted. "Like yours is better?"

I handed him one as Stephanie narrowed her eyes and watched. He looked at it. "This is beautiful," he said, put it gently in his pocket, and left.

After he'd gone we both breathed easier. "What a creep," Stephanie said. "I can't believe he works for Homicide."

"Maybe he has his reasons." I reached for the phone.

"Everybody has their reasons, Pete. That's no excuse for being an asshole."

I dialed the number and got what I always got: Celeste Vroman's voice mail. "It's Pete Ingalls, Celeste. A gentleman from Homicide was just here. Call me."

"So, who could have done this?" Stephanie said.

"Isn't it obvious? One of the editors at Taylor and Tackett. Start with lover boy Richard. She gives him his papers, he takes it hard, he says if I can't have you no one can."

"Nah. He's a wimp."

"Some wimps are land mines waiting to go off."

"Yeah, and some wimps are wimps. Forget it."

"Okay, then how about Dylan's boyfriend?"

"Because he's not getting a book deal? That's something you get drunk over, not kill someone for."

"Then what's your theory, doll?"

"Plus, if the Hotel Urbane is such a dive, what was Olivia doing there?"

"Use your imagination. Playing Hide the Spumoni with a charming tourist with an accent that she met in a bar."

"Forget it. She's not the kind of person to sleep around. She's seeing Litman and that's it." She shook her head. "Plus, it's Hide the Salami. Spumoni is ice cream. It's also hide the tourist. The bed hadn't been slept in. Who was the room rented to?"

"We don't know."

"Let's find out!"

"Dollface, this isn't our gig. We look out for Celeste and that's all. Which you did quite nicely while Thoreau was here. So let's not fall off the balance beam."

"You're right." She looked at me. "We have to find Litman's wife and talk to her ASAP."

I laughed. "You lost me, kid."

"Look, Pete, let's all admit something. We both know who could have killed Olivia and why."

"Meaning—"

"Meaning, Celeste. Out of jealousy. She's angry, she's volatile, you can hear her screaming on the phone from twenty feet away. She's strong. She could do it."

We were handing little jars of nitro back and forth. It called for special care. "Hypothetically." I gave a grudging nod. "But what's that got to do with Litman's wife?"

"The cop is going to find out all the obvious things. He knows that Olivia was seeing Litman, which means he'll talk to Litman and to his wife. Right?"

"Let's say."

"Which means we have to know one thing: does Litman's wife know about Celeste? Because what if she does? And what if Mrs. Litman is pissed about it? Then when the cops question her, she'll send them right to Celeste, whether Celeste is guilty or not. And what if the wife killed Olivia! She'd try to pin it on Celeste and save herself. So let's go. It's for the client, right?"

"Just a minute." I held up a hand. "Where does all this suddenly become 'we'? You're the hired help. You're the secretary. You stay here and powder your nose and answer the phone. I go out into the world and pursue the case. Nuff said?"

"Powder my nose?"

"I'm speaking metaphorically. Do your job."

"Come on. I'm into this."

"I work better alone."

"But I have good ideas. And two heads are better than one."

"I don't like your language. You have a foul mouth. It reflects poorly on me."

"I'll be really careful." Then she said, "It's not because I'm a girl, is it?"

I had to laugh at that. "Honey," I said, "you insult me. I have absolutely no problem admitting that you've got an excellent deductive mind even though you're a girl."

"Then let's go. We have to get to her before the cop does."

"Forget it, lady. Now excuse me, I have to go to work." And with that I got up, grabbed my hat, and walked out.

TEN

I had been walking up the street for about five seconds when it hit me: I didn't know where I was going. I knew nothing about Litman's wife, including whether or not she even called herself Litman or lived in New York. I went back inside and put the fedora back on the rack. Stephanie found a likely listing in the Manhattan white pages for Litman's residence, and we got mixed results: a voice message confirmed that "Jeff and Wendy" lived there, but no one answered.

"She probably works," Stephanie said. "So we have to find out where."

"Not so easy." I was gentle with the gal. She was green as a new blade of grass, that really green kind, but she was eager. It seemed like a good time for an instructive rhetorical question. "How do you find out where a guy's wife works?"

"Ask him!" She grabbed the phone and waved me away. I retreated to my office, because sometimes you have to create some space in which the young can make their own mistakes. A minute later she was leaning in the doorway, frowning. "He hasn't been in all day. His cell doesn't answer, and no one knows where he is. Both of which are unusual, they said."

"Maybe Celeste knows where he is."

"Yeah, right. Meanwhile, you'll notice she hasn't called back. We can't get to her, either." She bit her lip, thought hard, and snapped her fingers. "Got it." She disappeared. Seconds later, from the vantage point of having tiptoed to the doorway and eavesdropped, I heard her say, in a throaty, honey-covered voice of soothing but unyielding authority, "Jeffrey Litman, please, Dr. Constantino's office calling . . . Certainly." I walked out to join her and tried to make admiring eye contact, but the girl was in character and unavailable for nonverbal praise. "Is this Mr. Litman's office? Dr. Constantino's office calling, I've got Mr. Litman's results from the tests, is he there, please? . . . Oh, dear. . . . All day? . . . Well, might I please have Mrs. Litman's number, then? . . . Yes . . . Yes, I understand, but . . . Yes . . ." She rattled some papers. "But I've just been given the findings from the blood work, and I must say they are significant. Excuse me a moment. . . ." She held the receiver away from her mouth and called out into the thin air, "I'm trying, Doctor, but there's some resistance. . . ."

I picked up the cue. "Okay, uh, nurse—"

"Yes, I've said it's terribly, terribly urgent. . . . I will." She got back on the phone. "I really must ask you. . . . Yes, exactly, the patient's wife will want to know of it as soon as possible. . . . Yes, thank you. . . ." She jotted down a number and bailed out.

"Not bad, doll," I said. "I felt a twinge of medical concern myself." I reached for the number.

She pulled it back. "I'll call."

"I'll call, thanks."

"I don't mind."

"Give, baby."

"It's my job. Then we can—"

"Now."

Sulking, she handed me the number. I called. It was an art gallery on Fifty-seventh, and yes, Mrs. Litman was indeed in. I made an appointment to browse the wares in fifteen minutes and reached for my hat again.

"Okay, look." Stephanie came over and, while speaking, adjusted my tie, brushed smooth my padded shoulders, and generally policed my overall presentation. It wasn't unpleasant. "Remember to ask her how long they've known each other, if they have any kids and how old, how long her husband's been a partner, whether she knows Celeste, whether she's heard of Olivia, and what her husband thinks of the firm."

"Yeah, well—"

"And see if you can get a sense of whether they have financial problems."

"Okay, sure, but—"

"Like, if a kid has special medical needs, or their investments tanked when the market collapsed. Stuff like that."

"Aces, doll, but—"

"Oh, and this is easy. Find out how long she's been working at the gallery. Maybe she had to get a job recently."

I thought hard for a second, then made a decision. "I have a better idea. Why don't you come with me and ask her yourself?"

There was a telling pause. Then she smiled.

The gallery, in a high-rise, was one of those small, swank joints behind a single frosted-windowed door, where you walk into a big, bright, empty room, onto a gorgeous parquet floor, which feeds into several adjoining empty rooms, and you think, What's the setup? The wall decorations are nice, but what exactly is it they're selling? Then it hits you that it's the wall decorations that they're selling, if not exactly to you.

When we arrived there was no one else in the place. We strolled around and admired the art. The canvases seemed to be a series of related portraits. Each one showed a pair of people standing before mirrors. The gimmick was that each subject's image was not him- or herself, but someone else from the other paintings. So the paintings were linked by swapped likenesses.

No, I didn't understand it, either, but there were red dots beside a lot of the labels. Either people were buying these things, or someone was getting cute with the red dots.

Off the main room was a counter and a little office space. Seated there, paging through a magazine, was a petite, shapely looker with close-cut dark hair, conservatively dressed in a thin, luxe charcoal sweater over a darker, black skirt. She was in her early thirties but dressed older, and on purpose. She was one of those broads who when sixteen, in high school, already looked thirty: dark, seductive, and ready for action. She smiled as we bellied up.

"Wendy Litman? Pete Ingalls, P.I., and my associate, Ms. Constantino."

"How do you do?" She looked politely inquisitive. "Please, look around. Or do you have an appointment?"

"Not really." I smirked. "Unless you mean the appointment we all have. With the robed gentleman with the sickle."

Wendy Litman smiled. It was a cool disinterested smile. It was a smile that didn't offer much by way of revelations or cooperation. That was fine. I was about to make it turn hot and interested. "Mr. Ingalls, is there something I can help you with?"

"I've met your husband, Mrs. Litman. The attorney? Jeffrey Litman? He happens to be a friend of my client. I think you may be in a position to help me."

"I can help you acquire an original painting," she said. "Apart from that, I don't see what I can do."

"Put it this way. Do you know a woman named Celeste Vroman?"

She tilted her head just slightly to the side. It was a small gesture that spoke volumes, yeah, but I'd read them before and found them wanting. "I do, yes. I'm sorry—what business is this of yours?"

"As I said, I'm a private eye. Celeste Vroman is my client. I'm acting in her interests, and I'd like to ask you a few questions. For example, did you happen to know that your husband is having an affair with her?"

Stephanie started coughing—loud, hard, the kind of cough that's probably the worst of them all, that sounds fake and forced. Maybe it was an allergy, or asthma—or maybe it was a subtle message. I looked at her and got an eye-contact high sign signaling the need for a conference on the mound. I asked Wendy Litman, "Do you happen to have some water?"

"There's a fountain in the corridor just next to the elevator."

"Excuse us," I said, and took Stephanie's arm and steered her out. At the fountain I inquired into what was up.

Her whisper was urgent. "Don't tell her about the affair! She'll send the cops after Celeste! We just wanted to see what she knows."

I thought about it. The kid had a point. "My mistake," I said. "Let's go fix it."

"How?"

We returned to the gallery, where Wendy Litman looked, if anything, even more composed and ready to chat. "I seem to have misspoke," I said. "It's not your husband who's having the affair with Ms. Vroman. It's somebody else's husband."

"Mr. Ingalls—"

"Who, by the way, is having the affair with somebody else entirely."

"I see."

"Unless you already know that it is your husband." I was quietly pleased with that. It seemed to put the onus on her, although I should probably point out here that I've never been entirely sure what "onus" means. "Do you? Or isn't he?"

"Mr. Ingalls—"

Stephanie stepped up. "I think what Pete means is—"

"I know what Pete means." The dame's tone had lost its sweetness. We weren't talking about pretty paintings anymore. "Not that it is any of your business . . . regardless of who your client is . . . but I do happen to know a few things about the relationship between Ms. Vroman and my husband. Now shall we leave it at that? Good-bye."

That was good enough for me. "Good-bye, Mrs. Litman," I said, and turned to leave.

But Stephanie wasn't buying. "One more thing," she said. "How about Olivia Cartwright?"

Coolly, Wendy Litman said, "What about her? I know no such person."

"You said 'her,' " I volleyed back. The Ping-Pong was picking up. "How do you know she's a woman, then?"

"Olivia is a woman's name."

I absorbed this and gave a reluctant nod. Stephanie stood her ground and kept punching. "Then you don't know if Jeffrey is having an affair with her, either? Which, I mean, he could be, or not, but you, like, don't know, right?"

"What I know is that I would like for both of you to leave."

"Fine, right, but first, you also would therefore not know that Olivia Cartwright was found murdered this morning?"

Her eyes widened for a split second. "That's impossible," she said. "I mean it's impossible that I would know that." Then she turned away and walked back to a cabinet of wide, shallow short drawers built deep into the wall. Head down, stiff and distracted, she pulled one open and stood there looking down at what appeared to be, from where we were, some posters or prints lying flat.

I spoke to her back. "We heard it from the homicide cop on the case."

Her back was still to us. She was looking down into the drawer when she said, "God, that's terrible."

Stephanie said, "Your husband knew her, Mrs. Litman. I know that for a fact. They were . . . um . . . fond of each other."

She turned and faced us. She was solemn and poised and in no mood for sparring. "Oh really? And how do you happen to know this?"

"Because I spoke to Olivia last Friday."

"Then perhaps you should discuss it with Jeffrey. Assuming that this Olivia woman wasn't lying. Or referring to someone else. Or maybe you shouldn't discuss it at all. Maybe none of this is any of your business."

"It's all my business, lady," I said. "Literally business. Literally mine." I glanced around. The rooms were empty, except for a lot of painted pictures of people staring into mirrors and seeing someone else looking back. "I don't suppose you happen to know where he is."

"At his office, I assume."

"Not when I last checked."

She slammed the drawer shut and wheeled around to face us. "Mr. Ingalls, I hope you can understand how upsetting this is. If he's not at the office, I don't know where he is. Now please excuse me, I'm expecting a customer soon and I want to be prepared." She strode from that area through a doorway and into an office we couldn't see.

The postmortem took place on the street, surrounded by hustling shoppers and wandering tourists and methodical art gallery cruisers. I started the bidding. I said I believed Wendy Litman when she said she hadn't known anything about Olivia. It made sense.

"Not completely," Stephanie said.

"Why not? Olivia didn't know about *her*, remember."

"Yeah, but something seems off." She wrinkled her nose as though at a bad piece of fruit. "I'm just not buying it."

"Then put it back on the shelf. Meanwhile I'm not falling in love with her attitude about Celeste. It was clear as mud. If not clearer."

"Yeah, that's true. We can't explain it. It doesn't make sense."

"And let me take a crack at why." I was about to play a dangerous game. The possibility existed of my immersing the gal too deeply in the currents of my more speculative ruminations. But she was a bright kid and I thought she could handle it, so I gave her a full blast of the Ingalls metaphysical sensibility. "It doesn't make sense because, to us, it only seems to not make sense. Because it's some inscrutable female thing. It's one of those prerational gags that takes place on a level where feeling and intuition meet, which as rational creatures we cannot penetrate."

"No. It doesn't make sense because she's hiding something." I was busy pondering this when she went on, "So here's what you have to do, Pete. You have to call Litman tomorrow and talk to him. See what he knows."

"Maybe."

"Of course! What else?"

"Because—?"

"Because that woman's reaction to what we told her was extremely weird."

"So—"

"So we want to know what Litman says when we ask him what his wife knows."

I nodded wordlessly, implying that I agreed, that I really knew it all along, that she needn't trouble herself by telling me what to do, and so forth.

But, once back at the office, when I phoned Litman's firm, I was told he was still unaccounted for. He had never returned to the office the day before, and he wasn't there now, and the perky skirt working the horn had no clue as to where or when he'd reappear. I took this info in stride and asked to speak with Tad Phillips.

"Figured you'd call back," the lad said with an audible smirk.

We traded he-man/frat-boy small talk for a few minutes, during which he reminded me he was still interested in becoming my protégé if I was ever in the market. I strangled that baby in its crib and then asked about Litman. Where was he?

Phillips laughed, then told me to hold the wire. He shut the door to whatever little office he'd landed in, and resumed. "Jeffy's hiding," he said. "Mom and Dad are mad at him. Or maybe he's on some secret mission about the bonds."

"Slow down, ace," I said. "Who's Mom and Dad? And what bonds?"

"Megan Loomis and Greg Higgins. Managing partners. They're upset at Jeffy's handling of this estate disposition the firm got charged with. Like over a year ago. You know Thompson Fleer? Big rich guy? Low-income housing, government construction? So he croaks in February of last year and the widow and the two exes and the kids and the family cat start fighting over the estate. He's been with the firm since, like, forever, so the executor puts the assets, which include around nine million clams' worth of bearer bonds, in our care."

"Do tell."

"But wait, there's more. The case drags on and on. Then, like, six months ago, Kleinway International wins its final appeal against us. Some complex suit that's been pending for years. We'd hired Davilman Green and got sort of creamed. So now we're suing Davilman, plus we have to pony up to Kleinway some judgment in the low gazillions." Tad Phillips snorted. "Okay, we're insured, but word gets out. And the corporate clients? Their boards get nervous and decide they don't love us anymore."

"Which is why the moving men are there," I said.

"And why everyone's freaking out. It's *Titanic* time and the water outside is cold, man."

"So the bonds—?"

"So Jeffy's in charge of the Fleer estate. And he starts to stall. Big time. Delays, continuances, depositions in, like, Peru, and it's not clear why. But the other partners have their hands full with everything else, let alone everyone has to actually do work and make rain and conduct biz. So, like, last week Megan and Greg tell Jeffy to shit or cut bait. And he yells fuck you, I know what I'm doing, and they yell fuck you, this borders on fiduciary malfeasance, and doors are slammed and the kids are peeing in their pants and everybody's waiting for it to show up in *The Observer*."

"Got it. But refresh my memory. Bearer bonds—"

"Unregistered bonds that you can redeem off the street. Like cash. Not in anybody's name, no signature required. You find one on the subway, you can cash it in. The ones we've got are like ten-thousand-dollar bills. In piles. In the safe. Wait—" He covered the phone and I heard muffled conversation. Then he came back. "Listen, man, gotta go. Meanwhile you'll think about what we said, right?"

I said I would and that was that. Or was it? Suddenly the stage was full of law partner discord and a cache of negotiable securities and something I might be tempted to call fiduciary malfeasance. I made a mental note to remember it all and figure out the rest.

ELEVEN

The hack stopped in front of an apartment building, or what looked like one. There was a single set of double glass doors and a poker-pan doorman in charcoal gray livery. I drew the cabbie's attention to the fact that he'd made a mistake.

"No, no," he said. He was one of those Middle Eastern birds in a turban. "Jubilee Arms here. Right address." He pointed to a single brass plaque on the wall. If this was a hotel, it was going out of its way to hide the fact. I paid and got out, traded working-stiff nods with the doorman, and went in.

I came back out. "What's the gag?" I asked him. "Did they forget to build the lobby, or am I still in the rack and it's all a terrible dream?"

His eyes remained fixed on the environment. It would take more than a confused flatfoot to win his attention. "Fourth floor."

I shrugged and went back to the elevators, where a small waiting tribe of Euro-heps, modelistas, and show-biz mercenaries in black leather shuffled and snickered. One citizen, a skinny lad in a leopard-skin sport coat, nodded his bald head at my double-breasted and said, "Nice." I nodded back. No one talked in the elevator.

We emerged into a corridor, which at first looked like it had suffered a power outage and was lit only by the occasional emergency lamp. Then the truth dawned that this was as planned, that the emergency lamps were actually dim lightbulbs in misshapen, melted-looking sconces along the weirdly undulating wall, and that this was to a normal hotel what vermouth was to Seven-Up.

I shuffled through the darkness into what everyone was apparently agreeing was the lobby, where little unmarked desks and counters glowed like apparitions in separate, contained pools of halogen white. A slow scan of the area disclosed that Darius Flonger hadn't yet arrived, so I found a place to sit, on a chair molded out of resin and covered with burlap. It was paired with another of its kind and they were joined by a piece of furniture that had started out as a baby water buffalo and decided at the last minute to go through life as a table. I sat back, to the extent that I could, and waited.

I kept my attention on the entrance I'd come through. Nearby was the bar, lit like a crèche at midnight, a welcoming area of light and small tables and stools and other reassuringly identifiable objects. The staff all wore charcoal gray blazers and shared that look of attentive condescension and smug boredom that you always have to pay extra to find.

"Can I help you, sir?"

The lad offering assistance was a youngish black man, solidly built and nice and neat in a house uniform with a badge reading "Security" on his breast pocket. He was standing in front of me, leaning down in a way that suggested both deference and threat.

I gave him a collegial smirk. "Private talent, friend. On stakeout."

"Are you a guest?"

"Of Mother Earth? Aren't we all?"

"Of the hotel, sir."

"Not literally."

"Are you waiting for a guest?"

"I'm waiting for a visitor, chief."

"I'm afraid I'll have to ask you to leave."

"And why is that? I'm sitting here keeping my hands to myself."

"You've been here three hours, sir. This is not a public facility."

I nodded and reached into my back pants pocket. "Tell you what, soldier." I pulled out my wallet. "Why don't you have this discussion with Mr. Hamilton and get back to me with the conclusion."

"Sir, please, I cannot accept a gratuity. I must ask you to leave."

I admired the man's poise. I tried another angle. "We're both philosophers, brother—"

"Sir—"

"—so what say we reset the clock. I leave, turn around, and come back. My time starts over. Today is the first day of the rest of our lives."

"No, sir. Don't make me have to call my associates."

In my experience, when a mug starts invoking his associates, the wise man dusts. So I did the intelligent thing. I walked over to the registration desk, where svelte youngsters in charcoal cashmere jackets drifted about in solemn efficiency. Everyone wore a tag advertising their first name and their nation of origin. It was like a model U.N. run by a James Bond villain. Monica from Brazil asked Klaus from Germany if there were vacancies, got the nod, and signed me up. The per-night fee was half my monthly rent, but a pro does what he has to. I waved the room card at the security man as I returned to the chair. He nodded and moved off.

I'd been sitting there for a total of almost five hours and had begun to wonder if I'd picked the wrong joint when Darius Flonger walked in. He was accompanied by three other people: a man and woman obviously paired together, and a dwarf. Can I say that? A small individual, a size-deprived American, whatever the right terminology is. She was four feet, tops, in a pro-rata ultra-small ensemble of jeans and a white blouse. The other man wore a navy blazer and gray flannel trousers, his companion a black ladies business suit.

Flonger himself wore a dark suit and tie, and now is as good a time as any to ask: does it matter what these individuals wore? Let's just say they weren't naked, Flonger had come from work, and the dwarf was noticeably informal. They went to the bar.

I followed, palming my small camera. True, pix of hubby spending Happy Hour in a public place with a couple and a tallness-deprived human woman wouldn't exactly qualify as proof of an affair. But maybe my client would recognize the other couple and maybe that would help. I took up position at a little table near theirs and discreetly clicked away.

They were chatting about this and that, Flonger receiving the New York celeb's usual acknowledgment of furtive glances and studious avoidances from the surrounding customers, when I noticed that maybe my luck had begun to improve. They were all looking at me. What were the odds? This would give me the master shot I needed and spare me the effort of having to nonchalantly roam around their table, chasing dropped coins or continually tying my shoe, to nail all four.

Then the gent who wasn't Flonger muttered something and came over. He was a smooth-faced operator with silver hair. He didn't lower his voice. "What the hell do you think you're doing?"

Now, in my reading of the literature, when you're made on a stakeout and they start asking rhetorical questions, you roll the truth down the alley and see which way the pins fall. So I said, "Let me introduce myself," and walked him back to his table, where I addressed the ladies and gents. "The name's Ingalls. Pete Ingalls, P.I." Call it habit, call it reflex, call it the hard-won wisdom of a guy making a living, but as soon as I'd announced my name I had out my wallet and was handing around my card. Everyone's expression was unreadable as they each took theirs. "I've been hired by someone whose identity I am not at liberty to disclose—"

"Oh, for Christ's sake," the non-tiny woman sighed.

"—to snap some posed candids here of Mr. Flonger."

"Who hired you?" the silver-haired mug demanded.

"Ted—" Flonger began, trying to minimize and neutralize the event with a wave of the hand and an expression of eye-rolling resignation.

"No, Dar, I want to know. It's outrageous, this idiot lurking over there. Aren't we entitled to some goddamn privacy?"

"It's a public facility, chief," I said. "You accosted me, remember."

"Listen, you little parasite—"

Flonger stood up and held out open hands of mollification. "Ted, look, of course I appreciate your indignation. But let's settle this calmly. Mr."—he looked at the card—"Ingalls. This is a handsome card."

"Thanks." I looked blasé. "Others have thought so, too."

"I'm sure they have. In any case, I'm Darius Flonger." He held out his hand. I shook it. Five thousand years of Western civilization culminated in that handshake. We were two gentlemen, one of whom happened to be a world-famous journalist and the other of whom happened to be taking pictures of him. In that familiar thin, slightly nasal voice, well-known to me (and to the nation) from a thousand stand-ups reporting from the White House, he introduced the party.

The couple were Ted and Jeanette Eisenberg, who each answered my genial smile with a frosty grimace and a glance elsewhere. The little gal was Nora Thomas, a grad student in journalism at NYU. Her cursory handshake put a tiny bundle of twigs in my mitt.

Then Flonger said, "Why don't we all pose for one more shot, and Mr. Ingalls can get on with the rest of his business." The other three bristled but gave in. I shot one more as Flonger smiled with all-pro ease and the others glared like teens caught shoplifting. I thanked them and started to leave the area.

Ted Eisenberg suddenly leaped up and hustled over. He took me by the elbow and steered me out as he hissed in my ear. "I'm warning you, Ingalls. If I see you within a hundred feet of Darius, you are going to regret it for a long time."

"Go peddle your papers, Eisenberg," I said. "I already regret things for a long time. You do your job and I'll do mine."

He let me go and took a step back and said, "Oh, I'll do my job, all right. Don't worry about that." Then he turned and went back to the group.

TWELVE

I was standing on a podium in front of an orchestra, with a baton in my hand, and I was conducting. The musicians were sawing and blowing and banging, but the music was a tinny little beep-beep version of Beethoven's Ninth. I thought, " 'Ode to Joy.' If I only knew who Joy was, this would sound a lot better." And then I woke up—because it was all a dream, brother. I answered my cell phone. It was seven thirty in the morning.

"Mr. Ingalls? It's Celeste Vroman. I hope I didn't wake you."

"As a matter of fact, Ms. Vroman, you did."

"Listen carefully."

"You sound upset. Where are you?"

"Never mind. Just pay attention."

"I'm paying, lady. Retail."

"Something went wrong the other night. When Jeffrey and I were on the boat. It's . . ." In her pause I could hear an effort to control panic. "I need you to pick something up for me."

"Name it."

"I want you to go to Atlantic City. To the Sea Gull Harbor Marina. To slip number Fifty-three. Write it down. Fifty-three."

I grabbed the hotel's memo pad, thumbed the top of the pen, and complied. "Got it."

"You'll see a boat there, the *Sea Note*."

"Clever. I like it."

"On board, in a hold belowdecks, you'll find a briefcase. I need you to get it."

Fetching the problematic briefcase: Menial labor? Try a beloved classic from the gumshoe repertory. File under "courier," "safekeeping," and "valuable thing to be transported." Still, I hesitated. "Love to, Celeste, but a reasonable third party might wonder why you don't get it yourself. Some other poor lug might wonder why you left it there in the first place."

"I can't tell you that." She sounded impatient. "Call me and leave a message when you have it and I'll get back to you. Now repeat what I just said."

" 'Call me and leave a message when you have it—' "

"No, I mean the place, the boat, the whole thing."

Okay, I'm a literal person. There are worse character flaws. I repeated the specs and was just about to ask what this was all about when she said, "Don't look for me, Ingalls. You won't find me." And she hung up.

I couldn't drive to Atlantic City, because I couldn't rent a car, because I didn't have a driver's license, because I couldn't drive. Yeah, I know: "Gee, Pete. What kind of dick can't drive?" The kind of a dick who's lived in New York all his life, who appreciates mass transit, who just happens to give a damn about a little thing called municipal air quality.

So I did what people do. I went to Port Authority and caught the bus.

There are worse ways to travel. You read, you take a nap, you fall into a discussion with the gent to your left, who helpfully informs you that certain slot machines have retinal scans that can read your mind. You reflect on humanity and its boundless and manifold capacity for being nuts.

Atlantic City was its usual dolled-up doxy self. Arrive by raft from the east on the Atlantic Ocean, and it's all swank palaces and floodlit luxe facades. Drive in from the west, though, and you see behind the stage set, where they keep the humdrum streets of drugstores and gas stations, barbershops and beauty parlors, the haunts and dives and greasy spoons and watering holes of the locals. Farther inland, or what the natives, if there still are any, call "offshore," are the inlets, all branched out and narrowed down into marinas and piers and dry docks, like parking lots off an interstate.

I caught a cab at the station and we pulled into the crunchy gravel lot of the Sea Gull Harbor Marina at around noon. The sky was clear and the sun was warm—too warm. Midday would already be a bit late to be setting out. I strolled the slips and perused the vessels. The boats lashed to pilings and tied to cleats ranged in size from small canvas-topped dories to big multi-decked deep-sea cruisers, bristling with wires and cables and antennae like insects'.

I don't know what I expected to find at slip Fifty-three, but the *Sea Note* was a trim little one-engine outboard craft. On the other hand, hold the wire. Trim? Has any boat ever been described as *not* being trim? Then again, on closer inspection I realized that the *Sea Note* was, in fact, not trim at all. It was something of a mess. Certain poles and grommet-ringed tarps lay about in a distinctly un-trim manner. Whoever had last been out on this craft had not stowed anything upon return.

I stepped carefully down onto the deck and bent and examined what looked like an array of rust-brown blotches and spatters that started mid-deck and trailed toward the little wall of the deck, then up on top of it. The markings were dry, but slightly raised and freshly matte-like in texture, as opposed to worked into the wood and glazed over with polish and use. They were, in a word, new.

It didn't take long to discover that there wasn't any briefcase, either down below or anywhere else. I did the obvious thing— took out the cell and dialed Celeste's number. When I got the voice mail beep I said, "It's Ingalls, Ms. Vroman. I'm at the boat. There's no briefcase and some kind of paint blotches here and there. Call me on my cell with further instructions. I'll wait here for an hour."

Then it was time to ask some questions.

A man ten spaces over had just come in and, still in his vessel, was hoisting a cooler up onto the dock. I climbed onto the slatted walkway and strolled down toward him. He was a weathered old salt in a red plaid shirt and faded-to-white jeans, with a snowy grizzle of beard and a Sunoco gimme cap. The cooler must have been heavy; he set it down with a slam.

"Catch anything?" I asked.

"Flounder, mostly. Went out for weaks."

"That long?" Poor bastard, I thought. All that time and just this one Coleman chest to show for it. "You're what I call dedicated."

He squinted at me. "You're what I call peculiar." He looked at his boat, then looked back at me. "Wasn't out for weeks of *time*. Think you can do that on this little thing? I mean weakfish. Weakies."

"I stand corrected."

"You certainly do. Plus some blues, usual assorted junk. Skates like to drive you crazy."

"I hear ya." I found myself talking like him. I liked it. I liked trimming off unnecessary syllables and alluding in a word to a lifetime of wisdom and practical knowledge. "Ask me, though, don't quite understand why a man'd go skating on a fishing boat."

"Mister—"

"That some kind of technique? Roll around the deck on skates while you're reeling 'em in? Way I see it, the whole idea of the ocean is, you don't need skates."

"I wouldn't know."

He was threatening to clam up on me. I had to prime the pump a bit more. "Any idea why they call 'em blues?" A thought occurred to me. "Maybe because they're sad. Most fish look sad, don't they. When you catch 'em. Lay 'em out on that chipped ice and they all have that woe-is-me, I-got-caught look."

He picked up a mop that had been flat on the deck. "Is there something I can help you with?"

I pointed to Celeste's boat. "I was wondering if you knew anything about that craft there. The *Sea Note*. Or its owner."

"And why would you want to know?"

"Belongs to a friend of mine and something looks amiss."

"Ask your friend." He turned his back to me and began mopping.

It so happens I'm fluent when it comes to body language, and the current message was: Conversation Closed. But something inside me didn't like that. "Hey, soldier. It's a reasonable question."

The man stopped mopping and turned back toward me and squinted. His thin lips pressed together and got thinner. He turned his head back toward the marina. I assumed he was glancing at Celeste's boat. "There isn't much connected with that boat that I'd call reasonable. Not lately. What did you say your name was?"

"I didn't. The name's Ingalls. Pete Ingalls."

"And who's your friend?"

"That's not something you need to know."

He nodded slightly, then dropped the mop with a clatter, hoisted himself onto the dock, looked at me one last time, and said, "Excuse me, Mr. Ingalls." He walked past me and up the dock toward the marina.

I started after him, not at all sure what I should say. Ahead of us was a couple at another boat, a simple flat-bottomed job with a striped canvas sun roof. They were watching us and looking at Celeste's boat. I peeled off from following the fisherman and instead smiled a greeting at this pair. They were in their sixties, obviously married for decades, and wore identical maroon windbreakers.

The woman, big black sunglasses dominating her wrinkled, tanned face like welder's goggles, pointed with her chin to the *Sea Note*. "Are you asking about this one here?"

I nodded. "What can you tell me?"

"That it's a disgrace. Look at that. Makes me want to climb in and swab it down myself."

"She'll do it, too!" Her husband laughed and shook his head. He was rosy-cheeked and clean-shaven and roly-poly, and wore one of those floppy canvas caps with no brim, shaped like an upside-down peanut butter cup. "Don't get Lo started. She'll do it!"

She gave him a deadpan look. "I'll do it."

"I know you'll do it."

"I will. I'll do it."

I could have listened to this all day, but I had larger fish to fry. "Have either of you seen anyone on this craft?" "Craft" because I was playing the technical card, to flatter the audience and pry out some dope from them. "Today or recently or anything?"

"Last Monday," the man said. "We got here round sunset. They were just on their way out. I remember because it's an unusual sight, a woman piloting herself." He tilted his head toward the little woman. "Lois can do it, but we've been at this for forty years."

"I can do it," Lois said to her husband. "I pilot."

"I know you can do it."

"I can do it."

"Didn't I just say you can do it?"

I nodded and said, "Meaning, the woman you saw was younger than you folks?"

"Much younger." The husband held up a cautionary finger. "But no skinny ballerina, I'm saying. A solid-built gal around thirty. The man was below. Saw him through the curtain."

He pointed toward Celeste's boat. A white curtain hung in the port hole, a thin, almost translucent fabric you could see let light in while affording some privacy.

I turned to Lois. "Did you see the woman, too?" For a second she was lost in sour contemplation of the untidiness of the *Sea Note*. Then she returned her attention to me. "Saw 'em both. She was at the helm and he was sitting there below, kind of still. Probably reading."

"We found it here the next morning," Ed said, "looking like this."

"Like an eyesore, a real eyesore that we got to deal with." Lois looked offended. "Sitting there for two days. Terrible. Disgraceful, all that blood." She sighed. "But it's none of my business. . . ."

I blinked. "Wait a second. You're saying that's blood?"

"What'd you think it was? Paint? Tomato juice?"

I looked grim. "That's not funny."

"You got that right." Hubby managed to combine solemnity and outrage. "I mean if you want to clean your catch on board, you got to wash up after and get up the blood. It's common courtesy and good seamanship."

"It's also damn stupid," Lois muttered and pointed toward the parking lot. "When they got the table and sink over there."

I felt like an overmatched fighter being pummeled left and right by an opponent twice as strong. "Now you're telling me that's fish blood?"

Ed laughed. "Well, I sure hope so! What else can it be?"

I didn't want to condescend to these people. So I answered with a bit of simulated doubt. "Now I could be off base," I said, "but seems to me fish don't have blood."

"Get out."

"I'm serious." I shrugged to indicate: it's not my doing. "They're not mammals. They're fish."

"Of course fish have blood!" Lois snapped. She seemed to take this personally. "They're animals, ain't they?"

"Son," Ed said, not unkindly, "how long you been fishing?"

"Never."

"Uh-huh. Whereas Lo and I've been doing it since LBJ was president. You wanna argue over who knows more about fish blood?"

I threw up my hands and conceded the point. Then I thanked them and walked back onto land, drifting toward the tackle shop as I thought hard. What did I know? That Celeste and Jeffrey Litman had gone out Monday evening; that Celeste was expert enough to pilot the boat herself. That one or both of them had done some serious fishing, and then had failed to clean up after themselves. And that, as Celeste said, something had gone "wrong."

I heard a slow crunch and looked up to see a patrol car arriving in that languid, menacing way they have. Out of it stepped a muscular bruiser in a dark blue uniform and a belt studded with gear. He walked with a weightlifter's gait, slowly and methodically, as though he'd practiced it, arms held out at his sides like hanging parentheses. The cop got to where I stood at the start of the pier. He had a bushy moustache and wore dark sunglasses that I couldn't see his eyes through. He nodded and gestured with his chin toward the dual rows of boats. "You own one of these?"

I shook my head. "Just looking, Officer. Looking and asking. Is that against the law?"

He turned toward me with a start and seemed to stiffen a bit. The caliber of the conversation had just moved up a notch. "It could be. Depending." He pulled a pad out of his rear pocket and consulted a note. "Fifty-three . . ."

I joined him as we walked toward the *Sea Note*. "What brings you here?"

"Got a call."

We reached the boat. He scanned it quickly, frowned at the blotches, then turned to me. "This the one you've been asking about?" I nodded. "What kind of questions?"

"Oh, this and that."

He looked at me, eyes obscured by the black panels of his shades. "Sir. Don't play games. Tell me your interest in this vessel and what you've found out."

I reached behind me to get my wallet. He flinched instinctively but held off doing anything more. I got the wallet and handed him a card. "P.I. out of New York. I'm here on a case."

The cop looked at the card. "Not bad. Nice font." Then he looked at me. "I'm Officer Watley. Now tell me. Who's your client, Ingalls? What's the connection?"

I smiled. "Sorry, Watley. No can say."

He smirked and said, "You'll have to, if one thing leads to an-other." He added, "As it always does."

"All I can tell you is this boat went out on Monday evening and came back the next morning."

He jumped down onto the deck and walked around, jotting notes on the pad. "You touch anything?" I told him what things I could remember. When he'd seen all he wanted, he put the pad back in his rear pocket. "I'm going to call a forensics team. They'll be here in an hour, probably." Then he looked at me. "Any idea whose blood it is?"

I laughed. "Meaning, do I know any fish personally?"

"Come again?"

"It's fish blood. I don't know if you're aware, but it so hap-pens that fish have blood."

"Mm-hmm." He kneeled down to deliver a light, feathery touch to one corner of the biggest blotch. "I don't think this is fish blood, though. It's too thick. Unless they landed something big. Like a shark. Plus, you say it's sitting like this two days? It's been hot. You smell anything fishy?" He looked at me as though for the first time. "Speaking of which, what's your connection with all this, again?"

"I'll make you a deal, Watley. I'll tell you whose blood I think that is, but you promise to tell me when you find out if I'm right or wrong."

He considered it. "You wouldn't be here if you didn't know something," he said. He nodded. "You tell me whose blood this is, and I'll call you when we confirm it. Or don't. But that's it. You're freelance whereas we're the duly designated authority. Got it?"

"Try matching this batch to the blood of a Mr. Jeffrey Litman. Mouthpiece from Manhattan." I watched as he wrote it down.

"That's your client?"

"No comment. I'll be in touch, Officer."

I started to walk off, but heard him say, "If you're not, we will be."

During the nice leisurely bus ride back to the city I had plenty of time to contemplate the possibility that Celeste Vroman had killed her lover, Jeffrey Litman, and dumped his body into the Atlantic Ocean, and dusted for good.

It was probably Litman's blood on the *Sea Note*, and it seemed highly likely that my client had put it there. And if that were the case, I had a difficult choice to make, which wasn't terribly difficult at all. No, in fact it was Celeste who had the choice. She could turn herself in, and earn points with the DA, or stay on the lam, in which case I'd have to visit the johns and sing the whole aria. Because if I didn't, they'd find her, trace her back to me, and I'd be on the hook for aiding and abetting.

It was early evening by the time the bus arrived at the terminal. I killed an hour at a bar, utilizing some beers and seeing how many Happy Hour buffalo wings I could eat before the help got wise and grew vocal about it. By the time I reached my building it was dark. I was full, complacent, and tight.

"Ingalls! You son of a bitch!"

The assailant emerged from the shadowy stairwell that led to the building's basement. He was short and slim but a cyclone of energetic fury. He had to have been waiting there, possibly for hours, with the narrowest view of the approach to the front door. That was a lot of time to build up a head of frustrated, enraged steam. I was fumbling with my keys when he flung himself at me, sending us both into the row of thin, emaciated bushes that lined the front of the building on either side of the entrance.

Then things got nasty.

I don't know if you've ever been in a real fistfight—I know I hadn't—but they're not the clean, robust modern dance routines you see in the flicks, with compact, jazz-influenced jabs and broad, sweeping haymaker pirouettes. At least this one wasn't. We fell in a heap into the shrubbery, where the sharp twigs did an excellent job of raking and slicing my eyes. I shoved him off me with a kind of startled, resentful heave, powered by equal parts alcohol and adrenaline. He was a small, light man and it wasn't that hard. Then I tried to push off the landscaping to get to my feet and ended up slashing my hands and wrists on the branches. Once upright I was able to peer at his face. I couldn't make him, but I was able to discern a streaky reflection of something wet.

He was sobbing. I was all set to be deeply moved by the pathos of it all, by his snarl of "You couldn't have her for yourself, so you killed her!", and by his rigid, vibrating form as he stood there with the clenched fists and shuddering arms of an outraged child. Then he advanced on me, some other thing happened, and it occurred to me that I was no longer standing. I was sprawled on the sidewalk.

He stood over me, his face still in shadow, his breathing still a wet, sniffling mess, and practiced his placekick form with my ribs several times with a pointed hard shoe. I pulled into a fetal ball and shielded myself with my arms. Then I reached out. I grabbed for his ankle, grasped it, and yanked. He fell on top of me, scrambled wildly like an animal, drove an elbow deep into my gut, pushed himself to his feet, and stood there.

The jab to the stomach had driven out my wind. I struggled to take in air. I managed to say, "Tell Eisenberg I don't scare easily."

"She's dead!"

"Who? Jeanette? What—?"

"Which one was it, you prick!" He was crying. "Did you kill her yourself? Or pay someone!"

I hauled myself to my knees. It wasn't my final destination, but it was on my way, and a good place to stop for a rest. "Look." I was panting. "Tell Eisenberg . . . just tell him . . ." I tried to focus on my attacker. But my eyes were tearing and starting to swell shut. "Tell him to tell Flonger, uh . . ."

"I saw her give you money. That dyke." He must have found his own words enraging, because they inspired him to run around behind me, do some sort of thing with his arms, and somehow lever me back onto the ground. The pavement, no matter how often I was slamming into it, wasn't getting any softer. "And now I'm going to the cops."

He gave me one final kick and left. I could hear his weeping recede down the street.

THIRTEEN

It was fairly late the next morning when I transported my body into the office like a man carrying an armful of eggs. Stephanie was there, well into the day's labor of eating pizza-flavored Goldfish and circling ads in *Back Stage* with a black marker. She leaped up when I hobbled through the door.

"Pete! Jesus Christ!"

"Together again for the first time."

"Who did this?"

"I have no idea. All I know is, he left in tears."

She snapped her fingers. "I know who it was."

I have no beef with feminine intuition. Women, with their internal secret liquids and their monthly psycho visitations and their fabulous floral hair—they're not like you and me. Unless you're a woman, in which case you're one of them. "Do tell," I remarked.

"It was what's-his-name. The editor nerd." She approached and touched with gentle fingertips the Band-Aids on my face, wincing in sympathy. "Right?"

"It was dark."

"Okay, but, I mean, who else could it be?"

"I have my theories. You'll be informed on a need-to-know basis." I pulled back and headed toward my office. "Meanwhile just do your job and save the hunches for OTB."

"I am doing my job."

"You're doing my job. Back off."

I slammed the door to my office and gently flung myself onto the chair. Sure, it hurt. It hurt because that's what pain does. I called Catherine Flonger's number and got an earful of her voice mail telling me she wasn't in and that if I left a message she would call me back as soon as possible. I didn't believe it—what does "as soon as possible" really mean?—but I started jawing anyway.

"It's Pete Ingalls, Mrs. Flonger. You might want to know that one of Darius's pals sent a martial arts hard boy to bounce me off the sidewalk last night. Plus, I have some family snapshots of hubby and some close personal friends. Call me." And then I hung up and sat there. And I thought. Then I summoned Ms. Constantino in for some lateral thinking.

She arrived and stood in the doorway radiating enough attitude to roast peanuts. "Yes. What is it, sir?"

"Listen—"

In a tone as cool and sweet as ice cream she said, "Are you sure this is relevant to the performance of my secretarial duties?"

"Okay, fine. Very droll. I've been thinking about who waltzed me around last night—"

"I'm afraid I can't comment on that, sir. I wasn't present."

"Not present, yes, and would you like to hear what transpired in your absence, sugar?"

She tilted her chin up at me, plucky-skirt-speak for defiance. "If you think it's appropriate."

I stifled what I really did think and recapped the play-by-play of the recent past: the all-day stakeout at the hotel, Flonger and the Eisenbergs and the tinily dimensioned female, plus the events in Atlantic City, including the blood on the boat and the apparent, if not obvious, fact that Celeste and Litman had sailed out to sea together and only one had returned.

Stephanie's curiosity overcame her pique. By the time I got to the part about my getting creamed by a crybaby black belt in the comfort of the bushes in front of my own apartment building, her green eyes were gleaming and she had to force herself not to smile. She lost the struggle. "I was right. It was that guy. Richard."

"Eisenberg is the one who threatened me," I said. "Or doesn't that mean anything?"

"If the guy who attacked you said what you said he said, it's got nothing to do with Darius Flonger. Richard—"

"Wait a minute. What do you mean, if he said? Are you saying I don't remember it right?"

She shrugged. "How would I know? Plus you were totally mauled. So who knows what you remember?"

"It's just my body that was beaten up, sweetheart. Not my mind."

"Okay! Fine! So if you remember what he said, then I'm right!"

"Oh, that's slick," I sneered. "I like that. If my memory is accurate, that means you're right."

"Pete—"

"You want to be right? Try being there, doll. Try having your face make intimate contact with the sidewalk while the Karate Kid does flamenco on your rib cage."

"Look, forget it. You're too defensive."

"*I'm* defensive?"

She waved me away with a disgusted shake of the head. "Forget it, man. Fuck you."

She left. I sat there nodding, although to whom, about what, I wasn't sure. It was the perfect time for the phone to ring.

The phone rang. I stared at it, daring her to answer in the next room. It rang again. I picked it up. "Pete Ingalls, P.I."

"Mr. Ingalls? Harv Norrison with the Atlantic City Police. Calling from Forensics."

"Nice to meet you, Mr. Norrison."

"Yeah, look, I've got an Officer Watley here, asked me to call you when we had a make on the blood type on that boat? The *Sea Note*?"

"I'm all ears, Harv."

"Turns out it's type O negative. Same as your what's-his-name. Liptak."

"Litman."

"That's the one. They had it on file in the law office after some blood drive. Anyway, Officer Watley says he'll be in touch."

I walked slowly to the front desk, where Stephanie was, for some reason, noisily shoving some personal effects into a carton. You know the kind of thing I mean—the items a young woman would need to conduct the job of receptionist in a small office: a fully loaded makeup kit, a bag of low-fat wheat crackers, a binder listing casting agents, various back copies of *Daily Variety*, several little booklet-sized editions of recent plays. "It's Litman's blood type," I announced. "On the boat."

She paused long enough to reply, "No shit."

"Nice language."

"Whatever."

"You know, I'm thinking that maybe Celeste killed Litman—"

"Duh."

"Let me finish. Celeste killed Litman, and maybe she killed Olivia, too."

She surprised me by shaking her head—emphatically, hard. "No. No way."

"In fact, she killed Olivia to have Litman for herself. Then they go out on the boat, he says thanks but no thanks, and there she is: she's murdered once for his sake, and he's still giving her the brush. She sees red, reformats his skull, dumps the body, and returns alone in the boat. Makes no effort to clean the deck and dusts. And goes into hiding, where she is to this very day."

I was, despite the pain of the cuts, the aches in my pummeled ribs, the overall sense of bodily collapse and discomfort, buoyed by what I'd just said. I'd announced a scenario that fit all the known facts, on time and under budget. That must have been why it galled me in ways I didn't know I could be galled when Stephanie pressed her lips together and then shook her head no. "I don't think so. I don't think Celeste killed Olivia."

"Of course she did," I said. "It connects the dots like no-body's business."

"No, it doesn't. It's not right."

"And why not?"

She shrugged. "It feels wrong."

"Say what? 'Feels'?"

"Okay, for one thing, why would Olivia meet with Celeste at that awful hotel?"

"Maybe—"

"And she's too intelligent. Celeste. You can see it in her eyes. Killing Olivia is just too messy. There's Litman, there's you, there's everyone Olivia worked with. . . . It would be too easy to track her down. And what does she end up with? A guy—who's *married*—who dumped her in the first place! That's why it feels wrong. She's too smart to do something that dumb."

"You're making this up." I was angry, and I didn't know why.

"I am not! It fits the facts perfectly!"

"You don't care about the facts. You're just playing Madame Sylvia and drawing speculation out of the ether."

"It's called thinking, you . . . jerk!" She seized the box of pink Kleenex off the desk and rammed it into the carton and added, "By the way, I quit."

"Again?"

"Yes, fucking again!" She grabbed a small teddy bear and hurled it into the box. Then she looked at me with an air of sudden understanding. The clouds had parted and the sun had come out and you could hear the birdies singing. "You know what your problem is, Pete?"

"Actually—"

"You're threatened by a smart woman. Or a woman with power."

"Is that a fact."

"You bet your ass it is. The only way you can deal with women is to be this Forties sexist asshole who calls women 'angel' and gets to be in charge."

"You don't say."

"I fucking do say."

"Then how's about I tell you what your problem is, dollface. Does it ever occur to you *not* to talk back?"

"This isn't talking back! This is talking! What are you, my father?"

"I'm your boss."

"So? Can't I have an opinion?"

"An informed opinion, you work it out from facts and evidence and clues, that's jake with me. You make it up out of thin air, I want to hear Major Bowes bang his gong. Because then it's amateur hour, kid."

"You are nuts, man." She picked up the carton. "Life is too short to stand here arguing with a guy with Band-Aids all over his face dressed like an extra in *Guys and Dolls*. I am so out of here." She pulled back from the desk, then stopped. "But first I want to talk to Wendy Litman one more time."

"Be my guest."

"Thanks. I will."

And with that she walked out the door. The silence that settled in her wake was dense and absolute. I did what I had to do, what felt appropriate and necessary and wise. I ran after her.

We shared a cab to the gallery where Wendy Litman worked. Neither of us spoke. Instead we endured each other in irritable silence. It was like being married. Somewhere in the back of my mind, in the little room with the single naked lightbulb that never goes out, where the true things happen and the hard questions get asked, some voice was wondering why I had to put up with this. I did my best to ignore it.

The tension between us ebbed a bit when we entered the gallery. The same show was still in progress: people standing before mirrors showing reflections of somebody else. They were growing on me. I had paused to admire one in particular when Stephanie jabbed an elbow into my still tender rib and gestured with a nod across the room.

Wendy Litman was seated at the desk beyond the counter and not engaged in much of anything. She looked bad. Her clothes, like last time, were perfect: sharp black slacks, and a structured black silk blouse, gold accessories. But her face was puffy and her eyes lacked something. The clothes were wearing her, while her mind was elsewhere.

She bristled when she saw us but was too tired, preoccupied, or defeated to come out of her corner fighting. "What do you want?" she muttered. "I have nothing to say to either of you."

"Maybe we have something to say to you," Stephanie said.

"You have no right to harass me like this." She made a visible effort to summon what inner resources she had left. "If you don't leave I'll call the police."

"And tell them what?" I said. "That we haven't signed the guest book?"

"I'll think of something." She reached for the phone.

"Fine," Stephanie said, combative and spunky and looking for action. "But first you might want to hear what we've learned about your husband."

Wendy Litman put the phone down slowly, composed herself, and sat back in the desk chair. Her posture was equal parts defiance and resignation. She looked like a woman determined to face a firing squad with dignity. "Go on."

"Tell her, Pete," Stephanie said.

I told her about my visit to Atlantic City, the condition of the boat, the report of the couple about its comings and goings, and the cops' determination that the stains on the deck were the same blood type as Jeffrey's. As I delivered this last piece of news I studied the dame for signs of strain. But she took it without flinching. I couldn't tell whether she already knew all of it or simply believed none of it. The silence when I stopped was an engraved invitation for her to respond.

"I don't believe you," she said.

"Why would we lie?" Stephanie asked.

"You're looking for Jeffrey. You want me to say, 'No, it can't be his blood, he can't be dead, I spoke to him yesterday.'" She forced a wan smile. "Although I'm not saying I did. And I'm not saying I didn't."

"Like that makes sense," Stephanie snorted.

"Play Hot Butter Beans all you want, lady." I couldn't remember whether that was a game or a song. And I didn't care. What mattered was, I was talking with some heat. "I don't really care about your husband and I've had enough chinning with you to last a lifetime. But I'm looking at a client on one hand, and a dead woman on the other, and I think Hubster is somewhere in the middle. Now I've told you what I know and it's your turn to pony up. So let's you drop the veil and give up the skinny on Olivia Cartwright and Celeste Vroman, and then my associate and I can bounce."

"I don't know either of them."

"That's not what you said the other day," Stephanie said.

Wendy Litman blinked a bit more than necessary. "I said I had heard of this Celeste person. But I've never met either of those women." The phone rang. All of us jumped. "Now excuse me, I have work to do."

She turned her back to us and answered the call. Stephanie, meanwhile, grabbed my sleeve and dragged me back toward the entrance. Her whisper was urgent. "She's acting weird."

"Says who?"

"We just told her her husband may be dead. She should be freaking out more."

"Maybe he's not. Maybe she did see him yesterday. Maybe that's him on the phone."

"Then why doesn't she say that? She can say that and not tell us where he is. And why *not* tell us where he is?"

I knew there was a decent reply to this, and I had every intention of coming up with it. But it eluded me for the few seconds more that Wendy Litman needed to wrap up her phone call. When we looked around she had left the office and was approaching us across the bare, gleaming parquet floor.

I tried a preemptive strike. "Your husband may be dead, Mrs. Litman. But you don't seem all that broken up about it."

"The truth is, Mr. . . . I'm sorry, what was your name?"

Without a pause I reached for my wallet and held out a card. "Ingalls. Pete Ingalls."

"No, thank you, Mr. Ingalls. I don't need your card." She bestowed upon me a small smile of contempt. Sure, it hurt my feelings. But I get paid to have my feelings hurt. "And maybe I don't know where Jeffrey is. And you could be right. He could be dead, if you're telling the truth, and that really is his blood on that boat. But that is something I'll react to fully in private. Not here, in public, at my job . . ." She was inspired then to add, ". . . in the presence of two fools who harass me with questions when they have no right! Now either leave, or I'll call the police."

Several replies jostled in my mind for expression, but "Hey, fuck you, bitch" was not one of them. No, that was Stephanie's creation. She added, "We come here in good faith—"

"You represent a woman my husband's having an affair with," Wendy Litman said. "There's no way that qualifies as good faith."

Stephanie looked ready to throw a punch. "What are you hiding, Mrs. Litman? And wh—hey!"

I grabbed her arm and bum-rushed her offstage, toward the exit, leaving behind a crisp, all-pro "Thanks for your time, Mrs. Litman."

Out in the corridor I punched the Down button and released the prisoner just as Stephanie jerked her arm loose and wheeled on me.

"What's the fucking idea! When do you think we're ever going to get another chance to question her!?"

"A) Watch the lingo. There's no need to work blue. B) She was clammed and clamped, and we were getting nowhere."

"So you just give up?"

"You cut your losses and move on."

"Oh. Right. I get it." She put her hands on her hips. Is that "akimbo"? Or am I thinking of a Japanese movie? "You didn't like the fact that it was me who was talking to her. You would rather just walk away, instead of letting me take part. Just like you can't stand the fact that I know it was Richard who beat you up, and not some hired kung fu guy!"

"All right." I pulled out my cell phone. "Let's at least nail this. Stand by." I called my voice mail and was relieved to hear Catherine Flonger's return message. She was home and left her number. As Ms. Constantino bristled with the impatience of heedless, know-it-all, wise-guy youth, I called my client. She answered with a weary "Yes?"

"It's Ingalls, Mrs. Flonger."

"Oh God, Mr. Ingalls. I got your message. I'm so sorry. Although it's not like Darius to resort to such things."

"That's what I'd like to discuss with him. I don't suppose you have any idea where your husband is at the moment, do you?"

You could have driven a truck through the pause that followed—a big truck, with bad things in it. Her next reply came in a voice warmed and spiced like mulled cider. "You're going to go after him for beating you up, aren't you?"

"Let's just say I'm going to raise the issue."

"Do you know Frisson?"

"Some contemporary philosopher, right? What's his angle? The biggest victims of violence are its perpetrators? Maybe in the philosophy racket, doll, but not out here on the street."

"It's a department store on West Fifty-seventh. Darius is there in the men's department. I'm supposed—"

"Thanks, Mrs. Flonger. I'll be in touch."

I snapped off the cell. Okay, they don't go "snap." They make a little "tink" sound if they make any sound at all. I tinked off the cell. The elevator had arrived. I took Stephanie by the arm and hustled her in. Outside I flagged a cab, and we piled into the backseat. "Frisson," I said. "Department store owned by some philosopher. West Fifty-seventh."

Stephanie said, "Pete—"

"Who are you? *New York Times*?" The cabbie, a Middle Eastern gent with a moustache, glared at me and spoke more harshly than necessary and more rapidly than called for. "*Eyewitness News Consumer Fightback*? *Action News Hot Probe*? I do not need this!"

"You lost me, friend."

"Pete—"

"*New York Magazine* Undercover? Bureau of Consumer Affairs Fraud Squad? I am a busy man!"

And then it hit me: somehow, without my even ingesting anything, Wendy Litman had managed to slip me a Mickey, and I was spiraling down the rabbit hole to a nice warm place where nothing made sense and nasty people could do to Ingalls just about whatever they wanted.

Then Stephanie slapped my arm. "He thinks we're testing him. To see if he'd rip us off. For consumer news." She pointed out the windshield.

Half a block up, on our side of the street, a yellow awning stretched its canvas arch across the width of the sidewalk, tented up on slim poles and patrolled by a doorman in white. On it was the logo of Frisson.

"We blow an address, and he makes us for *Sixty Minutes*." I shook my head—in sorrow, and in amazement of the follies of this world. "Would it kill him to just point it out, then we all share a laugh at the human predicament?"

Stephanie shrugged. "Try auditioning. People don't see you for what you are. They see you for what they need you to be for them." She leaned forward toward the driver. "Sorry." She elbowed me toward the door. "Let's go."

"Good work, chief." I gave the hack the thumbs-up.

He gave me the finger and said, "Oh yes? Hey, fuck you, man, asshole."

FOURTEEN

The men's department of Frisson was on the second floor. To get there my associate and I had to battle our way across the main level, through a dazzling cosmetics bazaar of mirrors, lights, and glass. It's a rough place, if you're a woman, with ten thousand surfaces to show you what you look like, and a hundred drop-dead knockouts working the counters to suggest why it's wrong. Drag your eyes away from the creamy colors, the crystal fancy-ware, and your own incessant, perplexed reflections, and you've still got to make it past strolling spritz-whores, slinking like streetwalkers, packing perfume and shooting from the hip.

I got to the other side with a sense of relief. Stephanie, though, seemed unfazed. She meandered through this *Arabian Nights* marketplace without missing a beat, like she was taking the air in a nice, tame garden.

We stopped at the escalator and she looked at me. "What are you going to do when we find him?"

"Conduct a frank and open exchange of views," I said. After

the usual false starts and stifled terror, we did that thing that always seems impossible but that somehow, in spite of everything, you manage to do. I'm referring to stepping onto the escalator. We started gliding up. "On the subject of him hiring freelance muscle to sweep the street with my face."

"What if he didn't do it?"

"He did it." I pointed. "There."

The men's department was carpeted in gray, its various designer niches lit from the ceiling by strategically placed pin spots. Darius Flonger was standing on a little platform before a three-way mirror under the Giampietro escutcheon, sheathed in a new navy blue suit that fit him like an airtight alibi. At his knees a tailor kowtowed and flicked his soapy chalk. The newsman had the easy posture and air of informal beneficence of people used to being in the spotlight. We approached. Stephanie whispered, "Pete, forget it. Bail out." I ignored her.

"Well, well, Darius Flonger." I stood a few feet from him, my assistant hovering and fretting a yard behind.

"Please, sir, not now," Flonger said genially. "As you can see, I'm trying to buy a suit."

"You mean you don't remember me? I'm hurt, pal. I may bust out crying."

Flonger looked at me with genial condescension, and the bell rang. "Oh, wait a moment. I do know you. You're the man from the hotel. The man with the camera."

"There you go. Of course, the reason you didn't make me at first is on account of the facial reconstruction your tough boy did on me last night. But I assume he's reported back."

"I have no idea what you're talking about, Mr.—?"

"Ingalls."

"Yes, that's right. Mr. Ingalls. Are you saying I hired someone to beat you up?" He laughed and turned away, directing his attention to the button of his jacket cuff. "Why would I do that? And P.S., I wouldn't know how to even if I wanted to."

"Oh, I bet you could find a way, Dar."

I knew almost immediately that I hadn't said that. It was spoken in a woman's voice, a woman who didn't sound like Stephanie. I turned, and there was Catherine Flonger, in a casual tan skirt and a blousy beige shirt, with a trench coat folded over her arm. Stephanie stared, rapt, at the whole scene, as Catherine smiled coolly at her husband. "You know a lot of interesting people," she added.

"Hello, Catherine," Flonger said. He was using his formal, as-heard-on-TV voice. "You're right on time. Unfortunately I'm being held up by this gentleman."

"You may be held up a bit more," I said. "Your friend threatened me the other night, and you made good on it last night. So I'm here to settle the account."

"Mr. Ingalls," Flonger sighed. "If you're going to settle accounts, you should take it up with the man who attacked you. Or with Ted Eisenberg, since I believe he's the friend to whom you're referring. And who, by the way, is even less likely to hire a hit man than I am." He looked down at the tailor and said, "Do you have enough, Gene?" The man nodded and got up. Flonger stepped down from the platform. "Now if you'll excuse me, Ingalls, I have to change. My wife and I have a dinner engagement." He walked off toward the dressing rooms.

The women looked at me. Gene the tailor glanced over. In the three-way mirror, one Pete Ingalls looked at me, flanked by two others looking at whoever was off to either side. Did they know something I didn't?

"Lie number one," I said to Catherine Flonger. "You and your husband do not 'have a dinner engagement.' He has a broadcast in two hours."

"It's Friday. He doesn't do a segment on Friday."

I absorbed this with interest. "Fair enough. So he's buying clothes. And why do you happen to be here, Catherine?"

"It's Mrs. Flonger."

"Oh really? She's here, too?"

"What—?"

"Well why not." I indulged in a bit of sarcasm. It's fun, yeah, but like cayenne pepper: use sparingly or you get burned. "A guy goes shopping for a suit, he quite naturally brings his wife and his mother along."

Behind my client, facing me, Stephanie was waving her hands, either signaling me about something or drying her nails. "Uh, Pete—"

"I mean, Mr. Ingalls, I wish you wouldn't call me Catherine."

I took this in and added it to the mix. Things were threatening to spin out of control—and I wanted to be there when they did. "Noted. Meanwhile, Mrs. Flonger, if you've come here to do some shopping—"

"Not particularly. I came here to meet my husband."

"Join the club, doll." I spoke with a certain bitterness. "Sooner or later we all have an appointment to meet somebody's husband."

Stephanie stepped forward. "Okay, Pete." She thumbed toward the escalators. "You made your point. Now let's go. I'm telling you, he didn't do it. It was Richard from T and T. He was pissed about Olivia."

"And I think I told you that Darius doesn't go in for physical intimidation," Catherine Flonger said. "Why would he? What does he think you're doing?"

"He thinks I'm doing exactly what I am doing," I said. "Getting the goods on him for my client, who shall remain anonymous. Excuse me, ladies."

I walked toward the rear until I found the dressing rooms, a line of individual chambers with solid doors that locked. "Flonger!"

A muffled voice from one of them said, "Ingalls, what do you want?"

"One final word."

A door opened.

I didn't wait. Sometimes you have to grab the initiative and define the terms of the exchange. You act preemptively. You step up, you take over, you plant the flag first and defend it afterward. So I shouldered through the open door and barged into the little space.

Mirrors covered all three walls, affording me multiple-angled views of a short, bald, dapper gent in a white T-shirt and blue-striped boxers. He asked what the hell I was doing, and I apologized and said I'd entered the wrong room. I backed out onto the floor and saw another door open and heard, "Christ, Ingalls. In here."

I went in, and found Flonger in his trousers, buttoning a sport shirt. "Well? Let's get this over with."

He looked comfortable. It irked me. And I don't like to be irked. I got up close to him. At that distance, of a couple inches, his famous face lost its aura of importance and meaning, and became just one more pan on one more mug. "I'm onto you, ace," I said.

"I don't know what you're talking about," he said. "Whatever you or your client think I'm doing, you're both wrong."

Then he said, "Who did you say your client was, again?"

"Nice try, chum. I didn't. And I don't."

He switched on the wide smile and activated the eyebrows he'd trained at world leaders and government officials. "Ingalls, you're either certifiably insane or a brilliant performance artist. Whichever it is, can you say 'restraining order'?"

I had to laugh. "Spare me the softballs and let's go to the hard stuff. Can you say 'lemon liniment'?"

"You're out of your mind."

"It's the condition of modern man, pal. Meanwhile, let's you be advised that I happen to know what you're doing. And you know it. And I know you know it."

"Fine. Very eloquent."

"I'm not done yet. Because it doesn't stop there, does it. Eyeball this, friend." I grabbed him by the shirt and shoved his head toward one of the mirrors. "Look into the distance. See them? All the little Darius Flongers? Getting smaller and smaller out to infinity? That's what we have here. I know what you're up to, and you know I know."

"Ingalls—"

"And I know you know I know. And you know I know you know I know. We're two mirrors facing each other. Mirrors of mind. Mirrors of consciousness."

"Oh for God's sake . . ." Something had happened to all the little Flongers in the mirrors. The expressions on their hundreds of diminishing faces had slowly transformed from amused to grim. "Let me go, you idiot," they all said.

"I haven't delivered my message yet."

"Then get your hand off my shirt, and deliver your damned message."

I released the gentleman. "Here's the message, Flonger. I don't scare. I have a job to do, and I'm going to do it."

"Wonderful." He straightened up, smoothed out the shirt, and tucked it into his pants. "You don't scare, and you're going to do your job. That's what worries me, Ingalls."

"What's that supposed to mean?"

As he cinched his belt he said, "It means that it's dawning on me that you may be too stupid to do your job. You might need some help." He opened the door and walked out.

I did what you do when one man leaves another man alone in a dressing room. I went after him. "I'll ignore that," I said.

"You would."

"Meaning—?"

He stopped, and with a sigh communicating bored exasperation, turned back to face me. "Meaning, you might try taking your head out of your posterior. There's a great big world out there, and it's full of real things for you to discover and figure out. Look around, pay attention, and you'll learn what you want to know."

Somehow the conversation had changed. What had begun as a confrontation of adversaries had turned into a public service announcement encouraging kids to read. Meanwhile, Stephanie and Catherine Flonger were waiting, edgily ignoring each other and trading stiff smiles with the salesmen.

I wanted to get things back on track. As Flonger started to turn away, I grabbed his arm and kept him facing me. "Little addendum to the message, chief."

I hauled back and slugged him in the stomach. The wind rushed out of him and he doubled over with a strained grunt. "Call that a down payment," I said. I couldn't think of what it was a down payment on, so I walked past him and away.

Stephanie ran over to me. Her eyes were not quite as big as bar coasters. "Pete, Jesus, you *hit* him!"

"Once. Call it payback."

"Oh my God. Are you crazy? He has lawyers. His *lawyers* have lawyers."

"Send 'em my card. It's getting raves."

"Fuck." She linked her arm around mine and started escorting, some might say dragging, me offstage. "Okay, look. We'll go back to the office and write some bullshit e-mail apology."

I had to laugh. "I thought you quit."

"Yeah, but this is getting interesting. I unquit."

Ordinarily I might have been inclined to take her back. But I had just punched Darius Flonger. Something like that changes a man. "I don't think so, angel." I withdrew my arm and turned my back on her.

"Oh yeah? Like you don't need me?"

"Good luck with your career."

"You are fucking nuts!"

"And watch your mouth. This isn't Kmart. It's a department store in Manhattan."

"Okay, fine. Jerk." She stomped off.

It was then that I realized that Catherine Flonger was looking at me from about ten feet away with an expression of mesmerized fascination on her lovely face, yes, and just as her husband joined us, straightening his jacket and primping up his dignity. "Ingalls. Very funny. But if you think you're going to goad me into a fight, you'd better think again."

"I'm not thinking at all, Flonger."

"That's obvious. But hit me again and I'll have you arrested."

"Once is enough," I said. "Just keep your muscle boys on the leash."

He shook his head and turned to his wife. "Let's go. I need a drink."

"I think I'll skip it, Dar," she said. "I'm not really up for Jim and Emily."

The TV star hesitated. Married couples have their own private histories and secret codes and base-running signals; Flonger's pause, to his wife, must have been rich in content. "I'm not going to argue with you, Catherine," he said. He sounded like he was talking to History. Which is a neat trick, yeah. But is History ever listening? Somehow I doubted it. "I suppose I'll see you home later, then."

Flonger skipped, leaving a chilly breeze in his wake. Then his wife marched over and the temperature dropped ten more degrees—Celsius. "You actually punched him?"

"It's part of my job." I impressed myself with how unimpressed I thought I looked with how impressed I thought she looked. "He denied everything, of course. He said he didn't know what I was talking about. Believe me, I hear that a lot."

"And then you punched him."

"Once. It was enough."

"Mm-hmm." Color me surprised that she didn't break into applause or get misty with gratitude and concern. In fact, her thin, fine nostrils flared and her mouth pursed with what looked like distaste. "Mr. Ingalls, as long as I'm here, I'm going to do some shopping. But first . . . I can see I've made a horrible mistake. I want to conclude our business, and we can go our separate ways. So thank you very much for all you've done. Send me the final bill, and I'll mail you a check. I assume your letterhead is discreet enough not to attract attention."

She turned and headed for the escalator. I caught up with her. "What gives, lady? The jury's still out and the fat lady hasn't left Wardrobe."

She stepped onto the moving stairs and so I had no choice. I got on, too. Then she read me the riot act in words of one syllable. "I don't care about that anymore. I did not hire you to beat up my husband."

"No, that was my idea," I agreed. "Free of charge with my compliments."

"It's outrageous and appalling and disgusting."

"He signed up for it when he ordered me home delivery of some rough stuff."

"I told you. Darius doesn't do that. Nobody I know would do something like that."

"How about Ted Eisenberg?"

She laughed. "Ted? He's all talk. He's been living off her money for twenty years so he thumps his chest when he's out with the boys. He and Darius play poker on Thursday nights."

We were approaching the next floor, so I held my breath, because getting off an escalator is just as bad as getting on. I waited until my step flattened out at the apex of the ride, then bunny-hopped off onto terra firma. Then I said, "Look. I'm making progress. Pull the plug and you miss the payoff."

"This whole thing was a mistake." She drilled me right in the eyeballs. "I shouldn't have hired you. I can't have this. You're a thug."

"I'm a dick."

"Oh my God . . . Mr. Ingalls, you're violent *and* crude. And besides"—she gave a phony little laugh—"we don't even know if he's actually having an affair!"

I stared back at her. "Correct me if I'm wrong, but I thought Darius was the bad guy who's breaking your heart with both hands. You should be giving me a standing O."

"No. No. Not when you get violent. I don't live on that level." Her voice got tighter and took on some heat. "That's the world I *don't* live in. I have never lived in it, and I'm not going to start now. If I have to put up with his occasional flings in order to stay out of it, it's a price I'm willing to pay." And she walked off toward a smart little boutique where conservative, nice-lady clothes were prominently displayed.

I walked after her. "Wait a minute."

"Keep your voice down."

"Okay, sure, but here's a poser for you. What about the show-ers? What if this isn't just one of his routine little dalliances? Isn't that why you came to me in the first place?"

"I overreacted." Then she saw something and stiffened. "Oh shit." For some reason I attracted dirty-mouthed women. "Quick, come here."

She grabbed my arm and pulled me behind a rack of suits just as two other women cruised past. One was tall, in a long, black cowboylike duster. She wore no makeup and her black spiky hair looked like it had recently exchanged harsh words with someone. The other dame was shorter, in tan, doesn't-Mommy-look-nice slacks and a white blouse, neatly made up and with her light brown hair all bouncy and pert in a tidy, prim little do. Both car-ried wide, shallow Frisson shopping bags, canary yellow with the cursive logo in black.

Catherine Flonger watched them walk past while keeping a tight, admonishing grip on my arm until they'd turned a corner and disappeared. "What gives?" I said. "Think one of them's a candidate?"

"For what?"

"For the role of your husband's lover, Mrs. Flonger."

"Oh God no." She relaxed and moved out from behind the clothes. "The tall one is Karen Juracyk. Her husband moved out a year ago, and she's still pretending it's an experiment. The other one is Deb Corman. She has two kids and a house in Tuscany. Her husband's a radiologist. We think he's fucking her shrink."

"They sound like my kind of people. Didn't you want to say hello?"

"Actually they're my kind of people. So I do not want to say hello, not with you here." She gave me a strained smile, yeah, strained like baby food and just as nourishing. "But I think we're finished. So there's no reason for you to be here any longer. Thank you, Mr. Ingalls." She turned her back to me and walked over to a slanting chrome rack on which satiny gray blouses hung by hangers. Evidently I'd been dismissed.

But I wasn't buying it. I caught up with her. "Should I upgrade my hearing aid, or are you singing a different tune?" I said. "What happened to the dame whose life was falling apart? Who realized she'd been wrong about everything?"

"I was upset. I'm all right now. I don't want to change anything. I want everything to stay the way it's been."

"That's not what you said when you climbed that noodle shop wall," I said.

"That was a mistake. I was depressed and angry and acting out."

"That's a horse laugh. You meant it."

She didn't respond, but grabbed a blouse and swept off toward the dressing rooms in the rear. En route she seized a couple more tops. I followed and took up a position near the entrance to the line of little chambers, each with its own door, each harboring its own secrets, intimate secrets, the kind that maybe men don't know about, the kind that take shape when women try on clothes in private. Minutes passed. A salesgal gave me a look; I answered with my "I'm not homosexual" wink, to explain why I was loitering in the department.

Finally I called out, "I'm still here, Mrs. Flonger."

She sighed and opened a door and stood there in one of the blouses. It was unbuttoned and afforded me a glimpse of her low-cut, stylish white brassiere. It so happens I have a theory about brassieres. My theory is that I like to see women wearing them. I especially liked seeing her in this one: what little it pretended to conceal it subtly revealed through a sheer, translucent fabric.

"About time you dropped the veil, sugar." I leered. "Now we get down to where the rubber meets the road."

"I have no idea what that means."

"I think you know exactly what it means." I walked toward her. "Why did you tell me where Darius was? What did you think I was going to do when I found him? Shop for ties together? You sent me to him because you wanted me to do exactly what I did."

She hesitated. Then she said, "Maybe I did at the time. Until you actually did it. Then it was awful. I don't know why I hired you in the first place." She shut the door.

I allowed myself a small, bitter laugh. "Whereas I do." Then I opened the door a crack so she could hear better, and allowed myself another small, bitter laugh. "I think you started trying on the idea that turnabout is fair play. One goose, one gander, and everybody gets sauced."

"What?"

"That if your husband was doing certain things, then maybe you could do them, too. So maybe you wanted to find a guy you could do those certain things with. Certain personal things that you can only do with a guy you can be certain you can get personal with."

She opened the door. She was wearing a different new blouse, half-open. As she buttoned it up, once again I was afforded a glimpse of her brassiere-cupped breasts. I had the sensation of encountering two old friends. I wanted to say hi, how are you, but I didn't. I didn't because when a woman shows you her breasts one of the things you don't do is talk to them. At least not in public. Catherine Flonger said, "I think we're finished. Have a nice weekend."

"You don't have to pretend not to know what I'm talking about, Mrs. Flonger."

"I'm not pretending."

"Let's make believe that's true." It was my turn to lecture.

"So let me say it nice and slow in my own words. A guy in my position doesn't do that kind of thing."

Something behind me caught her eye. I didn't bother to turn around and see what it was. Then she withdrew back into the dressing room and shut the door. I didn't let that stop me. "What I'm saying is, if you read the literature you'll discover something I call the Code. It's a list of the acceptable and the unacceptable conduct for a man in my profession."

She opened the door. She had left the new blouses behind her, askew on hangers or messily collapsed onto the bench that fronted the main mirror. Now she was in her own clothes. "Excuse me," she said. "I'd appreciate it if you'd take the hint and leave me alone. I'm going to say hello to my friends now." She walked off.

I followed. Talk, Ingalls, I told myself. Talk or die. "Acceptable: Calling a client a liar and demanding the truth. Unacceptable: Taking the retainer and just going through the motions."

She was approaching Deb Corman and Karen Juracyk. They were busily murmuring picky-shopper critiques over a single pair of shoes on a pedestal, under halogen. My client must have thought taking refuge among the very two broads she'd been at such pains to hide from not a half-hour earlier would scare me off. How little she knew me. "Acceptable: Turning a client in to the authorities if she's done something illegal—"

"Cath! Hi!"

"Jesus Christ, Cathy Flonger."

"I thought I saw you two. . . ."

There was no explicit air-kissing. Karen, the tall one, looked arch and arranged her white, unmade-up puss into an expression of airy, humorless amusement. Beautifully done-up Deb beamed and laughed and twinkled. My client pointedly turned her back to me as I arrived. "Unacceptable," I said. "Betraying information obtained from a client in confidence."

The women looked at me. Karen Juracyk said, in a voice etched with frost, "Please. None of us have spare change. And you don't belong here."

I said to my client, "Acceptable: Keeping a client's secrets about a third party."

"That's all right, Kar." Catherine Flonger introduced us by name all around, then explained, "Mr. Ingalls has done some consulting work for me."

"Oh honey, what do you have to consult about?" Karen asked. "Unless it's sex. Ha ha ha!"

No, it didn't make sense and there was nothing funny about it. But we all laughed. We laughed because that's what you do when a woman says "sex" in mixed company, or when a man says it, in mixed company or in any company, or when anybody says it anywhere. We laughed, and everything was terribly merry and pleasant and congenial, not counting the fact that Ingalls was surrounded by three women who couldn't wait for him to leave. I said, "Unacceptable: Having sex with the client."

Karen's voice was throaty and her eyebrows arched as she said, "Oh, really?"

"Yes, really. With the client or with anyone else. Not while on the job. And the job never ends."

Catherine Flonger sighed. "Mr. Ingalls, I'd like to catch up with my friends, so if you'll excuse us—" She pointed to Karen's shopping bag. "What'd you get, Kar?"

"Sweetie," Karen drawled. "What do I always get? Highly overpriced footwear." She gave a deep, chesty laugh. "It's how I stay out of trouble until Gerald gets back. Shopping for shoes and everything that goes with them."

Catherine ooh'd to signal aren't-we-naughty and Deb beamed like a proud coach. Karen opened the tidy yellow shopping bag and withdrew a shoe box with an Italian logo. From it she pulled two high-arched, spike-heeled killers, all straps and gaps. She showed them around, then kicked off the shoes she was wearing, dropped the new ones to the floor, and like a rickety heron stepped into them. She instantly got two inches taller and had to bend over to tighten the works. Then she stood up and muttered, "If they don't hurt, it's not fashion."

I had two cents burning a hole in my opinion, so I spent it. "You're kidding yourself."

She staggered a bit and put a hasty hand on the nearby counter to find her footing. "Can't you take a hint?" she said to me. "You're supposed to be gone by now."

"Oh, don't listen to him, Kar," Deb said. "They look great."

"They look painful," I said. "If you're dressing to impress women, it's a mug's game. And if you're trying to impress men, you can take a tip from one who knows: it's a waste of time and money and a prelude to an appointment with Dr. Scholl."

Then a man's voice said, "Well, girls? Have we had good shopping?"

Karen Juracyk composed the elements of her face like a magician assembling playing cards for the next illusion. And then our happy little band was joined by Steve Corman, Deb's husband. He was a medium-height, smooth-faced swell in a black cashmere sport coat over a deep blue shirt, and charcoal slacks. His wife stammered her way through an introduction, and we shook hands like men. Then he pointed to Deb's shopping bag. "Get anything nice?"

She took out her own shoe box and produced some modest low-heeled item in beige leather with nothing flashy or sexy about it. Her husband took one in gentle, reverent hands as though receiving a newborn. "I love this!" he said.

"Karen got the fuck-me specials," Deb said, pointing.

Steve Corman glanced in the general direction of Karen's feet and said, "Fabulous. Very dramatic." Then he prompted, "We gotta go, Deb." His wife quickly boxed up the shoes, made chitchat farewells, and the couple left.

The two women watched them go. "Prick," Karen commented.

Catherine Flonger's tone took issue. "She's happy."

"Not for long."

A salesgal pulled in and parked a few discreet feet away, a fresh-faced cutie in her twenties, sublimely made up, her long dark hair corralled and lassoed in a just-business bun. She was holding something in her hand and she didn't look happy. "I'm sorry. Mrs. Juracyk—?"

Karen turned toward her. She was about to reply when she realized she'd been summoned for a tête-à-tête. She joined the young woman and said, "Yes?"

The girl held out a platinum Visa. She spoke in a murmur but in the upscale hush of the place we could hear everything. "There seems to be a problem with this card. We called the number and they said the account has been closed."

Karen barely reacted. "It's a mistake. Try again."

"Um . . . we did. We tried three times. Three different people said the account was closed by the cosigner."

"Try it *again*."

"Ma'am . . . do you have a Frisson card?"

"Of course! I have six different cards! But this has to be a mistake. He wouldn't have closed it. You're not processing it right."

"It may be a mistake at Visa, ma'am. But we can't complete the transaction—"

"How long have you worked here?"

The salesgirl paused for a second. You could see her shift from accommodating to wary. The help in joints like this, probably all had master's degrees in Prima Donna Management. "I've been here six months."

"I'll bet," Karen said. "Whereas I've been shopping here since before you were born. Do you know how much money I spend here in a year?"

"No, ma'am."

"Neither do I. But it's much more than your pitiful salary. Now give me the receipt, let me sign it, and then leave us alone."

"I can let you speak to the manager—"

A lightning bolt of rage shot through the older dame. Her white, shuddering fist slammed down onto a glass countertop with a thumping crunch and left a spiderweb crack. Her spiky black hair quivered as she screamed. "I don't want the manager! I want you to do what I say! I'm the fucking customer and you will do it! You bitch! You *bitch!*"

"Ma'am—"

"You lazy, incompetent little cunt!"

I stepped in between them and held up a hand. "Girls—"

The salesgirl said, "Ma'am, the manager's office is on this floor. She'll be happy to hold these for you and help you contact Visa to work this out."

"Oh, shut up." Karen bent over, did some adjusting, and suddenly lost two inches in height. When she stood up the shoes were in her hand, two exotic giant insects she had killed and was presenting for taxidermy. "Here. Take them and leave us alone." She slapped the pair into the waiting hands of the clerk.

The young woman said, "Thank you," raised her chin and floated off.

After five seconds of respectful, bruised, appalled silence, I decided to say something consoling. "Let it go, lady. You can wear designer fabulosos or flip-flops from Wal-Mart. Men don't really care."

"Oh please," she said. "You're not a man. You're a psycho who thinks he's Sam Spade. I can't imagine what Cathy has hired you for, although on second thought maybe I can."

"Cute," I said. "You tried to pay a hundred simoleons to torture your own feet, and why? To impress an audience who couldn't care less. Add this up and I'm the psycho? Check your math, sugar."

"A hundred? Where do *you* shop?" Then she let me have it with both barrels. "And, actually, if you must know, men do care. I mean actual sane, intelligent men. Whether they know it or not. They care how a woman looks. They may not notice the shoes per se, but everything works together to form an impression. And the impression is important."

"Karen, just . . . come on," Catherine Flonger said.

"I'm sorry, Cath. I don't know why you brought this idiot here, but let me have my say now." She burned her angry brown eyes into my receptive, mild baby blues. "The impression is your creation. It's like a work of art—"

"*Night Owls* is a work of art," I sneered. "Women getting dolled up is business as usual."

"The way you look, the way you smell, the things you say, the quality of your mind—"

"Karen—" Catherine Flonger looked upset. "Really."

"—the way you laugh at their jokes and the way you fuck—"

"Jesus, Karen, let it go."

"No, this is important. You imprint them with it and then everything you do builds on it. The shoes, the underwear, everything. Over years." She sighed. "Okay, sometimes they leave. But you're already inside them and that doesn't change. Sooner or later they come back. They have to."

Catherine Flonger started to speak, then changed her mind, shut her mouth, and waited.

Karen's eyes blazed. It was an interesting phenomenon. You'd think eyes are eyes. But hers had caught fire and she was shooting the flames at yours truly. "They have to come back because you're inside them. After a week or a month or a year or I don't give a fuck how long. And so you wait. And you stay in shape. And go to the goddamn gym. And avoid everybody's looks. Their sympathy looks. Their curiosity. And you watch what you eat and you buy new shoes. So you'll be ready when the man comes back and your life can get back to normal." She looked down and stepped into her original footwear. "So don't tell me how to dress. You of all people. In that ridiculous costume."

"It's not a costume, lady. It's what I wear."

"It's all a costume." She stepped toward Catherine Flonger and gave her a quick buss on the cheek. "Sorry, sweetie. You caught me on a bad day." Then she staggered off, shaken, like a victim emerging from a car wreck.

I looked at Catherine Flonger. She was staring at the diminishing form of her friend with an odd expression. Odd because it was with no expression at all: not pity, not disgust, not horror or wonder or concern. Then she turned to me, still with that blank, cool cameo face, until something inside clicked. She took my hand and said, "Come on."

We went back toward the dressing rooms and she dragged me inside one and shut and locked the door. With our image filling the three mirrors it felt like a committee had convened in an elevator. She unbuttoned her blouse, shrugged out of it, and turned her back to me. "Unhook me."

"Sure thing." As I undid the tiny metal hooks I leered. "But we seem to have forgotten to bring something to try on."

"I'm not trying on clothes," she said. Then she pulled the brassiere off her chest like a swimmer clawing at seaweed, and withdrew both her arms. And there they were. Except there weren't just two breasts in the room, small and endearingly pale, with a touch of middle-aged sag, each capped with a well-defined brown nipple. There was an infinity of breasts, on an infinity of half-nude Catherine Flongers, a chorus line of bared shoulders and flat midriffs and smooth backs, receding in ever-smaller versions to either side of the room. And there was an equal number of Pete Ingallses, too, in their identical double-breasteds and gabardine trousers and wide-brims tilted up and back on an infinite number of wary heads.

It was time to say something. "Catherine?"

She turned toward me. Her oval face was calm and her cool blue eyes were alert. "Don't call me that." She moved in closer. Then she was kissing me, her bare warmth pressed against my chest. Her kiss was beyond urgent. It was desperate. It was a kiss that ransacked you for all you had and then looked around for more, and if there wasn't any more, it waited.

And mine? Mine was tentative and polite and expressed regret that there wouldn't be any point in waiting. She stepped back and looked at me with a heartbreaking combo of perplexity and defeat. Then an idea dawned and she said, "Oh Christ. Don't tell me you're gay." She seemed to wilt before my eyes. "Of course. I should have known. With this getup." She sighed. "Just what I need." Then she offered a shopworn smile. "Sorry."

"Don't be," I said. "There aren't too many sure things in this crummy world, angel, but one of them is that I'm not gay. The key thing is, I'm a private eye. We don't do this."

"What do you mean, 'this'?"

"I told you before. We don't have sex with the client."

"Pretend I'm somebody else."

"There is nobody else." That threw her. I explained. "In this job, you don't have friends, you don't have relatives, you don't have a wife or a girlfriend or an ex or a fiancée. If you're lucky you have a secretary. Maybe she's a looker, but it's all flirty come-on and no follow-through and strictly, strictly business."

"You mean you don't have sex at all?" She bent, sighing, and rummaged around on the floor for her blouse. "What kind of a rule is that?"

"I told you. It's implicit in the literature and distilled in the Code. By which I mean, it's not written down. It's a tacit thing, an understood thing, handed on like folklore. It tells you what to do and what not to do in order to conduct yourself properly in the profession."

She sat wearily on the bench along the main mirror and held the blouse up over her chest. Then she shook her head in disbelief. "But that's . . ."

"Stern? Lofty?"

"Horrible."

I leaned against a mirror on the side of the room and got comfortable. I had rehearsed this, at home, a dozen times, in the shower and folding laundry and on the can. I knew it cold. "Try to understand something. People think a P.I. is a force for good, like a knight in double-breasted armor. Maybe that's still true. But in my book a dick is a professional, who does his job without fear or favor or feelings of any kind."

"I had no idea," she said. "And what does this have to do with women?"

"A woman comes along and says, let's make nice, and if you allow yourself feelings you think, what's the harm?"

"So? What is the harm?"

This was the setup. I had the punch line ready and waiting. "Because when a woman has a passionate liaison with a private investigator, she falls in love with him."

"Really?" Her eyes were wide. "Every time?"

"Read the literature. And then she's got you on a downtown

express to disaster. Sooner or later she'll come to the conclusion that you're not good enough. Which she won't be shy about sharing. Then nothing you do is ever right, and everything you do is just a little disappointing. It's what I call the wages of love. At which point, as a dick, you're a dead man. It saps your confidence and kills your nerve. You might as well hang up your hat and hock your suit and buy a chicken farm on Long Island." I added, with a kind of rough sweetness, "Listen. You're a sharp skirt and if things were otherwise I'd be more than hot and bothered. So don't take it personally."

"Really?" She laughed. "I take off my clothes and throw myself at you, and you decline, and it's not personal?"

"Not a bit. It's a matter of professionalism."

"Mm-hmm . . ." She rose, dropped the blouse, and moved in close again. "You know, you're involved in a very noble calling, Pete," she said. "But what you just said has a serious flaw."

"I can't wait to read all about it, Mrs. Flonger."

She leaned forward and kissed me very lightly on the line of my jaw. "A profession doesn't demand that you not have feelings. It demands that you do a good job no matter what your feelings are. I think you should revise your Code." She delivered two more light kisses to my jaw. I would feel the warmth of her face on my cheek. "Or throw it away." She pulled back and looked me in the eyes. "Because really, Pete. If you're afraid of having sex with a woman, then say so. But don't try to pretend that your job won't let you."

I said, "Is that what you think?"

"Oh yes. The thing you're describing isn't a code for professionals. It's a list of rules for a child." She shrugged. "Or a priest. And you're not either one. Are you?"

"Not the last time I looked," I said. "And what if the dame in question falls in love? And starts to find fault?"

"Let her." Her face moved past me and under mine and she spoke to my neck. "Tell her it's her problem." In the mirror opposite I caught a glimpse of her pensive face as she began to deliver soft little kisses here and there to my neck, experimental testings of the terrain. "Isn't that good news?"

I started to answer but had to pause when I realized she'd placed a hand on my zipper and had begun a gentle round of squeezing and caressing. Naturally, everything in me rose up in protest. But in spite of my reservations, in spite of my better judgment, in spite of my fear, it felt good. "And why would it be good news?" I was able to say.

She found my belt and with strong fingers slipped the pointy end out and unhooked it and pulled it open. "Because it lets you enjoy women." With two hands she unbuttoned the trousers, and there came that sudden release, that expansive give, when everything you've cinched tight and tucked in neat for action, for business, for professional behavior and discipline, is allowed to spread out and find its comfortable state of rest. "I can think of one in particular you can enjoy right now." Then she opened my trousers all the way and let them fall to the floor. She found my hand and placed it on her breast. It was a nice breast, all soft and warm, just like it's supposed to be. I had to fight an urge to scream, and the struggle caused me to grip her breast harder than maybe I should have. But she liked that and made a little noise.

"You may have a point, Mrs. Flonger," I managed to say. "But why me?"

"Because if I don't I'll turn into Karen Juracyk," she said. "You'll rescue me from that, won't you? Pretend you're a chivalrous knight saving a lady from turning into a witch." She stepped back, unzipped her skirt, and let it fall. Now she was wearing only panty hose. Her body had a touch of tan that made the breasts, my two old friends, look even whiter, more protected and precious. Then she did something that took me by surprise.

She knelt.

She pulled down my striped boxer shorts, and I had an oddly comical sensation of being entirely naked from the waist down and entirely clothed up above. It seemed like a metaphor for something but I couldn't think of what. Then I couldn't think of anything at all, because she took me into her mouth and I felt that first spasm of fear. Because you don't live your entire life devoted to a code of conduct and not get nervous when you find yourself violating it.

But Catherine Flonger's mouth was warm, and wet, and snug, and it wasn't so easy to focus on Codes and rules and the higher values, as that part of my body responded to all the things she was doing. The fear was still there, but other sensations began to build. And I couldn't come up with a reply to what she had said.

By the time she pulled her head away from me she had to lift up and shift back by half a foot. "That's more like it." In a second she had peeled off her panty hose and she was naked. Her long slim body gleamed in the flattering light of the expensive department store, light that had somehow become too bright and made me squint against it. Then she stood up and came in close. I could smell some light floral scent and, underneath it, a deep animal odor of flesh, sweat, and other things.

"You'll regret this," I said.

"I already regret everything. I don't care."

The room went on forever, in all directions, and it was filled with a series of half-dressed Pete Ingallses who said, "What if I care?"

"Shh." She made a ring of her finger and thumb and started stroking.

"Because somebody has to care," I said. When the body seizes control of the mind you say whatever comes into your head, like a drowning man grabbing for flotsam. "Somebody has to care, and somebody has to care that somebody cares."

"God you're weird." She took my hand and plunged it between her legs. "Touch me." I did what she said, and what my fingers shifted and contoured themselves to explore was not quite a thing and not quite a place. I was burning to know if this was right, to be sure that everything was as it should be. But I kept my mouth shut and did as I was told.

"Not so hard," she breathed. Her mouth was half open and her breath was hot on my chest. Her eyes were heavy-lidded and focused elsewhere. "Good . . ." She swooned into me. "Come on."

I had run out of ammo. The Code was a dead letter and I was responsible for its murder. I couldn't remember what my arguments were, and if I could, why I agreed with them. My resolve had been throttled. All I had now was fear and desire. They cancelled each other out. I couldn't move. "We shouldn't," I heard myself say.

"We have to. Come on."

She gave me a gentle push until my back hit the rear mirror of the room, and the lip of the bench beneath it chopped into the rear of my knees, and I slid down and sat. Then she straddled my legs and with a practical hand found me and positioned me and positioned herself, and then slowly lowered herself onto me. My hands held her sides until the fit was complete.

Then she began to move.

My fear swirled up before me and I steeled my nerve to face it. But it was like walking into fog: what seemed opaque and impenetrable kept giving way, sliding past and evanescing into nothing. Whatever I was afraid of kept failing to appear, and as the fog got thinner I caught a glimpse of openness and clarity. And then I was seized with the realization that I had made a lifelong, careerlong mistake.

This act of determined penetration was exactly like my work. It was like pursuing and finding clues, like searching out missing persons and putting the arm on them, like finding witnesses and getting them to talk, like every concerted and successful aggressive move into the world outside your office, your apartment, and your head.

Catherine Flonger swatted my hat off and wrapped her arms around my skull, her nails digging into my scalp. Her motion had shifted gears into a more focused and intense pumping. She had found a spot and was working it. "Oh God, don't move, don't move," she whispered. The air filled with the smell of urgency and the sound of insistence. With my cheek crushed against her chest, I had to fight to breathe. But that was all right. That was fine. I had gotten past every barrier that had blocked me for a lifetime. I had passed through everything and come out undamaged. A little strained gasping was a small price to pay.

"Oh God, I can't believe it," she whispered, and then shuddered, gripped harder, and convulsed in a spasm of stiffened muscles and tight grunts. That was when I knew I had broken through. I had slain the dragon and remained standing. And that triggered my own release. It seized up, focused, and burst forth in a silent pulsing of pinched muscles and loosed reserves and flaring nerve endings. I heard myself give a loud moan and gripped her with an almost vengeful ferocity. And all I could think was, "Well, well, Ingalls. So there really is a first time for everything."

I don't know how long we paused there like that, afterwards, skin cooling, scandalized whispers faintly audible from other dressing rooms and outside the door. When I felt her shiver and saw goose bumps on her arms, I lifted her off and pulled away, took my jacket off and put it around her. She gave me a wan smile and, dazed, sat on the little bench. Then she said, "I don't believe it."

"Kind of soon to get to the regret, isn't it?" I said. "Can't we at least enjoy this 'til tomorrow?"

"That's not what I mean." She frowned and shook her head, but more in puzzlement than unhappiness. "That hasn't happened in twenty years. I mean coming. Like that." I spread my hands in confusion. She had somehow grown demure and modest, and now spoke in a whisper. "I mean, by . . . insertion. Oh, you know. As opposed to orally."

I braced myself for what I knew was coming next: the tender softening, the flowerlike opening of vulnerability, the confession of love. I was called upon to do something the Code warns us may be necessary but that I had never done before. I had to let her down easy.

"Look, baby." I couldn't meet her eyes. This would be harder than I thought. "I care about you, sure."

"Not that Darius can't get it up," she said, chatting. She reared back her head and flexed her neck. "It's not him. He's all right. He functions. I've just never been able to get there with him like that. God. Twenty years."

"And it was special for me, too—"

"I mean, it's not you either, exactly. It's me. I can't believe it." Then she said, "For someone who had to be convinced, you did pretty good."

"Beginner's luck," I said.

She smirked. "Next you're going to tell me it's like riding a bike. So how long has it been?"

"How long has what been?"

"Since you last did this?"

"A lifetime. I told you. It was beginner's luck."

She stared. I stared back. Finally she said, "You mean this is your first time? Come on. How old are you?"

"Thirty-three."

"And in all that time . . . didn't you know any women before you became a detective?"

"Angel," I said, reaching for my trousers, "there was never a time when I wasn't a detective."

FIFTEEN

Having sex changes a man.

You wake up the morning after just a little more pleased with yourself than usual. You feel slim and trim and in tune with the larger forces, because you've done that ultimate thing and you've joined that secret club, the sex club of men, meaning the club of men who've had sex. Now you know what the excitement is about. Now you understand the songs and the movies and the dirty jokes. You can look the mug in the mirror in the face, and if the mug in the mirror doesn't like it, he knows where he can go.

But if the mug in the mirror says, "Not so fast, ace. The party of the second part just happened to have been a client," then you have a problem. You've violated the code of your profession. And that makes you something of an outcast, doesn't it? Because if the job can't trust you to keep your pants on, how can it trust you to keep a secret, or turn down a bribe, or take a punch to the puss when the occasion arises?

So you feel guilty, and exposed to judgment, and in a constant state of waiting for the hammer to drop. Naturally, then, when the phone rings, you grab it and yell, "Yeah?"

"Um . . . I think I have the wrong number. . . . Pete?"

"This is Ingalls. Who's this?"

"Oh. Wow. Hey, it's me."

"Everybody's me. Which me are you?"

"Like you don't know. Stephanie."

"Calling for your severance pay?"

"Huh? No, listen, I was thinking. Obviously Wendy Litman isn't telling the truth. So at first you think, 'Then she must know everything, but isn't telling us.' Like she's concealing stuff."

I wasn't listening. I couldn't focus. The idea of being on the outs with the profession had opened a truck-sized sinkhole in my stomach. At the bottom was a life of boredom, resentment, and blame, and I was plunging into it like Alice following that rabbit, without even a nice tea party to look forward to.

"But what if that's not it!" Stephanie went on. "What if she knows *some* things, but she knows that she doesn't know other things? Because that's how she was acting. She was being evasive. It's not that she knew what to withhold. She didn't know what *not* to say. Which means that . . ."

I didn't know what to do or what not to do. I had given in to temptation and now, like Adam, I was a man without a country, one hand holding an apple core and the other a one-way ticket out of Eden.

"Which means . . . okay, Pete, look," Stephanie sighed. "You're not saying anything. You're still mad at me, aren't you? Please don't be like this. I'm trying to make amends here. I want to atone for pissing you off in the department store. Okay?"

That's when it hit me that I needed to make amends. If I wanted to return to the good graces of the profession, to get right with the job and back on a solid footing with myself, something told me I had to atone.

"Anyway," the gal went on, "look, the thing about Wendy is,

this means that whoever she's working with isn't telling her everything. Or no, she's *afraid* they're not telling her everything. Because how would she know? Huh. That's interesting. . . ."

What sort of act of redemption was available to me? I had no idea. I was all fessed up with nowhere to go. All I could do was hope I'd get the chance—and that I'd be ready when and if I did.

But first I had to get off the phone.

"Listen, kid," I said. "On the one hand I appreciate all the brainwork you've put into the case. On the other hand, you're fired. You were fired, and you remain fired. Go do something else."

"Hmm? What? Look, tell me later. I gotta think about this."

You had to admire the girl's zeal. You also had to tell her to shut up and butt out, and you would have, if she hadn't hung up first. So you had to slam the phone down in irritation and find yourself wondering if drinking Scotch on Saturday morning, alone, right after breakfast, would be filed under "Knowing How to Live Well" or "Drinking."

I decided on both and that was all I needed. Halfway through the third I began to have interesting thoughts. A new angle on the Celeste/Litman/Olivia Cartwright case suddenly disclosed itself to me, all the elements abruptly shifting into a new pattern, like that optical illusion gag of the two faces which either are a vase or two faces, or not. I grabbed a pad and jotted some notes.

By the time I fell into the sack Sunday night I had compiled a picture of the Celeste Vroman case that surprised even me. It was a different picture than any I'd sketched until then, an ugly picture, a picture arguably even uglier than just murder.

You say to me, "Pete, what could possibly be uglier than murder?" My considered answer? Plenty. And there was Ingalls at the hub of it all, seated placidly like Buddha in those painted cloth banners you see at Indian restaurants. I was the hired jerk positioned squarely in the center for a lot of people—good people, bad people, indifferent people, and very bad people—to spin around. Not that I'm saying that Buddha was a hired jerk.

My idea involved passion. And if it happened to turn a hot, lurid, lavender light on Celeste Vroman, yes, on my very own client, with unflattering implications for yours truly, well, that was okay with Ingalls. You don't take a man's money unless you're willing to do certain things, and you don't take a woman's money unless you're willing to think of her as a closet lesbian— and a killer.

Shocked? Get in line. But the more I lived with the idea the more intimate with it I became. I started having certain thoughts.

I starting thinking that Celeste Vroman was secret lovers with none other than Wendy Litman. And once I started thinking that I was struck by how much it made sense. Somehow Olivia Cartwright had found out, so they killed her. And Litman didn't know any of this when Celeste lured him onto the boat and dispatched him, too.

Method? Both accounted for. Opportunity? In spades. Motive? How about Litman's estate, divvied up neatly between the missus and her girlfriend. Accomplice? Try Pete Ingalls, P.I., i.e., Prize Idiot.

There was a kind of calculating genius to it I had to admire. Celeste had used me like a border collie, a nice frisky work dog sent out to bring Litman back into the fold, to win back his affection and trust so she could get him onto that boat. He'd obviously not known about her and his wife's affair, their Sapphic entanglement, the love that dare not speak its maiden name. All he knew was, he wanted out, and was avoiding her. So she hired me to reel him back in. And didn't that mambo in step with Wendy Litman's demeanor at the gallery? She had acted secretive and evasive, and exactly like a woman with more to hide than a closet full of last year's passé fashions. Cute isn't the word.

Brooding on this, and figuring out how to work the coffee machine, were enough to keep me fully absorbed all Monday morning until I was inspired to make a phone call. It wasn't one I had planned to make when I got out of bed that morning. But then, it never is.

"Hello?"

"Ms. Constantino. Ingalls."

"Pete! Wow. Hey, why are you calling? What's up?"

"I was wondering if you wanted your old job back." She hesitated. Ten thousand years' heritage of the actor's craft had bestowed on her an ability to react in the moment. It left a void which I had to fill. "I don't have time to pursue the caseload *and* run the office."

"I thought I was fired."

"You were." I paused, then laid my trump card down with a slow flourish and a final snap. "But I'm experimenting with an idea. I call it serial employment. You hire someone, and you fire them when you want to, then you hire them back. It's lean, it's mean, it's just-in-time personnel management. It addresses the needs of the moment."

"Yeah. Your needs."

"Let's you be nice."

"Uh-huh. Okay, Pete, sure, I'd love to have a job. But not my old one."

I laughed. "How many positions do you think I need to fill, angel? Y—"

"The old one didn't pay enough."

"It's the only one there is."

"Then either you have to find someone else, or I'm doing my

own experiment. What happens is, you have the same job but you're paid more money for it. It's called getting a raise."

"After one lousy week of work?"

"That's why it's an experiment." She paused and added, with a sly little come-on in her voice, "Besides, I did some digging over the weekend."

"Now why would you do that?"

"I told you, Pete. Because I'm into this! And I had an idea."

I sighed. "Which was—?"

"I had a drink with Tad Phillips! He's kind of an asshole. But not stupid. Anyway, get this—the day Olivia was killed, Greg Higgins and Megan Loomis had a big yelly, shouty fight with Litman! Over his fucking up some case to where this old client of theirs fired the firm! And sought other counsel!"

"Interesting. That might give them a motive to kill each other. Or at least someone a motive to kill someone."

"And what about Tad himself?" she said. "Talk about disgruntled."

"Disgruntled enough to commit murder?"

She hesitated. "I don't know. But he seems to hate everybody there." She paused and said, "Pretty good, huh? So about that raise . . ."

I said nothing and let the air stop quivering. Then I suggested a figure. She doubled it. I died laughing. Then I suggested an alternative figure and she agreed to take slightly more. We had a deal.

Like a housewife tidying up for the arrival of the cleaning lady, I was policing the office prior to Stephanie's return when I heard a sharp knock on the front door. "It's open," I called.

It was Louis, the lad from the hospital room, in faded blue

jeans and a gray T-shirt. He had a little satchel on a strap on his shoulder. The lackluster moustache still lacked luster. He looked angry and simmering but he stopped dead when he saw me. "Sorry. I must have the wrong address."

"Not necessarily." I put down the paper towels and the Endust. "It's Louis, isn't it?"

He was wary. "Do I know you?"

"You thought you did."

"I'm looking for Peter Ingalls—"

"You found him."

He stared at me hard, his eyes frisking my features as though looking for hidden explanations. Then he found one. "You shaved. The beard is gone. You had it in the hospital."

"Go to the head of the class."

He nodded toward my suit, his face hardening, and the anger getting back on its feet. "And look at this." He surveyed the place and said, "What the fuck? Was the other guy like your secret identity? When you were at the bookstore? Do you work out of this office fighting crime?"

"Louis, that's almost exactly what I do."

"Ask me if I'm surprised. All right, look." He pulled something from the satchel. "Leonard was saying either you come and get it or he was going to toss it. So I said I'd bring it over. And you know what, man? Fuck you."

He slammed the item down on the desk. It was a jumbo version of those cardboard-covered school notebooks, with a black and white marbled front and a title plate reading COMPOSITIONS. Only the first quarter of it had been used, each page covered, on one side only, with a fine, meticulous script in thin black rollerpoint.

"Mind if I ask a question, son?" I looked at him and not the book. "Why the heat?"

"What, you mean why am I pissed? Because I read some of it at lunch before I came here, that's why."

"How much is some?"

"All. The whole thing. Fucking diary of a lunatic."

He threw this answer at me and waited for my take. I didn't provide much. "And? Stimulating ideas? Nice plot? Shapely narrative?"

"Calling me an idiot? And a cretin? And an imbecile? Is that what somebody like you needs? To feel okay? Coming in every day with your Abraham Lincoln beard and your pretentious, know-it-all, fussy bullshit? And *I'm* the idiot?" He shook his head and wandered around. I waited. When a guy needs to let off steam, all you can do is stand clear and hope you don't get scalded. He stopped and spun around and looked at me. "Jesus. Maybe you're a multiple personality. Do you find yourself being a different person depending on who you're with?"

"Don't you?"

"No, I mean, do you ever find yourself in a place and wonder how you got there?"

"Doesn't everybody?"

He looked sour and nodded. "Fine. Cool. So there's your notebook, Peter. Don't forget to take your meds."

I thanked him and watched him leave. As I put the notebook in a drawer I wondered if it held anything incriminating about oversized children. And just what was Louis's complicity in it all? Then Stephanie breezed in, a leggy knockout in tight blue jeans and a man's blousy white oxford. She looked around and said, "Oh my God."

"What."

"Nothing. It's okay. I'll tidy up." She started making noises at the sink with coffeemakers and related ordnance, and called out over the hiss of the water, "How's your face?"

"Healing."

"You talk to Richard yet?"

"When it's germane to talk to Richard, I'll talk to Richard."

It was around three thirty that a slow, heavy step sounded outside the door. Someone was transporting something weighty and ponderous, against their will. The door opened and a large, pale, hulking shape wandered in. He wore a big wrinkled London Fog, its belt missing and all the more vast because of it. "Hope I'm not interrupting anything," Det. Hank Thoreau snickered. He eyeballed me up and down. "Jesus. You look like shit."

"You should see the other guy."

"Turns out I have, Magnum!" Thoreau lowered himself into a chair. "Just came back from Taylor and Tackett."

Stephanie grew alert. "You talked to Richard?"

"Ding! Score one for the sexytary." He hauled a little memo pad out of his jacket pocket and squinted at it. "Richard Sternberger. Nonfiction editor. In person."

"How's he look?"

"Like Spenser for Hire here. Except not as bad." He chuckled. "It's pretty obvious who won *that* donnybrook."

"What makes you so sure it was Richard who came after me?" I said. "Your smart-cop's ESP? Some anonymous informant?"

"He told me." Thoreau fake-smiled. "He also told me he thinks you killed Olivia Cartwright. And boy does *that* set my toes a-tappin'."

"Why would I do that?"

"For pay, ace. In the employ of your evil client. So she could have unobstructed access to Mr. Jeffrey Litman, Esquire. Richard was in love with her. Olivia." He gave Stephanie a little smile. "But you already knew that."

"Richard's flipped out," Stephanie said. "Big time. Ambushing Pete like that? Beating him up on the street—"

I held up the open hand of not-so-fast. "I wouldn't say 'beating up'—"

"Attacking, then. Check Richard's medical history, Detective. I bet the guy's on drugs. Halcion or whatever. There's your killer. I mentioned him to Olivia and she rolled her eyes."

Thoreau shrugged. He looked like an albino walrus shifting position on an ice floe. "Maybe. I doubt it. He's falling apart, sure. But in a nice way. I don't see him on major league meds and I also don't see him whacking the beloved. Even on impulse."

I waved an airy hand and said, "Fine, so he's pure as the driven snow. Of course, I hear that and I want to ask, 'Who's driving?' But maybe that's me."

Thoreau smirked. "Believe me, it is."

"Point taken. Anyway, we know I didn't do it."

"Do we?"

"I was here, with my assistant, at the time of the assault."

"The whole afternoon?"

"Well, then I went out for lunch. We both did."

"And a witness will corroborate that?"

"Sure. The waiter at the Indian place. Plus the party we had lunch with."

Stephanie winced. "Pete—"

"Who would that be?" Thoreau asked.

I suddenly realized why Stephanie was distressed. I had to think of some way, fast, to avoid telling the cop whom we'd met for lunch with that afternoon. "I don't recall."

"No kidding."

"Indian food gives me amnesia." I shrugged. "Always has. I think. Who remembers?"

The detective sat forward, elbows on his knees. "Look, Ingalls. I don't like you for the Cartwright killing so don't bother trying to be clever. What I need to know is, do you want to press assault charges against young Richard?"

"Yes!" Stephanie looked thrilled.

"No," I said.

"Oh, come on, Pete! Please? He attacked you!"

"Nix. He was doing his job."

"His job? His job is to edit nonfiction!"

"His job as the heartbroken dumped boyfriend."

"Oh for God's sake."

Thoreau put his left foot on his right knee and kneaded his toes through his shoe. "My question is, how did his boss ever hook up with a piranha like Litman? I asked Richard and he didn't know."

"Neither do I," I said. I indulged in a world-weary sigh. Think there's nothing in this world to be weary about? See me after class. "It looks like we're destined never to know how and why they met. You want to call it Fate, be my guest. I can live with happenstance. But some facets of human existence are at bottom unknowable. Or, if you prefer, knowable only to God."

"She met him through a personals ad in the *New York Review of Books*," Stephanie said. We both looked at her. She shrugged. "She told me when I met with her. Litman placed an ad and she responded."

Thoreau frowned. "Why did she tell you?"

"I think because she was proud of it. She was bragging to another woman. It was like she applied for a job and beat out a lot of competition."

"She wouldn't tell me," I said. "Still, do the math. She lives in New York. She reads reviews. She reads books. She'd read a New York review of books. It adds up."

Stephanie gave me a sudden look but spoke to herself. "No it doesn't." She said to Thoreau, "Litman was a stud and a creep.

What would he want with the middle-aged college professors who read the *New York Review*? He'd want young, hot bimbos."

"Like you, you mean," the cop leered.

"Yeah, like me," Stephanie said. "Or like your mother."

"Ouch. That hurts."

"Fuck you."

"Blow me." He grinned to himself. His mouth was too small for his face and somehow pointed, like the beak of a squid. Do squids have beaks? Let's say they do. Let's say Det. Hank Thoreau's mouth resembled a squid's beak, the way his bone-white, unnatural skin reminded you of the underbelly of some grotesque fish that lives in the deepest waters, a mile down in eternal cold and dark, the kind that can't see and only comes out once a year, to be filmed for TV documentaries.

"So." I made an effort to wrap things up. "Are we all done?"

"Not yet." Thoreau's vast white face looked preoccupied. Some important distraction had taken hold. He looked around vaguely. "This is an office, right? You got any M&M's?"

Stephanie stared at him. "What?"

"Offices usually have stuff stashed away here and there. Little snacks and treats and shit. I suddenly have this craving for chocolate."

I looked at my assistant. "Ms. Constantino—"

"Forget it."

I signaled Thoreau with a gesture: I tried.

He looked bored and exhausted and waved it away. He started talking. "I spoke to an old friend of yours, Ingalls. Officer Dave Watley at the Atlantic City P.D. We're all in bed together now. It's a slumber party and we're in our jammies and our fuzzy slippers and telling scary stories about Celeste Vroman."

"I like stories," I said.

"Then bring your teddy bear and join in. Greg Higgins at

Hoffman, Ratner told me he'd spoken to Watley so I called him up. What we have is a triangle. Olivia to Litman to Celeste Vroman. Which you didn't tell me."

"It was an ethical matter," I said. "Reasonable people can disagree—"

"Reasonable people can suck my dick."

"Detective—"

He crossed his legs, right ankle on left knee, and started flexing the other foot, reciting some back story. "We asked around, me and Dave Watley, my new best friend. At Hoffman, Ratner lots of people have heard of Celeste Vroman, but no one has actually met her. There's an apartment in her name in Atlantic City, and a phone, and a checking account with a few hundred bucks. And some dealers in the casinos remember her, vaguely. But no friends or family. Meanwhile, the super at her place never sees her. Neither do the neighbors. Her mail must go to a post office box we don't know about. The boat is abandoned, she doesn't answer her cell phone . . . What can you tell me about her?"

"What makes you think I can tell you anything?"

The beaky mouth flapped in disgust. Then he looked irritated and bent over. There was the sound of a shoe hitting the floor. "Because . . ." He began to knead his toes. "Greg Higgins says you mentioned her." He sighed. It wasn't a pleasant sound. "Tell you what I think. I think she's your mystery client."

"Jesus Christ," Stephanie said. "Can't you conduct an interview without scratching your horrible disgusting feet?"

Thoreau smiled. "Sorry, pumpkin. These are the only feet I've got." He looked at me dead on. "So. Ingalls. Tell me about Celeste, or be booked for obstruction."

Classic? In spades. And if the case had still been open, or I had thought Celeste was getting a raw deal, I might have played foot-

sie with the cop and withheld some salient facts. But my work
was done and I had suspicions myself about the state of cleanli-
ness of Celeste's bony, strong hands. So I sang.

I told him everything, starting with our first meeting in the
restaurant, the phone calls, the temperament, the rage at Olivia
Cartwright. And the second meeting at the Indian restaurant, the
plan to spend some time on the boat with Litman, her telling me
to pick up the briefcase that wasn't there. The whole time
Thoreau had his mouth half open, his fingers dug into the toes
of his right sock-clad foot, and a glazed expression focused on
the inner infinity. Finally I finished and said, "That's it."

If he'd looked hypnotized and out of it, his reaction was
sharp. "Thanks. That helps." He put his shoe on, muttering to
his invisible friend, "It feels good while you're scratching but it's
a bitch afterwards. Like fucking drug addiction." He stood up.
"Last call for that chocolate, people. Anything. Hershey's Kisses?
Those little Milky Ways left over from Halloween?"

"Y'all come back and see us again real soon," Stephanie said.

"Oh, Ingalls. It goes without saying you'll contact me if you
hear from Celeste."

"Actually," I said, "it goes with saying. I don't think I will."

"Sure we will," Stephanie said.

I stared at her. Thoreau, of course, was pleased. "Smart girl.
Hey, let's go out on a date sometime!"

"What about your wife?" she said.

"She can go with Ingalls here. We'll double. We'll all go see
The Lion King and eat at some fucking Ethiopian place."

Stephanie said, "We'll tell you if we hear from Celeste—"

I said, " 'We'?"

"—but you have to tell us something. What's going on out
there? At Hoffman, Ratner or Taylor and Tackett?"

Thoreau stood there, huge and pale, mouth ajar, pondering. Then he shrugged. "I'll give you one." He licked his thin lips. "Do you intelligent people know what bearer bonds are?"

I nodded. "Like the ones Hoffman, Ratner were sitting on. Shake it up and pour it, pal."

"They're gone. The ones Litman was managing, from the whatchamacallit case. Higgins told me. When they heard Litman was missing they checked the firm's ledger. Turns out Litman had converted them to cash in a client trust account, which is perfectly appropriate. Only now the account's empty. Which isn't."

I said, "To the tune of—?"

"Eight million and change."

"Which means . . . what?"

"*Ob*-viously," Stephanie said, "Litman stole the money, joined Celeste on the boat so they could sail away to Aruba or wherever, she kills him, takes the money, and disappears."

Thoreau shrugged. "Maybe. I don't have Litman's body. I have Olivia's. That's my case. And I'm still wondering what she was doing at that dive."

"Having an assignation with Litman," I said. I might have glanced at Stephanie to see if she was buying it. Or I might not have. "What do they say at Hoffman?"

"Not enough." Thoreau moved toward the door. "I also talked to Richard and Randy and all the elves at the publishing house. Not everyone has an alibi but almost no one has a motive. It's a mystery, Miss Marple." He directed his dull gaze at Stephanie. "Look, Steph, if you don't have any chocolate, can I at least eat your pussy?"

"I'm offended, Detective. My pussy's better than chocolate," she said, meeting his eyes. "Next time you say something like that I'm filing a complaint. I'm sure I won't be the first."

"Not the first, and not the last!" He shuffled out the door. "Call me if Celeste pops up."

Once he'd gone we both breathed easier. But then, everybody breathes easier when the cops leave. Even when they've come to help, and not to sprawl around asking questions, attending to their athlete's foot, demanding candy, and tossing off obscene comments. Because cops are the guys you don't like to have to call and absolutely hate to have show up uninvited. Everybody's a furtive teen with something to hide when cops walk in the door. And everybody stands down and gets just a touch more comfy when they exit the premises. No wonder cops drink, and if they don't drink, no wonder they do whatever it is they do. Because don't kid yourself. They do something. We all do.

"Sounds like Thoreau and I are on a common wavelength," I said. Stephanie, still seated at her desk, was looking blankly at the wall. "About the bonds, Litman, et cetera." She again failed to respond. "Your thoughts on this important matter?"

"Huh? Oh. God, that jerk. I can't believe he ever solves anything."

"That's what you're pondering in the windmills of your mind?"

"No. I was thinking of something Wendy Litman said when we told her Olivia had been killed. Something Thoreau said— oh! 'It's a mystery!' What an asshole. But that's what I was thinking after we left Wendy. Remember what she said? We said Olivia Cartwright had been killed, and she said—"

"'Oh my God, that poor woman'?"

She laughed. "Yeah, right. No, she said, 'That's impossible.'"

"And? So?"

"And, so, what the hell does that mean? If she supposedly didn't know Olivia."

I stood up and stretched. This amateur girl sleuth thing: yeah, it was cute. To a point. We had reached and surpassed that point long, long ago. "Look, angel—"

"Hey. Pete. I have an idea."

"I don't need an idea. I need a secretary/assistant to do secretarial and assistanty things around the office. Haven't we been through this? More than once? I've hired you back, at an increase in salary, for an explicit purpose—"

"Yeah, I know, fine, but I have an idea. Just listen."

She started to tell me the idea. So I listened.

Yeah, it was a fun-filled day in my increasingly rich, full life, but it wasn't over. That night, around eleven, I was home, when the horn rang. Of the several people it could have plausibly been, it was none. Instead, a man's voice which I didn't recognize said, "Ingalls? Just listen. If you want to take pictures of Darius Flonger and his little girlfriend, go to Three twenty-two Thompson Street tomorrow before three o'clock. Apartment three C. There'll be a key under the mat. Don't get caught."

"Wait—hold it—One Twenty C Thompson—"

"Three twenty-two. Apart—look, man, write it down. Three twenty-two Thompson."

"—twenty-two, got it. Apartment . . . ?"

"Three C."

"What's the Zip on that, friend?"

"What difference does . . . Jesus, look, just don't fuck it up." Then the line went dead.

In the movies that's always followed by a dial tone, to signal "the caller has departed." But in real life you don't get the dial tone. You get silence. And that's what I got at that moment. The silence of real life.

SIXTEEN

The next morning was an unalloyed pleasure, if you liked waiting for a glacier. Stephanie asked if she could dust early and bang her pretty little head against the wall of an audition, and that was jake with me. I read the paper and played Minesweeper and fought off the thought that if the agency was going to make it past the first fiscal quarter I'd need more clients, sooner than later.

In the afternoon I went to work. I legged it up to Three twenty-two Thompson, a ramshackle apartment building in the West Village, where doddering ethnic grandmas in career-widow black poke down the street in their walkers past Italian bistros asking forty bucks for ziti. Okay, twenty, but add a salad and a glass of house red; now factor in tax, tip, title, dealer prep, and a buck to the gal who takes your coat. No wonder the mob's Italian. You have to be rich just to each lunch.

The building's main entrance was unlocked but the inner door worked on a buzzer. The roster of tenants in the glassed-in box to my left showed FRANKLIN in Apartment 3-C—a name that, like so many others, meant nothing to me. I pushed every button in sight until someone, trustingly but unwisely, buzzed me in. My destination was up a flight of white marble steps worn smooth and blunt-edged by four or five generations of immigrants who swarmed to Greenwich Village from Europe to exult in America's freedom and opportunity, and to see just what those beatniks were all about. Under the welcome mat, as advertised, was the key. I knocked, just in case. When no one answered, I let myself in.

The door opened onto a narrow corridor that led to a living room on the right, a bedroom on the left, then, farther down, a bathroom, then a kitchen off a dining room. It was one of those stifling New York apartments crammed with overstuffed bookshelves and a hodgepodge of worn furniture. No one in the framed photos on the tables or in the snapshots magnetized to the fridge looked familiar.

After a preliminary tour I cased the small bedroom. The layout bothered me. The bed stood barely three feet from the only possible place of concealment, the closet. The interior of the closet was dark, but I caught a break when its door proved to be a two-panel sliding job. Once inside I was able to crack it just wide enough to accommodate my inquiring eyeball and the lens of my camera.

But as soon as I settled in I began to worry. The light, from a window looking out onto an airshaft, was gray and thin and didn't inspire confidence in its ability to illuminate a decent mug shot, let alone a possibly challenging tableau of naked people frolicking amid obscuring bedclothes. And even if the parties in question got atmospheric and uninhibited and lit up the scene with strobes or candles or torches, I was fixed in place, stuck with a single vantage point with no guarantee my subjects would remain in range.

That's when it hit me: I'd been set up. Someone—never mind

who—had lured me into exactly this apartment, exactly this room, exactly this closet, in order for Flonger to find me and vent his outrage in more ways than I wanted to imagine. I was trapped. And it was zero hour. All I could do was wait, among the jeans and sport jackets and plastic-covered dry-cleaned dress shirts, and adapt to whatever happened.

It didn't take long. At three on the dot the door opened and in, chatting and laughing, strolled Mr. Darius Flonger and Ms. Nora Whatshername, the diminutive, tallness-deprived citizen from the hotel bar. As I watched, Flonger and the dame sat on the bed, touching and massaging one another and barely murmuring. He was six feet, in a black suit. She was barely four, in a white cotton shift. He shut the wooden Venetian blinds as she clicked on a bedside reading lamp. I snapped away. The surrounding clothes muffled the noise and my subjects didn't hear me.

Then he stood up and, with the slowly methodical moves of a man disrobing for a checkup, took off the jacket, the shirt and tie, the shoes, the pants, the underwear, the socks. His companion, meanwhile, found a boom box and turned on a CD featuring the kind of modern classical music that makes everyone feel just a little bit stupid. Flonger lay on the bed, face down, and the gal—now disturbingly nude herself—straddled his back and started massaging, a tiny rider atop a long, pale mount, working her little thumbs and fingers into his flesh.

With the music's angular, lurching sonic camouflage I could snap away with gusto, and found Flonger's mildly pleased, smugly smirking pan easy to frame. Of course, the photographs would be useless to my client, and a rebuke of my professional competence, without the identifiable presence of the lady. Lucky for me, Flonger was the affectionate type, and several times pulled her down to him so their faces were together for a quick nuzzle or smooch. I got plenty of those, too.

Maybe now's the time to nip in the tender bud of its spring-time certain people's distaste for what I'm describing—the act of spying on two adults having sex. Perhaps such people think it constitutes an invasion of the lovebirds' privacy. Except I wasn't invading their privacy. I was taking great pains to stay put in the closet and allowing them to do uninterrupted whatever it is they were doing. Certain people don't think of that, apparently.

Finally, after a notably restrained session of light petting and gentle caressing, Darius Flonger said in those on-the-air tones, "Mmm, that's good, honey. What do you say we take a shower?" Nora agreed, got off, and together they padded away toward the bathroom, a tall naked media star and his Munchkin-sized date.

I put my ear to the opening and listened for the hiss of the shower. When I heard it, I ventured out of the closet into the bedroom, with a burglar's paranoid tiptoe silence and a height-ened, thrilled sense of my own existence. I stuck my head out the doorway into the hall, and confirmed that the bathroom door was shut and the water running. I legged it silently down the central hallway and, with a sense of relief, scrammed, shutting the door gently behind me. In ten seconds I was on the street.

The drugstore's one-hour photo service came through as promised, and by tea time I was scanning an array of beauties. Flonger seemed to have gone out of his way to make his mug visible to the camera. There was no doubt who the nude gentle-man was, and even less that his companion was not Catherine Flonger, his legal wife. The couple did everything but pose be-side a vaudeville easel sign reading "A Spot of Adultery." It was almost too easy.

Sometimes it is. Life throws you a knuckler when you expect it to slide, then hangs a curve in the wheelhouse when you're looking for heat. All you can do is hang in, protect the plate, swing to make contact, and run like hell.

I stowed the photos in an envelope in the desk, then phoned Catherine Flonger and left a voice mail message informing her that I had certain documents she'd requested. Then I punched out for the day and went home. I had a date with a lady that night and wanted to be in peak form. And that meant a nap.

It was around nine o'clock when I walked into the lobby of Two Lincoln Plaza, a swank-if-undistinguished high-rise with stacked balconies like old-fashioned ice-cube trays. Stephanie had done some digging and come up with the address in question, and now it was my turn to play detective. When the security man at the command desk asked my name, I said, "Tad Phillips." I waved a briefcase at him and added, "Got some papers for him to sign."

"ID," he muttered.

I pulled out my wallet and handed him angry young Tad's card. It was all my assistant's idea, and it worked like a charm. The bored guard, a middle-aged man with unsmiling eyes and a faux cop uniform, lifted a phone handset, touched some numbers, and said, "Tad Phillips is here . . . From Hoffman, Ratner . . . Okay." He hung up and waved me in.

"Cool, pops," I said. An elevator ride and trek down a thickly carpeted hallway later, I knocked on 1704. A few seconds after that Wendy Litman opened the door.

She wasn't happy to see me. "My God. What do you want?"

"Can I come in, Mrs. Litman? Or shall we do this out here?"

"Do what? No. You can't."

"Play it your way." I loosened my tie and tilted the fedora back on my head. It was a cheap way to signal: I'm relaxed. "Why don't I start the bidding. I know what's going on. I could sing to the johns but I'd be a happier American if you and I did a deal." She hesitated. Then she stood aside and opened the door.

The apartment was broad, airy, and tasteful—all those things you'd assume about a place occupied by a rich Manhattan lawyer and his art dealer wife. The living room was a symphony of cream, oatmeal, and beige tones, with squared-off Danish-style sofas and tables and some spiffy oils on the walls. Wendy Litman wore an old shapeless blouse and sweatpants and slippers—but then, I hadn't exactly called ahead, and hubby was MIA. "What are you talking about, Mr. Ingersoll?"

"Ingalls. And I think you know exactly what I'm talking about, Mrs. Litman."

"I promise you, I do not."

And that irked me. When did "I promise" come to mean "I swear" with respect to states of being and not future actions? "I promise you, it's true." Or, worse, "I promise you, Napoleon was Catholic." It's disorienting. Not that I care. But let's face it. I do care. That's my problem. Wendy Litman, meanwhile, had her own problems. "Let me explain, then," I said. "May I sit down?"

"No."

"Good. I like standing. It helps me break in my shoes. Okay, here's the dope. Let's say there's a woman. Call her Wendy—"

"Mr. Ingalls—"

"Bear with me, it gets better. And there's another woman named Celeste. Now these two women are, for whatever reason, and I'm not here to pass judgment, homosexual lovers. Lesbians, if you will. And I have a feeling that you will." I paused to gauge the impact.

And it was immediate. What is it Freud says about laughter being the best medicine? Wendy Litman laughed. It was a sincere, spontaneous laugh, which was all the signal I needed to know I was on the right track. We laugh because we're nervous. We laugh because we're threatened by the approach of the truth, and because truth frightens us, and because being afraid really isn't all that funny, and so we laugh.

I continued. "And they wanted to go off together and be boyfriend and girlfriend, or girlfriend and woman-friend, or whatever it is such couples do. The only thing is, Wendy had a husband. That was the bad news. The good news was, hubby had access to a cool eight million in bearer bonds—"

"You are really and truly out of your mind, aren't you," she said.

"Maybe. Let me finish and then we'll decide who's out of my mind. So wouldn't it be nice if the girls got the dough in a way that could also ease Wendy's husband off the stage? And that's exactly what they did. Celeste, who maybe had been a special friend of Wendy's husband—let's call him Jeff—enticed him into stealing the eight mil and then joining her on a nice boat ride."

I paused again and saw that she'd gone from amused to amazed to ice-cold. "Go on," she said.

"Which he did. They took the boat out into the mighty Atlantic. A moonlight cruise on the romantic Atlantic. Only instead of celebrating their heist of the cabbage and the purity of the glory of the story of their love, Celeste bashes the Jeffster in the skull and dumps him overboard to sleep with the fishes. Then she goes into hiding with her ill-gotten gains until she can be joined by Wendy once the whole sordid business blows over. Am I getting warm?"

You could tell I hit a nerve. She could barely cobble together a sentence. "You're . . . crazy. This is insane! I'm going to sue you."

I smiled. "Now who's out of his mind, Mrs. Litman? You're not going to sue me. You're going to listen to my offer. I figure you have a couple of days at most until the authorities start to close in. And frankly, I don't care. But I do want to make contact with my client. It's not even to collect a bill, either. Because I've been paid in full."

The phone rang. She sighed, walked to the kitchen, and answered while I waited coolly in place. She said, "I'm not here . . . oh. Christ." She hung up with an angry clatter of plastic.

When she came back she was agitated. "Just tell me. Why do you want to contact this Celeste person?"

"To offer some advice. I've already stuck my neck out for her, and I want to wrap up our professional relationship with some honor. If that has any meaning to you."

"You must think it doesn't," she said coolly. "Since to you I'm just a thieving, murdering lesbian."

"Even thieving, murdering lesbians can have honor," I said. I wasn't sure if it was true but it sounded good. "The deal is, I don't go to the buttons and sing my little heart out, and you tell me how to get in touch with Celeste."

She sighed and sat on the arm of one of the sofas. "You do realize that this so-called theory of yours is ridiculous. I firmly believe my husband is still alive, and I have no idea how to contact this Celeste person."

"Come on, Wendy. The blood on the boat, the missing bearer bonds—and the dead Olivia Cartwright. Some people think Celeste killed her, too."

"There's no accounting for what some people think. I'm not responsible for what some people think."

"What if the people thinking are New York's Finest? Because make no mistake, sweetheart. Police think, too. They think and they feel and they have hopes and dreams like you and me."

She started to reply but then just gave up. "Do you ever listen to yourself?"

"That's a luxury I can't afford, lady. I'm too busy listening to everybody else." It somehow seemed inadequate. I added, "Except in the shower. I listen hard to myself when I sing in the shower. Maybe too hard."

There was a knock. She seemed to collect herself, then glided past me and went to the door. She peered through the peephole and then opened the door. Standing there was a clean-cut young man in his late twenties, in a sport coat and tie. I'd never seen him before. He smiled at her and said, "Wendy Litman? Is a Mr. Peter Ingalls here?"

I stepped forward. "You're looking at him, pal."

He held out an open wallet and I glimpsed some official-looking card. "John Garbus from Downtown, Mr. Ingalls. Your secretary told me you'd be here."

"You spoke to Ms. Constantino? At this hour?"

He was a smooth-faced lad with a dimpled smile. "I spoke to her this afternoon. She gave me your schedule for the rest of the day. I'm just now getting around to it."

"Getting around to what?"

"I'd appreciate it if you'd come downtown with me to answer a few questions." He turned to Wendy and added, "Sorry about this intrusion, ma'am. But it's rather urgent that we have a conversation with Mr. Ingalls."

I looked at Wendy Litman to generate some so-there eye contact, but she avoided my gaze. Instead she smiled at Garbus and said, "That's all right. Mr. Ingalls and I had just concluded our business." She gestured me toward the door. "Thank you for your proposition, but I think I'll pass."

I took a few steps but stopped before reaching the doorway. "And what if I don't feel like joining you, Garbus?"

"I'm betting you know what'll serve your interests in the long run, Ingalls. But I can get some paperwork, if it'll make you feel better."

"And what? Arrest me? On what charge?"

He laughed. "Oh, if I were to arrest you, it might be for—in alphabetical order? Start with aiding and abetting—"

"Try abetting and aiding, friend. B comes before I in this man's alphabet."

"I'll make a note of it."

"You do that. I'll be right there. Why don't you wait outside so the lady and I can wrap things up?"

Garbus shrugged and stepped into the hallway. I went up to Wendy Litman and said softly, "I can stall these birds for tonight. I suggest you think about my offer."

"We have nothing to discuss. Good night."

"Free ride tonight only. I'll be in touch." I stepped out into the hallway, and she shut the door behind me.

Twenty-four hours later I was seated on the passenger's side of a white Daewoo Lasagna at a meter on Ninth Avenue in front of Two Lincoln Plaza. I had been there for half an hour, watching the ebb and flow of this nonstop reality show we call life. Finally a young woman came out of the building carrying a tote bag. It was Stephanie Constantino at her most alert and revved-up. She hustled over to the car. I made the window go down and said, "How'd it go?"

"I think good. She didn't admit a thing, but she kept listening. And at least I got in. Beats being hung up on three times in a row."

I unlocked the door, and she got in behind the wheel. "Nice car," I said. "Good choice."

"It was the cheapest thing they had. It'll do."

"The thing I don't get is, why call it a Lasagna?"

"What?"

I had to chuckle. "And you a dame of Italian extraction. Lasagna, kid. Broad, flat noodles—"

"I know what lasagna is. I just don't know why they'd name a Korean car after it. Hang on."

She got out and walked to the rear of the car and scanned the trunk and the bumper. Then she shook her head and came back. "Look, I know it's hard to read that scripty writing," she said, "but it's Leganza."

"Point taken. In my own defense, let the record show that unlike some people, I don't read Korean. Just tell me how it went upstairs."

"Fine. She didn't recognize my name when the security guy announced me. But she let me come up anyway. I mean that's how freaked she is by all this. Once she saw me she remembered."

"Aces. And?"

"She asked why I was here now, at night. I said I hadn't heard from you all day until an hour ago. Then I said, Look, I'm here to tell you that my boss has been arrested. And it got to her. You could see it. She said, 'Of what interest is that to me?' Which, obviously, if you're talking in that Jane Austen way, then something is extremely wrong and you're making a major effort to stay in control."

"Okay, so you had her hearing steps. And—?"

She smiled broadly and made with a coy lowering of the sultry green eyes. "First of all"—she touched fingertips to her breast in a modest bow—"I was fabulous." She looked back at me, exuberant. "I said, 'If Pete's arrested, it means he has to tell the cops what he knows.' I told her you wanted to be loyal to Celeste and be professional and all, but once the cops get involved, you have to tell the truth. 'It's what detectives do,' I said. Don't you love it?"

I nodded. "So you told her what detectives do. Good. And I suppose you went on about me being the one clean man in a dirty world who walks these mean streets but is not himself mean?" I had an afterthought and added, ". . . although sometimes understandably irritable?"

She shrugged. "Nah. Not really."

"Maybe you should have."

"Whatever. I mean that's your line. What I said was, 'They don't talk until they're arrested. Then they tell what they can. I mean, a hundred dollars a day only buys you so much loyalty and discretion.' "

I liked the gal—in spite of her relentless snippiness and mouthy presumption. And I liked myself. Approving her idea to send her to put the fear of God into Wendy Litman had been one of my better ideas. "Nice," I said. "And now . . . we wait."

"There's more. She asked what I thought you would talk about to the cops. I said, 'Everything. Everything he knows about Celeste, and your husband, and you, and the bearer bonds, and the blood, and the law firm.' I said, 'Pete thinks Celeste killed Jeffrey. He also thinks she sold *him* out, and that's what he's going to say.' "

"Great. And you told her we know that she and Celeste are very much in love."

"Nah," she said. "That's your theory. I don't buy it. Anyway, I said, 'Pete made his one call to me. He said Celeste hadn't gotten in touch all night last night or all day today, and he feels used. And he thinks she killed Olivia Cartwright and that you're probably complicit.' "

"Excellent. And that's when she collapsed in tears and sobbed out a touching confession."

"Are you kidding? She's tough. She got all tight in the mouth and had this whole body-armor tension thing going, and she said, 'That's ridiculous.' I said, 'Maybe, but it sounds good to me, and it'll sound good to the cops, who don't have squat and are looking for leads.' That got to her. Which I called, remember?"

I did remember. Stephanie had said the day before that simply telling Wendy Litman my theory wouldn't be enough to pry anything out of her. Only seeing me being hauled to headquarters would impress on her the possibility that the bulls were wise and the party might be coming to an unpleasant end. "Brilliant. Well done. Give yourself a gold star."

She smiled. "Thank you. Oh, then I improvved some new thing. I told her that your theory was way plenty to have the cops move in on *her*. At least with wiretaps, which she'd never be able to detect. Like, tomorrow. You could see her get freaked. Then she said, 'Why are you telling me all this? What do you want?' I said, 'Because if you come forward, you'll not only get my boss off the hook, you'll save yourself major grief. The sooner you turn yourself in, the better it'll be for you. Because get real. They're going to catch you, they're going to catch Celeste, and they're going to turn the two of you against each other."

I nodded grimly. "And now, let the waiting commence."

" 'Meanwhile,' I said, 'Here's where you can reach us.' I gave her the number and said, 'Plus, if you talk to Celeste, tell her my boss needs to talk to her.' And then I left. *Now* we wait." She sat back and sighed, "God, this is so much more fun than scene work."

We both turned to look at the apartment building's entrance, as though expecting Wendy Litman to come waltzing out on cue. When it didn't happen my assistant and I settled in for what might be hours. I said, "And she bought the whole Garbus thing."

"Yeah! See? Wasn't I right about that, too? I figured as long as he was hauling *you* in, she wouldn't challenge it."

"And he wasn't bad. The lad had presence."

"Oh, David can do that in his sleep. He was on *Docket One*. Although as a rich guy's son who gets his fiancée addicted to pills. Not as a cop. Still, I mean, he's great."

"Do I detect boyfriend material?"

She laughed. "Right. For a dancer named Phil. David's totally gay, Pete. We're in acting class together." She reached into the tote bag and pulled out a paperback copy of Joe Orton's plays and a little battery-powered reading lamp that clipped onto the pages. "So, here we are. I'll go get sandwiches later." And she settled in to read.

I had my own in-flight entertainment. I pulled out the notebook Louis had brought, and hauled up from the floor a big, boxy, stand-alone emergency flashlight. I clicked it on and positioned the notebook. I had no idea what to expect. There was no title or author's name anywhere, just dated entries in that fussy, elegant script. I opened to the first page.

> *VOLUME XXVII*
>
> *The first pristine page of the next new notebook: bliss! The padding provided by the full complement of untouched future pages is absolute; the pen sinks ecstatically into this (firm, pliant) bed of paper and seems to luxuriate in the very grooves it inscribes. The edges of the notebook have that die-cut, sharply hewn sculptural quality, which henceforth can only degrade, increasingly attenuated and made shiny, blunt, and soiled with use, with the repeated openings and closings and scuffings that come with daily journaling. How I'm tempted to stop at the bottom of this page and buy a new book for each page to come!*

I looked up. I had to. You can only read so much of this kind of thing before you want to get drunk or slug somebody. Preferably both. I skimmed a couple more paragraphs about the writer's "love affair with journaling," and then slowed down to note the following:

> *Of my continuing work at the bookstore, the less said the better. As I have suggested here, it is a job, no more, no less. That my colleagues, without exception, remain imbeciles and assholes goes without saying. Just today Louis, a moron of the first water, leaned over my table and said, "Look, Peter, Leonard is getting antsy with all these piles. I need you to process them faster."*

The guy obviously liked to hear himself speak, or read himself write. But I did manage to glean a few useful facts. He worked at Seaside Books, which he described as a huge, musty cavern of a place on lower Broadway, where reviewers' copies go to live out their days at half-price, and you thread your way around stacks of remainders with prices low enough to make you think you really want them.

This particular mug's job was to maintain a database of incoming books purchased from estates, libraries and colleges. He sat at a big table in the labyrinthine basement, way in the back, under white, cold fluorescents, entering titles and authors on a computer. He got an employee discount and wasn't afraid to use it, so every Friday, this Peter Ingalls, like many of his co-workers, dropped a good chunk of his take-home on more books.

He read whatever looked interesting in the next new shipment. And he had no other life whatsoever.

> *At home it is the same: Mother, too, urges me to "process them faster." "Peter, for the love of God, what are you going to do with all these damn BOOKS?" (I, in my imagination:*

"Read them, Mother.") *"Why don't you put them down and take a nice girl out to a movie?"* *(I: "Why would I? 'Girls' have become a distraction to which I am now thankfully indifferent.")* *"One of these days I'm going to throw them all out!"* *Then comes the head-shaking disavowal, the tutting withdrawal, the aggrieved lament for the deceased father-husband, the ritual condemnation "God damn those Chesterfield Kings!" et passim. (To think that until the age of thirteen I assumed that my father had been killed by a claque of homicidal British monarchs who, for some unknown reason, had determined that Donald Ingalls, sales manager for Kwal-i-T Specialty Plastics of Flatbush, Brooklyn, must die.)*

But enough of the dull quotidian. To my reading! Am currently absorbed in Talking Trash: Curse Words and the Degradation of Public Life *by Djimmini, along with* The Gods of Ancient Egypt *by Kraquie,* Roommates: The Erotic Life of Gertrude Stein and Alice B. Toklas *by Gumm,* Telepathy, Hypnosis, and Channeling *by Bayhlove, and* Teach Yourself French Already! *by Gahdd.*

You get the feeling this guy never did anything but work in the store, read his books, write in his notebook, and bicker with his mother.

Yeah, you get that feeling—and then something happens.

Stunning turn of events.

Today I was at the table, entering titles while inwardly fuming about Steve's shortchanging me on lunch from the deli—I asked for no chips, yet he charged me for half of HIS when we "just split it"—when the sound of a female's, "Uh, excuse me," captured my attention and brought me face-to-face with the most enchanting girl I have ever seen. I felt my expression go slack with wonder.

She is in her late twenties, about five foot seven, with a round, amused, inquisitive face framed by an efflorescing bouquet of honey pre-Raphaelite ringlets. Her eyes are the richest brown, her skin delicately and heart-stoppingly pale. Her voice ("Um, I'm looking for Meet Me at the Morgue by Ross Macdonald?") was music itself. Incredibly, no one else in the area stared, as I did. Everyone—staff, customers, cretin Louis, sneaky Steve—went about their idiotic business, while this angel from Heaven itself stood among us in our vast, bleak basement.

I started to give my usual brisk, unappealable reply whenever anyone asks me for help ("Busy! Working the catalogue!") but found myself, as though in a trance, rising from my chair and actually thinking about how to assist her! I brushed some crumbs from my beard and said, commandingly, "This way," and led her back upstairs to the main floor, avidly shouldering customers aside without scruple. I'm sure she shared my pleasure in ignoring the hostile stares and expressions of "Hey, watch it!" stimulated by our passage. She said something I was too excited and nervous to understand but which, once I had ushered her to the proper stacks for M in the fiction department, proved to be, "I've already checked the fiction department."

How I laughed and laughed! As did she, to an extent.

I asked about the title she sought. "It's a private eye mystery," she said informatively. I confessed that I had heard of the genre but not sampled it. She smiled (my heart fairly stopped) and said, "Well, it's not for everyone."

I knew at once I had to see her again, and so told her to

return in a few days, when, I promised (rashly), I would have the book. Under pretense of offering to reserve the tome when I found it, I managed to ask her name: Sally Feingold. Fine gold indeed!

I must find Meet Me at the Morgue. *But moreover I must familiarize myself with the detective school of mystery fiction. If it is the royal road to her heart (and mind), I shall learn its every curve and rest stop!*

I skimmed. Our man Peter spent the next few evenings and lunch hours casing the general interest book stores and the smaller fanatic boutiques in search of Sally's request. He also grilled clerks and innocent bystanders about putting together an introductory sampler from the *Hit Parade* of the literature.

The chains were useless for the Macdonald title, but he got close at a couple of shops specializing in mysteries. Finally, the night before she was to return to the store, he found it—a dog-eared, beat-up paperback. He was ecstatic—at first:

I intend positively to bask in her pleasure when I hand it over—as my gift, of course. "How can I repay you?" she'll ask. "Permit me to stare at you for an hour," I'll reply.

He sits at his desk all day, barely working, fending off Louis's gripes and prods ("The piles are getting out of hand, Peter. Then Leonard gets pissed and I'M the one who gets shit!") and keeping a hard fix on the steps leading down from the upper main floor. The book is on his lap. He giggles out loud with excitement.

Finally, late in the afternoon, she shows. She spots him, waves, and winds her way through the shoppers and tables and towering shelving units toward him. Then a sudden surge of acid shoots through his belly and he realizes his mistake.

> *It then occurred to me, in a horrifying flash, that I must not give her the book at all! Once she had it, she would be free to thank me very much, insist on reimbursing me (should I recoup the tax?), and drift out the door and away—forever! I could hardly allow that. I must see her again. I must make certain she returned only after I had had time to learn the genre!*
>
> *So at the last second I concealed the book in one of the piles on and around my desk, where it would be safe for the duration. (Taking it home was unthinkable; any day now Mother may begin her rampage.) It was The Purloined Letter writ large. I composed an expression of regret (modified by a smile of undimmed hope) as she arrived. "I almost had it," I reported. Her dear face fell. I then said, to banish the clouds, "But I have a lead on another copy. I'll know—" I thought fast. "—in a week." She forced a smile, thanked me, and said she'd come back then.*
>
> *Triumph!*

You had to wonder about a guy whose idea of victory consisted of blowing fib dust in the eyes of a decent, foursquare skirt whose only agenda involved obtaining a book. You also had to ask yourself how he'd managed to pursue a lifetime of reading, and years of working in a bookstore, without exposure to the literature. But I envied the poor sap. He had it all ahead of him, for the first time.

I paged through descriptions of the crash course he gave himself while waiting for the gal's return. He made full use of a week's worth of mornings, subway rides, lunches, dinners, and late, late evenings. He also stole hours during the workday, when Louis and Steve and the rest of the basement crew were off visiting homes and libraries to purchase and box and bring back their collections. Then this Peter Ingalls—the other one, the one who isn't me—had his big table in the back of the basement to himself. He could hide behind the towers of volumes waiting to be catalogued, fend off customers asking for help, open the novel on his lap, and keep on reading.

He read the classic authors and the classic titles. He read the secondary titles, and the essays, and the short stories. It wasn't clear how much, or even if, he slept.

And wouldn't you know it—it changed him.

> *I am humbled—and upset. In my recent immersion into the world of the private eye ("eye," I realized, being a homologue for the initial of "investigator") I have encountered a personality so unlike my own as to make clear to me, for the first time, what I am.*
>
> *For is it not so, that we do not see ourselves in those who resemble us nearly so vividly as we are shown what we are, or are not, by those who are not, or are, otherwise?*
>
> *The tall man serves us notice: "Behold. You are not tall. You are short." The fat man's girth demonstrates—to us, and to the world—our lack of fatness. The jerk who cheats us out of lunch money shines a bright light on our admirable honesty, even as the stupid man gives testament of our intelligence.*
>
> *Thus does the private eye act as a kind of anti-mirror, revealing to myself all my shortcomings, all my lacks, all my weaknesses. One thinks of Kant reading Hegel (or was it the other way 'round?) and "awakening from his dogmatic slumbers." I have awakened from mine, with a vengeance.*

If I am to win the heart and mind of Sally Feingold, I must become a new man. To do that, I must change my life.

A bookworm mama's boy gets a snootful of the literature and undergoes a spiritual awakening, like that gentleman on horseback in the Bible, Simon called Peter on the road to Mandalay, or Peter called Paul giving his sermon on the Mounds. Cute? As a litter of puppies. It's possible that my Bible studies need a brushup.

Before that week had passed, Mr. Peter Ingalls had given notice to his mom and found an apartment in The City in the West Forties. (By now I was beyond surprise at reading how this bird, with a name identical to my own, found digs in my own neighborhood.) He'd lived rent-free, date-free, car-free, and restaurant-free for a dozen years, and so had more than enough savings to contract for the place and to furnish it. Dough wasn't a problem.

And he was motivated. He had a muse to inspire him. And he had an image in his mind of a model, an imaginary but compelling mentor to guide him: the private detective.

She returns tomorrow. I'm ready. I will produce the book, bestow it with charm, and chat knowingly about others in the field. Then I shall ask her out—yes, on a date! "I live in the City, too," I will cry with joy. "And I'm a new man—thanks to you!"
And so to bed.

(ADDENDUM AT 3:47 A.M.: Sleep impossible. Too excited. Was struck by disturbing thought: What accomplishments have I to show for myself? With what can I impress Sally other than the fact that I found a copy of M. M. a. t. M.? *Ans.:*

THESE VERY FRUITS OF MY JOURNALING. I will bring this volume to the store tomorrow, leave it lying about, and tempt her curiosity.)

(ADDENDUM AT 4:26 a.m.: Still can't sleep. Thrilled!)

SEVENTEEN

That night I became an expert on the particulars of stakeout as Stephanie and I sat in the Daewoo Leganza and waited to see what, if anything, Wendy Litman would do.

You know how it is when you're in a car waiting for someone. You look around. You read the store signs. And you watch individuals engaged in the activity of being themselves. You find moments of amusement or pathos in the quirks and foibles of regular people in unself-conscious pursuit of their everyday affairs. You watch the passing parade of this cockeyed caravan, the rich panoply of this gorgeous mosaic we call life—you watch, and you admire.

Not me, brother. I concentrate on reality and think deeply about my immediate concerns.

You'd think that would be enough. You'd think that would be valid. Ingalls minds his own business and broods without comment in the still fastness of his inner being. Maybe he pulls out a nail clipper and polices the fingertips. Maybe he produces a copy of the *Daily News* and works the Jumble to increase his word power.

You have to. This is stakeout, where you leave all the glamour and excitement of the P.I.'s work back at the office, and dig yourself a hole and climb in for an unregulated staring contest with Boredom itself. You're not making something happen. You're not reacting to something that's happening. You're hoping something will happen so that you can, in secret, watch it happen. So you do what you can to keep alert.

But since when does that include interrogating your partner? I ask because gradually I became aware of the fact that Stephanie had put her book down and was staring at me. In fact, she could have been staring at me for minutes on end. Fine. It's a free country, and if it's not free, it's offered at a discount, with the savings passed along to we, the people. Suddenly she said, "You really couldn't tell that David was gay?"

"How could I?" I said. "He was playing a cop."

"Cops can be gay. I mean, I'm just asking because it's kind of obvious."

"Not to me, angel. But I was on the job."

"I know." Then she gathered up her moxie and said, "Pete? Are you sure you should be a private eye?"

"Positive. Why do you ask?"

"Okay." She turned in the seat toward me and settled in. "We're going to be here a while so we might as well talk, right?"

"Let's say. For the sake of argument."

"So is it okay if I ask you some personal questions?"

"You can ask whatever you want. I'm free to not answer, in my own words, as I see fit."

"Good." She spread her hands, groped for the right words, and finally found them. "What is with you? I can't tell if you're serious, or if this is some big put-on. Don't you see how other people react to you?"

"And how is that?"

"They think you're nuts! This suit—these aren't clothes. It's a costume. You don't speak in a normal way. You speak like an actor in a detective sketch. But you're doing this every day, in the real world! You're charging people money, you're tailing people and getting beaten up, you're talking to cops. . . . But the way you talk, the way you dress . . . You're just very weird."

She was challenging my very existence, my authenticity as a person and as a self. But then, they always do. Who's "they"? Put it this way: Who isn't?

"You've got me all wrong, doll," I said. "I'm the most sincere guy on the block."

"Look." She ramped up the seriousness. That was okay, yes, that was fine. Ingalls is nothing if not a man with whom you can be serious. "You want to wear retro clothes, fine. You want to talk funny, no problem. You want to put the whole world on, that's cool. But don't put me on. Because it's just you and me in that office, every day. And we're going out, and solving cases—I mean, look at us, cooped up in here all night. It's like we're living together."

I smiled. "Mercy. Ms. Constantino? Is this a proposition?"

"You wish. No, it's me being pissed at someone, a co-worker, who won't be honest with me. I just wish you would just fucking come off it so I know which end is up and where you're really coming from."

"The right end is up. And I'm coming from where we all end up coming from, lady, sooner or later. From the heart."

"Oh, fuck you, Ingalls."

"Hey. None of that."

"I'm trying to connect with you and you treat me like you treat everybody else. So just kiss my ass."

She flung the door open and got out and slammed it. Then she walked off, with the brisk stride of a dame whose high heels

would have made a sharp, angry staccato on the sidewalk if she
hadn't been wearing sneakers. I sighed, because that's what you
do when a woman walks out. It's also what you do when a
woman walks in, now that I think of it. But that's a different
kind of sigh.

I could have gone after her. I also could have hailed a cab,
gone home, and enrolled in a technical institute to begin a new
career in air conditioner repair. Instead I stayed put, keeping the
stakeout and waiting for Wendy Litman to make life more interesting. She didn't comply. I ransacked my brain for diverting
things to think about and came up the clever idea of using my
cell to call the voice mail for office and home. The former came
up empty. There was one saved message on the home system:

"Peter. It's Louis. You know, I gave you the journal the other
day . . . and I was pissed off . . . but now I think you're really . . .
you need some help. Like therapy, professional psychiatric
help . . . Anyway, I remembered that the journal stops the night
before your accident, and I started to think you may not recall
what happened, because of your injury. So listen and save this,
because I'm going to tell you what happened. You came to work
late and said you had overslept. I was already there and Leonard
had already given me shit about your table. So pretty soon that
woman showed up. Sally Whatshername. And you and she were
talking, and you sort of casually laughed and then looked over at
one of the piles on the table. And you know how these old estate
lots are, none of the books have dust jackets and they all look
alike, all dark and worn—I mean one pile looks pretty much like
another. So you hadn't noticed anything before. You went over
to the table and looked over all the piles, all the titles, and you
began to completely freak out. That's when you ran up to me
and said, like, 'Where is it? Where's that book? *Meet Me at the
Morgue* by Ross Macdonald? The whole pile is gone.' And I told

you I had just finished putting some piles in boxes and stowed them on the shelves, because Leonard was giving me grief. You said, like, 'You idiot shithead! Which shelf?' So I said, 'Over there, on top of Large Overstock.' So you grabbed a ladder and took it to the shelf and climbed up. I had put them on the very top just to get them out of the fucking way, four big cartons full of stuff you hadn't catalogued yet, that I had put up there *so you wouldn't get into trouble either, remember.* You said, like, *'Oh my God, which box is it in?'* and reached out for one of the boxes. Anyway, you grabbed a box, the ladder started rocking back and forth, so you, like, lunged at the boxes, and the ladder fell, and you fell, and three or four boxes full of books came crashing down on top of your head. Which knocked you unconscious. And that's when we called the ambulance and they took you to the hospital.

"I don't know if you remember any of this. But there it is. So maybe it'll help. Okay." Then a dame said, "End of message."

I deleted this monologue with a sense of regret that the other Peter Ingalls might never hear it and learn about that fateful night. Then I figured, the hell with it, what he didn't know wouldn't kill him and what didn't kill him would make him stronger. So he was already better off.

Then I thought about this and that. I must have dozed, because sometime later a slam of the driver's side door jabbed me like a beat cop's nightstick and jolted me awake. Stephanie had climbed back in.

"I'm waiting for an apology." She didn't look at me, but just stared out the windshield.

"Who from? I'll help you wait."

"Who from? From you! For still not coming clean."

"Angel, this is as clean as I get. You—"

"Okay, fine. I figured you'd say that. I came back because I want to finish this case. After that, I fucking quit."

"Please. Airbrush the language."

"We'll stake out Wendy, see what happens, finish this up one way or another, and that's it. You can be a hard-boiled dick or a hard dick with a boil, for all I care. Okay? Fine."

"I fell asleep."

"I know. So?"

"So I don't know that she didn't leave while I was out."

"Don't worry, she didn't. She's still up there."

This was another eerie, almost inexplicable aspect of this human being we call woman: her ability, from a distance and without any identifiable means even remotely familiar to physics, to simply *know* things about her fellow women. Call it telepathy, call it intuition. In any case, I marveled. I shook my head. I said, "I'm sure you're right, sugar, but how can you possibly know that?"

"Because I called and she answered and I hung up, okay? Jesus. Look, you sleep. I'm too pissed. I'll take first shift and wake you up at three."

"Suit yourself. If you want me, you know where I am."

She rolled her eyes.

When she prodded me awake my teeth had that grainy film that comes from not brushing them, when you feel just a little homeless and all the hyped-up mints in the tin can't bring back that clean, fresh feeling. So you do what people do. You run your index finger along your teeth and then you chew gum. Stephanie made sure I was awake, then climbed into the backseat, pulled a little inflatable pillow from her tote bag, blew it up, got comfy, and sacked out.

It was then that I began to wonder: how is it that we are suddenly surrounded by a variety of super-strong peppermints? Where were they twenty years ago? Is everybody more sophisti-

cated now? Or has the American palate become so jaded, so enervated with its exposure to the wasabis and jalepeños of the
world that it needs the promise of bigger thrills and sharper stim-
ulation just to get out of bed in the morning?

Thoughts like these kept me occupied until dawn and beyond. During that time a couple of people left the building, but
our gal Wendy wasn't one of them. Around eight I turned on the
radio. The pop hits, the deejays' loudmouthed leering—they had
the desired effect. Stephanie woke up.

I went out to the deli to stretch my legs and get some coffee.
When I returned I pointed out that we'd soon have to contend
with parking restrictions and morning traffic. "And for what?" I
asked. "So we can follow her to the art gallery?"

"No, man, don't you get it?" She blew across the top of her
joe; whatever done-up, nicey-nice makeup she'd worn the night
before had somehow disappeared, leaving her face looking
touchingly naked and vulnerable. "As of last night Wendy thinks
the cops have you. She doesn't know what you'll tell them."

"Good point," I said. "Or how it will get back to her girlfriend."

"Yeah, you're still into that lesbian theory, aren't you?" She
shook her head. "I don't buy it. They may have teamed up to get
Litman's money, but they're not lovers. Wendy's straight."

"All dames seem straight, kid. Then one day they show up
with a lady on their arm."

"We'll see. But I guarantee you she didn't get much sleep last
night."

"That makes three of us," I said. "But what if she's doing it
all by phone? What makes you think she'll be forced to go anywhere?"

"Ooh, yeah, you're right. We gotta smoke her out of there."

She furrowed her brow and thought. Then she whipped out the cell, punched some digits, and then said, "Hi, honey . . . Fine . . . On stakeout with Pete . . . Yeah, really . . . Well that's why I'm calling. I think she needs a push . . . Right. Great. Perfect. You're the man! Thanks a ton. Bye." And she hung up. She looked revived and amused. "Watch this." She turned to look at the doorway, so I did the same.

By now the production number of morning was going full tilt. We observed the nonstop exodus of well-dressed citizens marching off to their day's labors, and the smartly trim or sociopathically sloppy kids on their way to the day's private schooling, the natty oldsters in their porkpie hats and pastel clothing, the freelance artsy wiseguys in ten tones of black, and the stylish housewives without portfolio, all pouring out of the building and striding off to wherever it was they were en route to for pleasure or profit. It was a nice day, if you liked mild temperatures and moderate relative humidity, clear skies and a light breeze. I was just about to offer a pithy comment about this teeming hive of energy that is New York when Stephanie grabbed my arm and said, "Holy shit, there she is."

"Wh—"

"Get down!"

We hunkered low but a discreet glance up, toward the building entrance, made our concealment hardly seem necessary. Mrs. Jeffrey Litman was clearly a dame out of sorts, nervous and edgy and preoccupied and in no shape to scan the environment and suss out surveillance. She wore a stylish black leather jacket over sharp black jeans, casual suede shoes, and carried a small, snazzy purse. "No suitcase, so she's not lamming," I murmured.

"But she's not dressed for work, either. See? Let's follow her."

I was about to inform my associate that I was well aware we

were to follow her, but then the pace picked up. A white Mercedes, driven by a valet, appeared from around the corner and pulled up with a pricey hush. Wendy Litman ransomed the car with a dollar tip, got in, belted down, and pulled out.

Stephanie had her game-face on. "Let's roll." Then she giggled. "This is *so cool!*"

We pulled into traffic behind the white car. Any doubts I'd had about the utility of this scheme disappeared as Wendy circled around in a series of rights until she was heading north. Wherever she was going, it wasn't downtown to work. At Seventy-second she turned left and led us to that endless construction project known, for lack of a better term, as the West Side Highway. Stephanie kept one car between us, and if that meant cutting off a bakery truck or passing some muscle-bound SUV along the wrong lane, then that was what it meant. "How'd you get her to move?" I asked.

Stephanie kept her hard stare at Wendy Litman's car and said, "I called David and had him do his Garbus from Downtown character. He called her and asked if she'd be in for the next ten minutes, because he had some questions. That got her out the door."

We followed our quarry over the George Washington Bridge, when she bailed out onto the Palisades Parkway. Traffic thinned and we had to be more circumspect.

It was then that my cell phone started ringing.

I whipped it out of my inside jacket pocket, but Stephanie reached over and took it from me before I could answer. "Leave it," she said.

"Easy, doll," I said. And yeah, maybe I allowed myself a little chuckle. "If memory serves, aren't we in fact waiting for various parties to phone up and reveal their whereabouts?"

Her eyes were on the nice white sedan as it eased around the curves and past the dense, trim foliage. "If it's Celeste, she'll hear we're in a car," she said. "That might spook her into running."

"Who's 'we'? I'll be on the horn. You'd be a nonspeaking extra. And I could tell her I'm on my way somewhere else."

"Pete, Wendy probably called Celeste and told her something was up. She could be talking to Celeste right now. The less obvious we are the better." She pointed. "Wow, look, she's turning."

Wendy Litman had taken an exit off the curving Palisades and there was nothing we could do to prevent cruising right behind her as we both curled around on the offramp. We were in one of those many leafy semisuburban enclaves that hover outside The City like multiple moons around a planet. Stephanie slowed so we'd fall a bit behind her as we drifted to a stop sign, crossed railroad tracks, and wound into a small, old community of narrow asphalt roads, big heavy trees dense with leaves, and modest houses up streets that lacked sidewalks. We passed a sign reading WELCOME TO TAPPAN as we turned a couple of times and crept with melodramatic caution up a quiet street to a house two or three in from the cross street beyond.

It was as average a little getaway as you could imagine, with cool blue clapboard shingling and white wood. A handsome bay window dominated the front, the room beyond only partially concealed by a diaphanous white curtain. Wendy Litman pulled her purring ritzmobile into the driveway that angled down into the closed garage, stopped, turned it off, and got out. I expected us to veer toward the curb. But Stephanie didn't slow and we breezed on past.

"What's the idea?" I said. "Isn't this our stop?"

"She'll notice if we pull over. We'll come back."

As we drove past, I could see that Wendy had a key out and was working on the front door as we drove by. "Take a look," I said. A second car sat in the driveway. "The girls are having a get-together. We can make four for bridge." We reached the stop sign at the end of the street and turned right, then reached another turn and made a right. We were halfway down this street when Stephanie hit the brakes and we sat there while a mom in an SUV the size of a tank waddled out of her driveway as empires rose and fell.

That's when the cell rang again. I gave Stephanie a look; she replied with a nod and handed me the unit. I hit TALK. "Pete Ingalls, P.I."

"Ingalls." There was no mistaking the voice. "It's Celeste Vroman."

I winked at my assistant and said, "You sound lousy, Ms. Vroman. Too much single malt last night?"

"Please. I mean yes, I'm a bit under the weather. Where are you?"

"On the phone. The real question is, where are you? The line of people asking goes out the door."

"I'm . . . I'll tell you the truth, Ingalls. I'm in hiding. And I think you know why. Apparently something's happened to Jeffrey, and people think I had something to do with it." The big rig had successfully left its own driveway and had cruised away. Stephanie resumed driving, but with a paranoid's stealth and silence. "Ingalls? Are you there?"

"Yeah. Sorry, doll, my assistant just came in with some important documents. Look, Celeste, I don't have to tell you the heat is on and everybody's getting sweaty. I need to see you and clarify a few hundred things."

"That's impossible. Let's do it now. I have things I want to ask you, too."

We reached the end of the street and stopped at a T intersection where traffic was tooling in either direction. "Now?"

Stephanie looked both ways. "On the phone? Absolutely not."
Stephanie's eyes went big as hubcaps. She made a face of hysteri-
cal horror and gestured with vigorous nods and a rolling hand:
keep going. "On the other hand, most things in life are relative
and not absolute. Let's talk about your boyfriend. Mr. Litman."

"What about him? And where are you? Do I hear traffic?"

"Yeah, outside the office." We turned right and crept forward.
"As for Jeffrey, I'll tell you what about him. I have reason to
think he's dead. So do the cops. And not just any cops. The
homicide boys, with their forensic team, and the little plastic
bags, and the DA on the speed-dial. Your comments?"

"I haven't seen Jeffrey. Why do you say that?"

We had come full circle and were again at the street where
Wendy Litman had turned in. Half a block down, she and the
woman I was stalling on the horn were planning to flee the juris-
diction and discuss what silver pattern to buy with their eight
million clams.

Stephanie took a right as I said, "Don't play games with me,
Celeste. I want to know why you're in hiding. Meanwhile the
johns have hauled me in for tea, and I found a little blood and a
lot of no briefcase on the boat. It's your boyfriend's blood. People are starting to talk." I glanced at Stephanie: she was laughing
silently and gave me a big thumbs-up. Sue me, but it felt good.
"It would be nice if you said something meaningful about all
this."

Stephanie pointed to her left: we had arrived at the house in
question.

"Look, Ingalls, our business is finished, isn't it?" Celeste Vroman said.

As we parked I said, "Not if the cops call Litman's disappearance a homicide. In which you're implicated. Bearer bonds, lesbian love affairs, the death of Olivia Cartwright: discuss."

"I . . . look, you fool, I had nothing to do with any of that—"

My associate shut off the motor and thumbed toward the house, then rolled her hand around as though opening a car window manually: Stall her, she mouthed, keep talking. "Okay, Celeste, let's review the bidding," I said, and Stephanie and I each opened our doors quiet as mimes. We crept toward the house as I improvised, "Jeffrey knew that his wife and you were having an affair. He was having an affair with Olivia and everybody was jealous of everybody else. . . ."

"What? Jesus, Ingalls, are you insane?"

"Yeah, insane like a fox." I was on the driveway, not yet in range of the bay window, which hung about two feet off the ground, on either side of which were shrubs about five feet high. "Why don't you drop the veil, angel. Jeffrey's dead and the bonds are missing." Stephanie stepped lightly up to the bush on the right, dropped down low, crept under the window, and slowly rose to peer inside as I said, "Wendy acts guilty as sin and you've disappeared from sight. Connect the dots and get a nice picture. A picture of murder."

Stephanie's head jerked suddenly toward me. Her eyes were wide—and not "as hubcaps," which had been a theatrical take done for effect. No, this was spontaneous and sincere. She had seen something incredibly shocking. She waved me over with frantic scoops of her hand as her head jerked toward the window.

I hotfooted it toward her as the voice in my ear said, "Ingalls, whatever you're accusing me of, I deny it completely."

I had reached the first bush. I bent over low and legged it like Groucho until I reached her. "Then why did you call me, Celeste?" I said.

"I heard you were arrested," she said. I was beside Stephanie, under the bay window. She jabbed a finger toward it. I rose slowly, like a sniper, as Celeste Vroman said, "And I wanted to know if that was true, and what they asked you—" I peered into the living room.

Pacing rapidly up and down in jeans and a sweat shirt was Jeffrey Litman. He held a cell phone to his ear and was saying, ". . . wanted to know if they've charged you with anything, and what you've told them." Oddly, the identical words were coming into my ear through my phone, in the voice of Celeste Vroman. "You and I have a relationship characterized by an expectation of professional confidentiality, and I assume you have told them nothing of what went on between you and me."

The human mind is a fascinating thing. Give it an opening premise and a final conclusion, and in a second it'll come up with something to get from Point A to Point B. Or put it this way: mine does. And it does so without my having to lift a finger. It took merely an instant for me to devise a theory that explained the tableau before me. It was wild and improbable; morally it smelled, and legally it looked as dirty as a drug dealer's soul. But it explained the otherwise inexplicable.

Celeste Vroman had somehow managed, not simply to mesmerize Jeffrey Litman into doing her bidding, but to control him from a distance, remotely, to use him to psychically relay her thoughts and her voice to third parties. Call it coerced channeling, call it hypnosis. From whatever distant location served as her hideaway, she was beaming her words—maybe by some small transceiver implanted in Litman's skull—to her willing slave, who was shuttling them on to me, and in a damn good approximation of her voice.

I looked at Stephanie. She widened her eyes again and whispered, "Now what?"

"Celeste? I'll call you back." I clicked off my cell and handed it to Stephanie and said, "Now comes the good part."

I got up and started toward the front door. Stephanie grabbed at my jacket and managed to clutch a handful, enough so I felt the tug and had to stop. When she started to speak I seized her wrist and pulled her out of the range of the window and away from the house.

"Are you crazy?" Her voice was an urgent hiss. "What are you doing?" She started ticking off items on her fingers. "He probably killed Olivia. He could have a gun. Wendy's in on it with him. They could *both* have guns. You can't go in there. Let's just get out and leave it for the cops."

"Sorry, angel. No can do. This is the chance I've been waiting for. This is how I get square with the job and pay off my debt to the Code."

"Huh?"

"All right, look, I haven't told you this but you might as well know. I had sex with a client."

"*What?* Who? Not that Flonger!"

"Yes. And—"

"Jesus Christ! Pete!"

"I had my reasons. Only it turns out—"

"Yuck!"

"—turns out it's not that simple. There's a—"

"Why her?!"

"Please?" She clammed and I managed to squeeze in edge-wise the revelation of a lifetime. "Yes, I did it the other day, with Catherine Flonger. And I'm not exactly proud of it."

"I'll bet! She's so—"

"But some of that's baloney. Because I *am* proud of it. I did it willingly, and we scaled the peaks of ecstasy, and I finally got my merit badge in Human Sexuality."

"What—? You're kidding—"

"But it was against the laws of the profession, and nothing's for free in this strip mall of life. If you don't pay as you go, the interest charges'll kill you. Maybe by walking in there and facing off against the bad guy I can appease the flatfoot gods and win back the right to wear the suit and the hat." She started to speak but I cut her off. "Go home, go back to the office, go take in a matinee. This is your day job, and you've got other priorities. But this is what my life is all about."

I chucked her under the chin and then hotfooted it over to the front door. When I got there, I knocked.

EIGHTEEN

I have often admired, in the literature, how the gumshoe in question offers himself up as a kind of truth-teller provocateur. He doesn't sneak into buildings and put stethoscopes to walls. He doesn't plant bugs and chortle, later, concealed in a van amid tape decks and headphones. He walks calmly into the lions' den and announces his presence. He tells the lions why he's there, and he waits to see what they're going to do about it.

There was a glass peephole in the door, a primitive bit of security apparatus that I took pleasure and professional pride in not covering with my hand. I wanted my quarry to know who had come calling, and I wanted to see what he would do. I found out one second later. Litman flung the door open, snarled, "You! You fucking *fuck!*" grabbed me by one of my large lapels, and hauled me into the house. The door slammed behind me. With a look of savage fury he hauled back a fist. I had just enough time and instinct to do the same. We both let fly.

Like that exhibit in Gettysburg of a Union bullet and a Confederate bullet that had collided in midair and fused to form a symbolically heartbreaking lump of lead, Litman's fist and mine smashed into each other with a meaty, crunchy noise, followed by his bark of "Shit!" and mine of, I think, "Ow!" Then it seemed like a good idea to squirm and writhe in pain. I was rubbing the back of my right hand when Litman recovered, spun me around to face him, and shot a right cross against my jaw.

This was the second time in a week I'd taken part in a physical altercation. I hadn't cared for it the first time, and wasn't crazy about it now. I was hurled backward against a wall, then slid down the wall onto the floor. A touch of a knuckle to my face came away wet and red. I dabbed a fingertip to the spot and on impulse felt other places, and my hunch was confirmed: this one slug had undone whatever healing my previous scars had enjoyed and I was spouting the red stuff like a man attacked with a garden claw.

Then Litman went to work, venting whatever rage and frustration he had been saving up, slamming me with punches in the gut. I tried fighting back and may have landed a lucky swing or two, but he was in better shape, and more motivated. When at one point I spun around, he drove a good one into my lower back and I felt something give inside. If I had been fully conscious it would have hurt more.

I sat on the floor, slumped against a wall, my general sense of awareness and physical being gently bobbing on a sea of pain. Litman stood over me as his wife hovered in the background. She looked lousy, pale and distraught and paralyzed. Litman shook his head in bitter disbelief, said to me, "You asshole," then turned to his wife and said, "I told you not to come here. Now we have to deal with this."

She made a visible effort at dignity. "I thought he was in jail."

With his trim physique and short hair and bald pate, Litman looked compact and efficient and almost amused by it all. He turned back to me. "Ingalls, how the fuck did you ever get this far? Hold it." He took two strides back toward the middle of the room. A fireplace was set into the main center wall. He grabbed a poker and returned, waving it around like a tennis racquet. "Wend. Come here." She inched forward with faltering steps until she was close enough for him to grab by the wrist and fling at me. "Check his coat for weapons."

"I'm not packing, Litman," I said. "With your psychic swami powers and mental abilities, you should know that."

"What?"

"Your mental link with your girlfriend. You'll need it, too, once the cops get wise. She'll go up for murder two and you'll go in for accessorizing. Also grand theft, fraud, and your choice of two sides."

He did a damn good imitation of a man who doesn't understand what another man is talking about. "Ingalls—are you really that dense? What girlfriend?"

"Dense as an owl, chum. I'm referring to Celeste Vroman." I got to my feet, an act that caused Wendy Litman to recoil and her husband to plant himself and waggle the poker in warning. "Of course," I said, "you could roll on her. The DA might give you a Get Out of Jail Early card in exchange for serving her up. In any case, the ballgame's over. You're going inside, pal. You, too, Wendy. Unless you learn to sing loud and long."

Wendy had retreated until she was once again behind her husband. He half turned toward her and said, "Do you believe this?"

"Jeff . . . why did he say murder before? Mr. Ingalls—"

"Wendy. Call me Pete."

"—why did you say murder? Murder two? Was that it?"

"Because somebody killed somebody," I said. "And I think your husband and I know who it was. Right, Litman? The jealous mistress. The dark, alluring lady you still dream about. The one you went on the boat with, so you . . . wait a minute . . . you . . . uh . . ."

Several thoughts had arrived COD in my mind and I was having trouble paying for delivery.

Meanwhile, Wendy looked baffled and said, "Jeff, what is he talking about?"

Litman laughed. "Unbelievable. Sit down, Ingalls, while we figure out what to do with you." He shook his head and said, to himself, "But we have no choice. There's only one thing we can do."

"Jeff, what did he mean—?"

"Who cares what he meant! It doesn't matter what he meant! Isn't it obvious? He's an idiot!"

"Come on, Wendy," I said, snapping out of it, my eyes burning into hers. "Who do you think killed Olivia Cartwright?"

"I don't know."

I paused, because that's what you do when you drop the bomb, when you proclaim "gin," when you pull the name from the envelope and announce who gets the statuette. "Your girlfriend, sugar. Celeste Vroman."

Litman turned to his wife and said, "Well. Now you know."

Then the two of them burst out laughing. And I thought, Ingalls, you're in the presence of a kind of remorseless evil you can barely comprehend. For the first time I began to wonder if maybe the literature had led me on a nice stroll down the garden path. I was in this house, alone, with two laughing killers. One was an attorney and the other was a lesbian. As they laughed, Litman handed the poker to his wife and walked off toward the kitchen. In a moment he returned, carrying a roll of duct tape.

"Ingalls," Litman said, sighingly, pleasantly spent from his spell of laughter. "No matter how fucked up things have gotten, now I know I'm a genius. I needed an absolute fool to make this work. So I shopped around and I chose you. And I couldn't have done better." With that he zipped off a length of tape, nicked the edge with his teeth, tore it off the roll, and said, "Hands behind your back, tough guy."

"What if I don't, Litman? What if I elect another option?"

"Then I'll beat you with this poker till you look like salsa."

"Jeff—" Wendy Litman sounded repulsed.

"Shut up. Let's go, Ingalls."

I put my hands behind my back. Litman wrapped them tight in the tape, and all I could think about were those times in childhood when I had a bandage on a playtime scrape or abrasion, and how difficult and painful it was to remove the adhesive tape or the Band-Aid, and how this would prove much, much worse, because of my adult male body hair.

Wendy Litman's face was pinched and crumpled in distress as she watched her husband wrapping my wrists. Maybe it was in sympathy with the pain she knew, I knew, we all knew was inevitable when I finally got a chance to take the tape off. Maybe it wasn't. Finally she said, "Jeff, what are we going to do?"

Litman looked grim. He started pacing, nodding as he watched the floor. "We have to get rid of him."

"Get rid . . . how?"

"Knock him out. Dump him in some woods on our way out."

Tight-lipped, she turned away from both of us and took a few steps away. Without looking back she said, "I thought we agreed no one would get hurt."

"Wendy, Jesus Christ, we're doing damage control here!"

"I know . . ."

Sometimes you make your own opportunities, and sometimes, if you're lucky, the other guy makes one for you. When he does, and he shows up at your door to hand it over, you have to be there, awake, sober, and dressed, to take receipt. Don't expect the other guy to leave a little note sticking out of the mailbox saying he'll come back tomorrow. Because the other guy doesn't come back tomorrow. Wendy Litman had just revealed herself as that other guy. It was time to welcome her into the apartment.

"It's not too late to save yourself, Wendy," I said. "You've been victimized by some nasty people. Now your husband wants you to join him. Join him where? On the bad side of the street. Where the sharpies and the hustlers play. Where the thugs slug it out with the dirt-eaters and the pimp-meisters, where the men breathe through their mouths and the women have long finger-nails, and everybody wants something for nothing, and nobody has a valid photo ID."

"Mr. Ingalls—"

"Just listen to me, Wendy." I spoke with some heat. This might be the last chance I had to save this woman from a destiny of jail, death, or the squalid, low-prestige existence of the failed criminal. "Jeffrey here is going to run off with his killer girl-friend—who's actually your killer girlfriend, which is even worse—and his eight million, and where do you think that will leave you? And even if they let you go along, and the three of you got into some kind of kinky international fugitive three-way situation, it won't end there. They'll come after you."

"Who?"

"Who? The Special Cops. The guys in suits. The guys who show up in a Ford Taurus with a Glock in one hand and a calcu-lator in the other. The Bureau, the insurance companies. The Feds. The DEA. INS. OSHA. The FDIC. Cross a border, try to hide out where the offshore banks are, and the world's best come looking for you. Scotland Yard. Interpol. The Sûreté. The Hague. The Stasi. The Fonz. The Justice League of America. The League of Nations. The League of Women Voters—"

"Ingalls—"

"It's no life for a dame like you, Wendy. Bail out. Be smart. Save yourself. Hit your husband with the poker and help me get loose."

Litman looked deadpan at his wife. "We've got eight million safe and sound, and all we have to get past"—he thumbed toward me—"is this. Okay?"

You could see her make up her mind. She straightened up two inches and said, with finality and poise, "Okay." She looked around. "What do we knock him out with?"

"Wait here."

Litman skipped into the kitchen as Wendy faced me with the poker. I tried another ploy. "Yeah, 'wait here.' He'll wait—until the two of you have gotten away. And then he'll dump you, sweetheart. He'll dump you for her."

"For who?"

"Who else? For Celeste! Where is she right now?"

She shook her head. "You know, he told me about you, but I didn't believe it. . . ."

Litman came jogging back into the room carrying a cast iron frying pan. He hefted the thing, getting a feel for its weight and balance as he approached me. Then he said, "Sorry, Ingalls. But it's your job, isn't it? To get beat up and knocked out?"

So I did the one thing I thought had a chance of working.

I collapsed onto the floor.

"Get up," he said. "Get up or I'll start practicing on your knees."

I got to my feet as slowly as possible. As I did I looked around for a way to escape. By sheer bad luck I had ended up cornered in the living room, with both Litman and his wife blocking any way out, either into other rooms or to the front door. Once on my feet I drew myself up and said, "You'll never get away with it, Litman."

"I already have, asshole," he said, and raised the frying pan. I collapsed again, slumping to the floor in a heap.

Litman took a swipe at me as I fell. He missed, spat, "Shit!"

then leaned over me and raised the pan. I curled up and hunched my shoulders and veered my head away from him. He swung and I took a hard one to the thigh, but the pan hit flat, and while it hurt, it could have been worse.

He flung the pan onto the floor, where it landed with a dull clang. Then Litman leaned down and dragged me to my feet and slammed me against the near wall. For good measure he drove a fist into my stomach. Since my hands were taped together behind me, I had no way to shield myself. The wind flew out of me and I couldn't breathe. "Let's get this fucking over with," he muttered. Then he bent down and retrieved the pan, reached out his left hand to steady me, and reared back.

A sharp bang reverberated at the front door. Litman jerked his head toward his wife to go see who it was. She peered through the peephole and turned back toward us. "There's nobody there," she said.

"Son of a bitch," he muttered, and strode to the front door and flung it open.

A wide, curved blade on a long pole lanced in through the doorway and speared Litman in the gut. He cried out and recoiled, jerking back into the room. Then the person who speared him came in: it was Stephanie, wielding a snow shovel. She raised it up halfway, like a cricket bat, and whacked Litman on the side. But it was a light aluminum job with not much heft, and she was a svelte young thing with minimal beef. In the end the shovel hit him with barely more impact than a fraternity paddle. As they struggled over it I did the one thing I could do, under the circumstances: my hands still bound behind me, I flung myself at Wendy Litman and the two of us collapsed onto the floor.

Stephanie was game, but Litman was a decent athletic specimen and was driven by every bad feeling in the book. She never had a chance. Finally he got one of her arms behind her and one of his around her neck. He hissed, "If you don't want to die right now, put your hands behind your back." She did what he said. He held them with one hand, tore off a swath of duct tape in his mouth, and wrapped her up, too. He ran his hands over her body, and I thought it was an unnecessary bit of sexual exploitation until he said, "Fuck," and pulled something from her jacket: my cell phone. He pocketed that and flung her at me and the two of us shrank back toward some furniture. He gave his wife the poker, pointed to us, said, "Just keep an eye on them while I pack. We don't know who she's called. We have to get out of here." Then he hustled upstairs.

I looked Stephanie over for bruises or bleeding and asked, "Are you okay?"

"Fine," she said, then mouthed silently a word I couldn't quite make out.

"Um, small . . . tall—"

"Never mind." She called across the room. "Hey, Wendy! All set to run off with your murderer husband? Gee, hope he doesn't kill you, too! What a bummer that would be. I mean we all know he killed Olivia, right, so he has nothing to lose."

Wendy Litman glanced toward the top of the stairs, then replied without conviction, "Shut up."

"I mean I'm sure he told you someone else did it. Like some guy where she worked, right? Out of jealousy over him and so forth."

I leaned toward Stephanie and said, softly, "Good angle, kid. But I thought we agreed that Celeste killed Olivia."

She glanced at me, said, "Later, Pete. Just back me up on this." Then she called out, "But the thing is, Wendy, why was Olivia's body found in that dump? That's what nobody can figure out. If she was having an assignation with anybody, why not do it at her own place?"

Litman's wife shrugged. "She liked the thrill of it. She liked the squalor."

You had to hand it to the kid—she had moxie. She laughed. "Yeah, right. You never met her. I did. She was a petite little brainy-type mouse who probably needed a support group to get up the nerve to let a guy go down on her. Forget 'the squalor'."

Wendy Litman replied to this with a face of stony indifference. "If you don't stop it I'll have Jeffrey tape your mouth shut." Then she put down the poker and looked around until she saw the duct tape, retrieved the roll, and headed toward us. "In fact, I'll do it myself."

"Fine." Stephanie's hazel eyes flashed; she was in overdrive, scrambling for something to say. "Just don't come crying to us when old Jeffy decides he'd rather have eight million and all the babes he can buy, than share it with his tired old wifey."

Wendy said nothing but picked at the edge of the duct tape with a nail, trying to get it started off the roll. I said, "Or he'll have Celeste do it."

Nobody reacted to that, but then, of course not. These were two women engaged in a struggle to the death. Show me the man who can truly comprehend the intricacies and hot buttons of a dispute between two skirts, and I'll show you a man who doesn't exist.

Wendy got the tape going. With the sound of a ripping, throaty twang she yanked out a length and tried to tear it off. Instead it wrinkled and stuck to itself. So she put the edge in her mouth and tried to tear a little starter rip. We were all on this day becoming intimately acquainted with duct tape. This gave Stephanie a chance to say, "No, sooner or later you're going to have to ask yourself, 'What was a nice conservative lady like Olivia Cartwright doing in a third-class dump like the Hotel Urbane?'"

And then something happened. Wendy Litman stared at us. "Where?"

"The Hotel Urbane. Upper West Side, like Broadway and a hundred and something. Not exactly an SRO but still . . ."

Wendy let the tape drop to the floor. Her focus was elsewhere. She said, "But that's—" and stopped, just as her husband came bounding down the steps, carrying a stuffed canvas travel bag. "All set?" he said.

She faced him and didn't look like she was remotely all set. "Jeffrey, you didn't tell me Olivia Cartwright was killed in the Hotel Urbane."

"So what?" He glanced at us.

"Don't tell me so what. That—I know—"

"It's a coincidence."

"I didn't see it in the paper," she glanced away and murmured, then looked back at him. "I didn't see the paper at all. That was the day the Metro section was missing, wasn't it? The day after she was found. You used it for something, you said." She was talking to herself at this point. "And I said, 'Since when do you use the Metro section?' and I thought that was so odd—"

"Wendy, for Christ's sake. Don't collapse on me now. We've got to get rid of these two and then we can discuss this." He looked around. "We can't do it here."

Stephanie looked up sharply. "Do what here?" She turned to Wendy Litman, who was adrift in her own inner ruminations. "Are you listening, Wendy? He killed Olivia and now he's planning to kill us. With your help. So sure, what the fuck. One murder, three murders—go for it."

Litman went over to his wife and laid a gentle hand on her arm. "Listen, babe. We're all set. We take care of this one last thing, it'll look like Celeste did it, and we're home free."

"Urbane . . . Why would you take her to—?" And then her

expression seemed to collapse. She took two sudden steps back, recoiling from him and leaving him grasping air.

"Shit," Litman said. He spied the duct tape on the floor and bent down and grabbed it. He yanked off a strip and placed it over Stephanie's mouth just before she could yell a protest. While he did so he spoke to his wife. "Goddamn it, don't crap out, Wendy. We're almost there."

I chuckled. "How are you going to make it look like Cel—" The rest was lost as Litman plastered a swatch of tape over my mouth.

"Now let's go. You start the car—"

"I'm not going," Wendy Litman said. "The Hotel Urbane— that's the place you were using. The only way that woman could have ended up there was *if she followed you.*"

Litman absorbed this, his jaw clenched. Then he said, in a voice utterly drained of affection or concern, "You have three seconds to change your mind."

His wife said, "There's no way I can go with you now." And then her composure collapsed and her expression curled into anguish. Her face twisted slowly, like a child's, as she started to cry. "You said no one would get hurt!"

"I was wrong. Things happened."

"You killed her!" She was suddenly possessed by rage. Wendy flew at her husband and beat him with little, ladylike fists of fury. "Fuck you! Get out!"

"Goddamn it, this is going to work!" Litman shoved her away and spun madly around, looking for something. Then he found it. He leaped over to where the snow shovel lay on the floor, grabbed it, and came up swinging. The flat of the blade hit Wendy square on the side of the head and she collapsed in a heap. I did what I had to do: I flung myself at him like a free safety making a last-ditch tackle. My hands were still taped behind me so I had about as much maneuverability as a CPR dummy. Still, he went down, with me on top of him. I maximized what advantage I had, which is to say, I went completely limp. Think it's easy to crawl out from under a lifeless human body? Call me up; I'll come over and you can try it. He pushed and jabbed at me until I rolled off him. Then he leapt up, seized the snow shovel, and brought it high over his head like a man about to split a log with an axe.

That's when Stephanie broadsided him, flinging herself at his back and bringing the whole unbalanced extravaganza—Litman, herself, the snow shovel—crashing down on me. He clawed his way out while we did what we could to jab elbows into him and kick any part of him within range. He drove a fist into my ribs, practically threw Stephanie across the room, and then got to his feet. He must have heard something, because he ignored us, grabbed the travel bag, and ran to the bay window to look outside. "Shit." He dashed past me into the kitchen in the rear. I heard the back door open and slam shut. Then silence.

Then came a rapid, hard banging on the front door. "Open up! Police!"

I hobbled over to the front door, turned my back to it, and tried to open it with one of my taped-up hands. But while I managed to grab and turn the knob, the door stayed shut: there was a dead bolt at eye height. I tried raising my arms behind myself to unlock it but they hurt like hell, and I couldn't see what I was doing.

I faced the door and yelled, "Around the back!" But it came out "Ahhbk," because my mouth was still taped.

Stephanie limped over to join me and said, urgently, "Lmm tkff yrgg."

"Hhm?

"Lmmf tkff yrgg!"

"Open the door! Police department!"

I nodded and brought my face down to her own bound hands. She managed to take hold of one end of my gag with her fingers. I tore my face away from the tape, then yelled, "We can't . . . It's . . ."

"Open up! Police!"

"We're tied up! We can't!"

"I'll get it," someone said.

I spun around. The huge, pale, hulking form of Detective Hank Thoreau shuffled past me, unbolted the door, and opened it. Two local cops spilled in, guns drawn and held in two fists, pointed up, just like on TV. I looked back toward the kitchen: there, in handcuffs and chaperoned by a third uniform, was Jeffrey Litman.

"Here." Thoreau gently turned Stephanie toward him. "Gotta get that tape off you," he drawled. "Gotta save that pretty mouth for what it's meant for." With surprising delicacy he peeled the gag off.

"Thanks," she said. "Dickhead."

NINETEEN

On the way back, while I basked in triumph and pain, Stephanie made an unscheduled exit off the highway and insisted I check in at the E.R. of West Side Medical. I made a token protest and then agreed. No one asked about health insurance and everyone treated me as if I was what I looked like, a marginal survivor of a newsworthy car wreck. They kept me overnight in a semiprivate room, which I shared with a gent in post-op recovery from appendicitis. "You *look* like I *feel*," he wheezed, many times.

The next morning a young doc breezed in with a clipboard full of jargon and specs. He rattled on about contusions, spleen compromise, hairline fractures, and other ailments, made sure I'd taken a painkiller, and said I could check out in twenty-four hours after tests and observation. I said I felt fine and started to get up.

I came to in the midafternoon of what turned out to be the next day. Sunlight flooded in through the window, and my roommate had been released. So I was alone, flipping through magazines and taking note of all the fine consumer items I didn't own. A knock at the open door made me look up.

It was Stephanie, snug and artistic in chinos and a black turtleneck and carrying, as she crept into the room with tentative baby steps, a bouquet of red and white tulips. "Pete? Are you up for a visitor?"

"I'm always up for you, kid."

She handed me the posy and I was touched. A nurse found a cheap little milk glass vase somewhere, and we set it up on the side table. Stephanie sat in the visitor's chair nearby, took a good look at my face, and two glimmering tears leaped into her eyes.

"You're so beat up. Does it hurt?"

"I'll live. Any news from the outside world?"

She looked naughtily thrilled and nodded, wiping her eyes. "Litman and Wendy are under arrest. They haven't found the money yet, but Megan Loomis thinks it's offshore somewhere. Thoreau thinks they'll get at it."

"Aces, doll. And what about Celeste?"

Stephanie bit her lip and looked very solicitous toward me. Is that what I mean? Solicitous? Like she felt sorry for me. Or does that mean she looked like a door-to-door salesman? In any case, she leaned toward me, put her hand on my knee, and said very gently, "Pete. Thoreau interviewed me this morning. We figured out the whole thing. Are you ready?"

A year ago, when Thompson Fleer died, Litman's firm was given custody of the bearer bonds pending the resolution of the disputes over the estate. Litman was put in charge. Within six months he realized the firm was in trouble; because of other cases and judgments against it, it was in danger of going under completely. It was an LLP, which used to be a kind of record people listened to before the onset of the fabulous digital age, but which now meant Limited Liability Partnership. So Litman wasn't all that exposed to personal financial risk—unless, that is, it turned out that he was, the rules governing LLPs being somewhat porous and the damages against Hoffman, Ratner being of both the compensatory and the punitive variety. And who, once the ship sank, would want to hire one of its disgraced crew? Litman was contemplating a future of professional ruin, possible personal penury, and a distinct loss of social prestige.

So he decided to steal the bonds.

There are many ways to steal something. You can just take it and run, and try to get away. But "get away" means one thing to a kid boosting the contents of the register at a bodega, and another to a sharp attorney swiping eight million from a firm with resources to go after him, a police force willing to give it the time of day, and insurance companies lacking a sense of humor. So Litman decided that the best form of getting away would be for everyone to think he was truly and permanently away, i.e., dead.

Assuming you want to be thought dead without actually having to incur death, you're stuck with a restricted menu of options. You can fake your own suicide, and yeah, that appeals to the self-reliant American in us, but it's tricky. The absence of a body—especially coupled with the absence of eight million in bonds—raises questions. So you're left with the project of faking your own murder. It's dramatic, it takes the issue of motive off the table, and it can include a plausible reason for the absence of a body. "Which, of course, was the whole point," Stephanie said.

So Litman needed a story as to who would want to pop him, and why. He could hire someone to masquerade as a murderous enemy or a kidnapper, but it would be like borrowing money from the Mafia: the after-sale customer service gets increasingly problematic. The so-called killer could shake Litman down whenever he felt like it. And there would still be the problem of assuring that the so-called killer got away.

Then he hit on the idea of Celeste.

"Thoreau and I agreed that was sort of genius," she said.

"You become your own killer. When you split with the loot, your body disappears, and the killer disappears."

It was easy to create a false identity among strangers. Litman went to Atlantic City, rented an apartment and opened a bank account, got himself up in drag, and made appearances around the casinos. Nobody cares. They've seen it all and their main attention is elsewhere. It was the perfect place to be vaguely remembered.

But it wasn't enough. He needed family and friends and colleagues to know about Celeste so they could confirm the story once it was set in motion. But he couldn't take the chance of actually having anyone meet her. How do you accomplish that?

Stephanie said, "Litman needed someone who would not only believe in Celeste, but who would have a reason to go around to everybody else, talking about her and referring to her. So, who could he get to do that? With a minimal exposure of Celeste. What kind of person moves around in your whole network of colleagues and family and friends? Spreading the belief that this so-called Celeste Vroman actually exists, like an e-mail carrying a virus from computer to computer. Which everybody believes because this one person—who, remember, is a stranger—believes it. Someone you can hire and whose job it is to talk to everybody who knows you. A private eye."

Of course, the P.I. in question had to meet this fabricated *femme fatale* at least once. So to minimize the risk that the P.I. in question might see that this woman was actually a man in makeup and ladies' clothes, the meetings were held in dark places, for as brief a time as necessary. And everything else was done by phone.

She continued, "Then the question is, why would people think she wanted to kill Litman? What was her motive? Simple: jealousy. Because it's private but everybody knows it makes people crazy and capable of murder. Okay, but jealous why? Jealous of whom?

"That's where Olivia came in."

Jeffrey Litman needed a frail eager for a relationship and knew he'd find one in the personals column of the *New York Review*. Once he cast the unwitting Olivia in the role of his new girl-friend, he had Celeste hire me to go to her and tell her to back off. I was not only establishing Celeste's existence, I was spread-ing the word about what would ultimately be her motive for off-ing Jeffy.

And that's what would have happened. Celeste—and Lit-man—would have hinted to me that they'd reconciled, that they foresaw an exciting new life together, that they would "go away." Then Litman would have staged the boat ride, with the blood and the disappearance of himself.

"Hold it," I said. "The couple at the marina saw two people pilot the boat out to sea. Who were they?"

"Celeste, and probably a mannequin," Stephanie said. "A blowup figure like some women use when they drive alone? As fake passenger? Didn't you say they only saw the man below, in the cabin? Sitting still and reading?"

I nodded.

After the staged killing, Celeste would have "gone under-ground with the money." Olivia Cartwright would step forward, heartbroken, and tell everyone how her boyfriend had been killed by the jealous bitch that everyone, by then, would have heard of. When they realized at the law firm that the bonds were gone, they'd conclude that Litman took them, and that he'd been ripped off before walking the plank. Celeste, of course, would literally vanish forever. And it would have worked, if the unfore-seen hadn't happened.

The unforeseen took the form of Olivia acting on the news

that Litman was married. I hadn't mentioned it. Why would I? I was working for Celeste, and could have compromised my client if Olivia had decided to tell Litman's wife about his lively and expanding harem. But my assistant had felt no such compunction.

"Maybe I was wrong," she admitted. "Maybe I shouldn't have told Olivia all that. I was working for you. I could have gotten you in trouble with the client." She shrugged. "Sorry."

"Don't talk out of school next time."

She smiled. "Next time I won't."

When Olivia learned the truth from Stephanie, she felt betrayed. A wife she didn't know about—what else was he hiding? She followed him from his office one morning to the Hotel Urbane and confronted him in the room. Maybe she thought she'd catch him with Celeste. What she couldn't have anticipated was catching him *becoming* Celeste, getting into makeup and into character for his lunch with me and Stephanie at the Indian restaurant.

He couldn't allow the secret to get out, of course, and so he strangled her. And then showed up for lunch, shaken and rattled but in costume and on time.

"She died because of what I did," Stephanie said.

"She died because of what she did and what Litman did," I said. "You told her the truth. You didn't make her get mixed up with him, and you didn't make her follow him and trap him in the hotel room. Your conscience is clear and is released with the thanks of the court."

She gave a little smile and shrugged. "I know. Still. Anyway, you know the rest. Wendy didn't know he'd killed Olivia. But she knew about everything else. I don't know what they'll charge her with, but she's ready to spill her guts regardless."

I sat back and sighed. "You were ahead of me on this one," I said. "You knew Wendy was the weak link, you knew how to pry her out of the house and send her running to Jeffy. Good work, doll. Give yourself a pat on the back."

"It's about all I'm going to get," she said. "It's not like Celeste is going to finish paying her bill."

"You let me worry about the financials. Let's sign me out, and we can go back to the office and see where we are."

"Pete. Listen." She paused, an actress finding her rhythm. She had rehearsed this. "That stuff I said? All that fuck-you and come clean? I take it all back. I don't know whether you're putting on the world or what, but I don't care anymore. When you got up and went to that front door, and knocked, and Litman dragged you in and beat the shit out of you, I thought: Jesus Christ, he's the real thing. It was brave and solid and extremely cool. So that's what I think. And I'm sorry for being such a fucking jerk about it."

My pain must have shown on my face, because although I said nothing, she looked suddenly upset and concerned. "Is all this too much? Should I just shut up? What's wrong?"

"Do you have to work blue, doll? We're in a hospital, for God's sake. The language."

"Sorry. Go get dressed."

I did, and got a nasty surprise as I was tying my shoes: a nurse, confirming my release and presenting me with a bill. Then I checked the bottom line and enjoyed a little laugh.

"Glad to see you're recovering so quickly, Mr. Ingalls," the nurse said. "What's so funny?"

"This typo, ma'am." I pointed to the total. "For that kind of dough I could stay at the Pierre for six months."

She peered at the sheet. "No, I'm afraid that's accurate." She indicated some printout boilerplate I had overlooked. "It's itemized right here. They can discuss it with you at the cashier window."

I didn't know hospitals had a cashier window. In fact, I didn't know you actually had to pay hospitals real money. I always thought that somehow somebody caused money to be directed to them in exchange for their services. Turns out that in this case, that somebody was Ingalls. I handed the lady at the counter my plastic, traded some wisecracks about needing the Demerol now more than ever and, with Stephanie strolling beside me, left.

It was around four in the afternoon. I said I had something back at the office I wanted to give her. We hailed a cab and she chattered brightly about Litman, Wendy, and the ordeal we'd all just been through as we drove downtown in lurches and pauses.

Finally, as shadows claimed all of the streets and the edgy, throbbing rush hour din picked up all around, we got back to the office. There was a message on the voice mail, but before checking it I had something to do and something to say. "Sit down, doll." I pointed to her chair at the reception desk. I went back into the rear, got what I'd come for, and returned.

"What's up, Pete? Oh, listen. I forgot. Tuesday I have to take a long lunch. I'm meeting with a new agent."

"Take as long as you want, kid."

"Really? Thanks."

"Starting tomorrow."

She began to speak, but something in my expression tipped her off. "What."

"That medical bill ate up my grubstake, angel." I held up the checkbook I'd retrieved from the back. "I have just enough to pay you for this week, and that's it. I'm out of business."

"But what about Catherine Flonger? Has she paid?"

"I'll get enough from her to cover the utilities. I thought I could stretch it out for six, seven months. But that tab uptown just wiped me out."

"Pay it off over time! You put it on plastic, right?"

"Debit card. The dough is gone."

She fell silent. "Fuck." She fell silent again. "Sorry."

"You were great. You have a knack for this. And there may be enough clients out there to make this work. But unless they show up tomorrow, I'm finished." I wrote a check and tore it out and handed it to her. "Don't worry. It'll clear."

"I know it will. I know you're a square guy." She stood up. "Well, it was fun while it lasted, wasn't it?" Women's faces get distorted and disfigured when they start to cry. So do men's. Maybe that's why Stephanie turned away from me and said, to thin air, "What are you going to do now?"

"Beats me. I'll think of something."

She turned back toward me and came over and kissed me on the cheek. "Good luck, Pete." Then she turned, grabbed her tote bag, and hotfooted it out the door before the tears actually started.

I sat and looked around and waited for reality to change its mind. It never does, but it can't hurt to offer the opportunity. Finally I remembered the voice mail and dialed in. "Mr. Ingalls, it's Catherine Flonger. I'd like to meet with you at your office. Call me. Any time."

I decided I might as well close out all the accounts at once. She answered on the first ring and said she'd be right down. I knew, of course, why she was coming. I rehearsed my lines and got the Kleenex ready.

Catherine Flonger arrived in an outfit of plain off-white canvas slacks and a loose, unsexy, unstylish tuniclike top. She wore no makeup. Her hair looked somehow chopped and tied off like a sheaf of something agricultural. She carried an old briefcase instead of a purse. She had an odd air about her, a blend of hushed watchfulness and fearless, almost defiant calm. I couldn't decide whether she had become transformed into an exalted, higher form of her previous self, or just lost it completely and enrolled in Fruitcake U. I ushered her into my office, sat her down in the customer's chair, and waited to see which. I hoped I'd be able to tell the difference.

We got past the inevitable expressions of dismay over how terrible I looked, with my facial Band-Aids and my limping gait and my general display of abrasions and purple bruises. I put them down to a "rather physical case, recently resolved," and then observed, "But never mind me, Catherine. You look fairly lousy yourself."

"Please, Mr. Ingalls. Mrs. Flonger."

I laughed. "After all we've meant to each other, and considering what you've come to say, don't I get first-name privileges?" I paused. "Or didn't all we meant really mean all that much?"

"What do you mean, what I came to say?"

I recited my monologue. "After what happened in the dressing room . . . well, let's just say, I know you have strong feelings for me. Feelings, yeah, let's call them love. Feelings that a dame like you would naturally experience after an intense sexual experience like the one you experienced. And I want you to know that I have affection for you, and yes, it goes beyond the normal feelings a dick feels for his client. But it isn't love, Mrs. Flonger. And I hope you can accept that, and we can both move on."

For a second she looked as though I'd slapped her in the puss with a cream pie. Then I had to straighten the items on my desk and wind my watch and look around the room while I waited for her to finish laughing. I reached into the bottom desk drawer and brought out the office bottle and two paper cups. Gasping, she reached for a Kleenex and dried her eyes. "Scotch?" She declined. I poured myself one and took a slug. The Scotch arrived in my gut to warm applause and a feeling of uplift.

Finally she said, "Thank you for being so sensitive, Pete. But I'm not in love with you."

"Glad to hear it."

"Do you know why I wanted to have sex with you in that dressing room?"

"You told me," I said. "You were slumming. You wanted to convince yourself you weren't as boring and bored and silly as Karen and Deb and the other class skirts paying in the high three figures for a pair of shoes designed by a Chinese foot-binder."

"Partially. But it was also because it was your idea."

"Do tell. What—?"

"I stood in that store, listening to Karen being so horrible to that poor girl—and so oblivious of the truth about her husband—and I felt like I was suffocating. But I remembered that doing what you had suggested had worked before. The rock climbing. Which I quite enjoyed. So I dragged you in there."

I shrugged with what I thought was probably sincere modesty. "So okay, yeah, you never know where wisdom's going to come from, is what you're saying."

"Oh God no. You're not wise. You're beyond wise, or no, you're *before* wise. If that makes sense."

"Listen, sugar—"

"And then that orgasm." She leaned toward me a little and perhaps blushed. It looked good on her. "I'm telling you I hadn't come like that in twenty years. I was like Sleeping Beauty. I woke up."

"Because I'm Prince Charming."

"Because I didn't care what you thought. I've said that all along. You're so odd and absurd and from another world, I just couldn't be bothered to care what you thought of me. I hope that doesn't hurt your feelings."

"What if it does?"

"Then I apologize. But I don't think it really does. I think I'm as exotic to you as you are to me. And if you want you can take it as a compliment. I felt absolutely uninhibited with you. Imagine that."

"I'm trying."

"But that isn't the best part. The best part is, afterwards, in the cab going home, I sat there feeling this . . . this release, this immediate *joy*. And then, it was as if I could feel myself coming down with a disease." She paused. Maybe she was distracted by the memory. She licked her lips and swallowed and forced herself to keep talking. "This horrible sensation came seeping in, and I felt just squalid."

I took another sip. It tasted good, although not good enough.

"I couldn't believe what I had done—acted out the most obvious cliché of the rich bitch, banging the hired help in an upscale public place because it was so declassé and transgressive."

"Okay, but—"

"And right there, in that stupid cab, I got it. Is that what they mean? Those people? When they say 'I got it'? It doesn't matter. I got it."

"Catherine. Mrs. Flonger—"

She sat forward again. Now her eyes were bright. She was thrilled by what she was explaining. "Do you see what I'm saying? One minute I'm ecstatic and free, and *my body, itself*, is doing something I couldn't get it to do for twenty years . . . and the next minute I'm disgusted and full of sophisticated contempt. How is that possible?"

At last, a question Pete Idiot could answer. "I'll tell you how. It's because you're a woman. You—"

"Please. This is deeper than that. I sat in that cab and thought, 'Look at you. Look at what you just did. How tacky. How cheap. Aren't you better than that?' And I could see for the first time that this disgust with myself came from the *best* part of me. Or what presented itself as the best part. The part that had standards and good taste and moral principles and all that . . . that . . ." Her hands splayed open, fingers wide, as she groped for the *mot au jus*. Which she found. ". . . all that *shit*, that makes up the prison I've been living in. Living in it and not knowing it! Dressing for it at Frisson. As Darius's wife. As someone who is so worried and vigilant about what other people think of her, she has to impress her fucking shrink! As someone who worries that if she approves of the wrong wine at a tasting she'll somehow have to go to Hell. And this was supposedly the best of me! That wanted me to despise and disown that . . ." She shut her eyes lightly. ". . . that beautiful, wonderful come."

Then Catherine Flonger sat forward and reached for the Scotch bottle, poured a little into the second paper cup. "Mr. Ingalls, I'm telling you—" She sipped a bit, grimaced, and shivered. "Hmm. Awful. But not bad. I'm telling you, by the time I got out of that cab I could see that my whole life I had been a model prisoner. My best impulses, my worst impulses—they were all the impulses of a prisoner. So I'm leaving. I'm getting out of jail. I'm letting myself out, in fact." She sat back and looked at me. "You haven't the faintest idea of what I'm talking about, have you?"

"Maybe I like to think I do," I said.

"I hope not, Mr. Ingalls. Because your purity is a gift."

"Okay, fine." I had had a long day and was reaching the point where my good sense was handing the torch to the booze. "Message received. We made the beast with two backs and you had a moment. Now, what would you like me to do about your husband, and the dwarf, and this whole messy business?"

"Nothing. Your work is done. You've done an excellent job." As she opened the briefcase she gestured toward it and said, "My old one from college. It's like coming home to a favorite pet."

She pulled out a checkbook and a pen. "How much do I owe you?" I told her. As she wrote the check she smiled. When she tore it out and handed it over, she said, "This has helped me more than any therapy I've ever had. Thank you."

"Thank you, Mrs. Flonger. Catherine."

"Mrs. Fl . . . Miss Binney. Miss Catherine Gail Binney. That's my maiden name. I'm a maiden again, Mr. Ingalls."

"Whatever that means." I folded the check and put it in my pocket. Then I opened the flat main drawer and pulled out a yellow envelope. "Meanwhile, I have these photographs of your husband in various compromising positions."

She waved them away. "Destroy them. They're irrelevant now. I'm getting out of the marriage as quickly as possible. Darius has already agreed to terms."

"And then?"

"Then I'm going to travel. One suitcase. Second class. Not like a TV star's wife and not like a student. Around the world. I spent my first forty years avoiding and discrediting most of reality. Now I'd like to respectfully observe it." She stood and held out her hand. I shook it. "Thank you, Mr. Ingalls. You've been a tremendous help. Good luck with your other cases."

"Well . . ." I spread my hands. "There aren't going to be any other cases."

"Oh, how sad! Why not?"

I explained how recent events had required me to expend all my startup funds. She expressed regret and assured me that she would be happy to refer other prospective clients if I did manage to stay afloat. I thanked her.

"Don't thank me, Mr. Ingalls," she said as she headed for the door. "I'm the one in your debt. You have a very special skill, and I hope you never find out what it is."

TWENTY

I came in the next day to an office full of no assistant, a schedule full of no clients, and a bank account full of no money. I put in some time doodling on a legal pad and daring the phone to ring, and that's when I started to wonder about one final puzzle.

Who had tipped me off to Darius Flonger and Nora Shortie's tryst at the Thompson Street apartment? Some enemy of Darius's, probably—they had to number in the low five figures, with his grating personality and unchained ego—but why? And who, besides his wife, knew I was on the case to begin with?

It was think about this or drop by Vince's liquor store for moving cartons and phony sympathy. So I pondered a bit and played Solitaire on the box and waited for it to be lunchtime. Then, at about eleven thirty, the phone did ring.

"Pete Ingalls, P.I."

"Mr. Ingalls?" The voice was preoccupied, distracted, and reverberating in an echo chamber. The caller was using a speaker phone.

"Himself."

"Sir, my name is Anthony Muir Smith. I'm an attorney representing a Mrs. Catherine Flonger. You've done work for Mrs. Flonger?"

"Yeah. Is there a law against it?"

"I hope not, sir, or we're both in trouble. The reason I'm calling is, Mrs. Flonger has made an appointment for you to see me later today at three thirty. It's extremely important that you attend this meeting, so I'm calling to make sure that time is convenient. If it isn't we can reschedule."

I hesitated. A rich dame's lawyer calls and invites you for a chaw and a talk: the heart races in panic and fear. "Mr. Smith, what's the gag? Am I being sued by your client?"

"I think it would be better for everyone if we discussed that when you arrived. Can you make the three thirty?"

I told him I could and he gave me the address. That provided me with a comfortable three hours in which to lose my appetite, stare at the office bottle, decide not to drink that early in the day, wait another hour, and knock back a restorative snort. Then I walked the thirty blocks to the guy's office. My body would be that much more toned and exercised for when they strapped it to the rack and started turning the wheel.

The Scotch had been a bad idea, but the walk, the air, and the sight of citizens going about their business came as a tonic. By the time I arrived at the specified midtown address, any misgivings or worries I'd started out with had been quietly sedated by the energy, drive, and uncontainable scope of the city. There were eight million people swarming all over these boroughs. Somebody had to need a gumshoe.

Smith's office was on the twenty-third floor of an older highrise, the kind that seeks your respect as an institution of professionals instead of, as new buildings do, trying to intimidate you as a capital of the Galactic Federation. There was black marble on the lobby floor, with brass insets of a compass rose, and elevators that weren't automatic. The law firm's reception area was presided over by an older broad with champagne-colored hair who had left her sense of humor in her other pants. The place had the realistic-but-dead air of a diorama at the Museum of Natural History. She announced my presence, listened to the reply, and indicated an opaque door of black leather quilted with brass studs. It buzzed as I approached. I went in.

A young gal in a fluffy white blouse and a navy blue skirt met me, smiled, said, "Mr. Ingalls? This way." I followed her past a phalanx of paralegals and other worker bees to an office in the rear. A door was opened, I was gestured in and found myself facing a familiar figure.

"Well, well," Darius Flonger said. "Ingalls, if I weren't in such a good mood, I'd return what you gave me. With interest."

"Flonger," I said. "I'm in a bad enough mood to hope you try."

"Still the tough-talking asshole, I see." Flonger turned toward the rear of the room and said, "Is that it, Tony? Are we done?"

Farther in the room, at a large desk, sat a thin, white-haired, clean-shaven gent in a nice suit. His blue eyes looked friendly but reserved the right to destroy you in a court of law, and his healthy pink complexion suggested that even if it came to that, it was all for the best. "That's it, Darius. Sic transit."

"Splendid. Out with the old, in with the new." Flonger turned back toward me and smirked. "How's your client, Ingalls?"

"Which one?"

"You have others? Will wonders never cease."

"You know, Flonger, you're pretty chipper for a man whose wife has just left him."

Flonger gave me his camera-ready robo-smirk and said, "Now why do you think that is?"

"I'm sure I wouldn't know."

"I'm sure you wouldn't know either, Ingalls, so why don't I tell you. I happen to be in an excellent mood, because the last laugh is on Cathy. And you, I might add. Who do you think tipped you off to that apartment? Who do you think left the key under the mat? A friend of Miss Thomas, whose flat we borrowed for our little imposture."

I may have gulped. "The dwarf?"

He laughed. "We say 'little people,' as everyone on earth except you seems to know. Yes, the dwarf."

"The tipoff came from you?"

"That's right. I could see at the department store you needed everything handed to you on a silver platter."

"You wanted me to take pictures?"

"Of what? Giving massages? A bit of chaste necking? Which is all we did, if you'll recall. Nora is a grad student at NYU and was happy to give me a rubdown for some money. We went to the shower to give you an opportunity to leave. Nora was very glad you were smart enough to use it. But yes, I did want you to take pictures. Although they turned out not to be necessary. Cathy was entirely ready for a divorce without them. Whatever meetings you and she had, they did wonders for her. And for me! I was dying to end it."

Something connected in my brain. "That's why you left the matchbook," I said. "And mentioned the hotel. You wanted me to catch you. Why?"

"Isn't it obvious? I wanted out of the marriage. But if I told Cathy that, she'd have raked me over the coals and taken most of my assets. This way, the photos would be embarrassing, she'd decide that she was more motivated to get the divorce than even I was, and I'd get away cheaper. Which I did. Lots." He slapped me on the shoulder. "I don't know how you did it, but it worked out beautifully for me. Thanks, pal. Take care. And if you find a spare moment in your busy career, go fuck yourself. Tony? Regards to Beth."

Flonger left. Smith stood. "He really is obnoxious, isn't he? I don't think you can learn that. It's innate." He offered his slim, pale hand. "Tony Smith, Mr. Ingalls. Have a seat." As I did he added, "I don't represent him, by the way. I represent Catherine. He was here to sign some papers."

"The more I see the guy, the more I don't want to be married to him myself," I said.

"I'm surprised it lasted as long as it did, frankly. I've represented her father for years. When she married Darius Flonger I raised my eyebrows but kept my counsel."

"Kind of chatty, aren't you, Smith? To a total stranger?"

He smiled. "Arguably. But Catherine thinks highly of you, Mr. Ingalls. As you'll see." He shook his head, still bothered by the memory of Flonger. "That marriage—they raised Hannah, of course. . . . And I suppose now is when I'm supposed to say that Catherine is a strong woman, that when she sets her mind to something it takes a powerful force to divert her from it, that she was committed to the marriage for a long time." He made a throwaway gesture and a moue of disapproval. "But I don't think that's why she stayed. I don't think it was that deliberate. Or praiseworthy, frankly. It was something else."

I asked the gent what any of this had to do with me. The bland expression of bemusement disappeared and the sharp-eyed mouthpiece mug emerged. "The settlement of the divorce proceedings for Mr. and Mrs. Darius Flonger will leave Catherine Flonger with a lump sum of approximately twenty million dollars. She has indicated to me that she wants to make a gift of one million dollars of that to you."

I looked down at my lap, I scratched my jaw, I did the things you do in such a situation. Then I said, "Catherine Flonger is a daffy broad, counselor, but this joke borders on the sadistic. Where is she?"

He looked at his watch. "Over the Atlantic Ocean. About halfway to Amsterdam."

"So she's willing to pull the gag even without being here to enjoy it? That's artistic." I looked around. "Or is this being taped?"

Smith smiled, showing his little white teeth. "Oh, this is no joke, Mr. Ingalls. She is perfectly serious. Of course," he laughed, "I don't mean I'm going to go into the back and bring out some bags with dollar signs on them stuffed with cash."

I smiled a stiff smile of skepticism. "Of course."

"But it's a cool million, Mr. Ingalls. And it's essentially yours."

"Smith. Why? What gives?"

He blinked several times, fast, and then consulted a sheet of paper on his blotter. He read, " 'To make possible your continuing service to the people of our fair city in your capacity as confidential advisor and private investigator, so that others may avail themselves of your unique qualities of patience, tact, and understanding, and so improve their lives as mine has been improved.' " He indicated the document. "It's all here. Have your representative review it, and if everything is kosher, we can establish the fund next week."

I took the papers but could barely breathe, let alone scan them. "So I get a million clams? Just like that?"

He waggled an open hand back and forth. "Not quite. There are certain restrictions. I suggested to Catherine that, rather than give you the whole amount in cash, which you—or anyone, of course, even I—might be tempted to squander on pleasures and luxuries, she should use the money to create a trust fund, the yearly dividends from which will go to pay your various expenses and underwrite your detective work."

"Aces."

"She thought so. Of course, you could still use the money for nonprofessional purposes, but at least there would be some check on that." He handed me the papers. "I suggest you have an attorney review them."

I reached for a pen on his desk. "Nix. I trust the dame." I signed, then reached into my pocket and said, "Excuse me a minute." I pulled out my cell phone and punched a pre-programmed number. After two rings the other party answered. I said, "It's me, doll. Recharge your Metrocard and be at the office first thing Monday. We're back in business."

"Pete! No shit? Fabulous! Oh. Wait. Monday. I can't. No, yes I can. But I'll be in late."

"Don't—"

"Can't we make it Tuesday? Although I have that lunch."

"Monday is the start of the workweek, angel."

"But I have a callback and then a lunch!"

"Okay, but we all—"

"Oh! I know. I'll reschedule the lunch to Wednesday. Okay! See you then. Bright and early Monday! But like late."

"We're out of cookies."

"Got it. But, Pete?" She hesitated. "This may be a stupid question, but what'll we do?"

I laughed. "We'll do what people do, sugar. Wait for the next client."

EPILOGUE

Stephanie still hadn't shown by midmorning on Monday when the next client walked in. At least I thought she would be the next client. I was wrong.

"Um . . ." She was confused. It looked good on her. I put her in her late twenties, five seven, slim, in a pressed white blouse tucked into nice clean jeans and trim navy blue sneaks. What sold the whole package was her hair, a full, bushy explosion of little ringlets in a sunny, glinting blonde that set off her sweet round face and clear pale skin. A big purse hung on her shoulder. She looked around. "I don't think I'm in the right place."

"Join the club," I said. "It's the human condition."

"You may be right. Anyway, I was looking for someone who used to work at Seaside Books. I called there and they gave me this address."

"What's this someone's name?"

"At the store they said Peter Ingalls. He had an accident trying to find something for me, and I wanted to see how he was."

I had to laugh. "I wouldn't know, miss. This Ingalls gent and

I share a name, and down at the Seaside they like to confuse the two of us. What's he look like?"

"Well . . . kind of weird. Hermity? With a big beard and sort of dorky clothes. Nothing like you." She shrugged and smiled. "Anyway, thanks. Sorry to bother you."

"No bother at all," I said. "I'm here to help."

I watched her leave the office. She shut the door behind her, and in a few seconds she was out on the street, with the rest of New York, going about her business.